PRAISE FOR
THE KEEPERS OF METSAN VALO

"Wendy Webb once again spins a magical web in *The Keepers of Metsan Valo*, weaving Nordic folklore, family legacy, and the bonds that unite us to each other and to the natural world. She is the sorceress of Lake Superior. Get ready to be ensnared!"

—Carol Goodman, two-time Mary Higgins Clark Award–winning author of *The Lake of Dead Languages* and *The Stranger Behind You*

"A novel taut with threats and secrets, family lore, and folktales. Who—or what—truly guards and keeps the magnificent house and grounds of Metsan Valo? That is the question that thrums through the novel. And who—or what—is threatening and haunting the family who calls it home? Dark, brooding, and mysterious, as all good gothics should be. Loved it."

—Kim Taylor Blakemore, author of *After Alice Fell* and *The Companion*

PRAISE FOR
THE HAUNTING OF BRYNN WILDER

"The action builds to a satisfying and uplifting ending . . . Webb consistently entertains."

—*Publishers Weekly*

"Endearing and greatly readable . . . [a] tale that is both warm and poignant."

—*Kirkus Reviews*

"A haunting tale of grief and loss that is beautifully layered with new beginnings and woven into a gothic ghost story both bone chilling and heartwarming."

—Melissa Payne, author of *The Secrets of Lost Stones*

Praise for
DAUGHTERS OF THE LAKE

"Simultaneously melancholy and sweet at its core."

—*Kirkus Reviews*

"Well-delineated characters and a suspenseful plot make this a winner."

—*Publishers Weekly*

"*Daughters of the Lake* has everything you could want in a spellbinding read: unexpected family secrets, ghosts, tragic love stories, intertwined fates."

—Refinery29

"Perfect for anyone who loves a good ghost story that bleeds into the present day."

—*Health*

"*Daughters of the Lake* is gothic to its core, a story of ghostly revenge, of wronged parties setting history right."

—*Star Tribune*

"*Daughters of the Lake* provides an immersive reading experience to those who love ghostly mysteries, time travel, and lovely descriptions."

—*New York Journal of Books*

THE
WITCHES
OF
SANTO
STEFANO

OTHER TITLES BY WENDY WEBB

THE
WITCHES
OF
SANTO
STEFANO

A NOVEL

WENDY WEBB

LAKE UNION
PUBLISHING

Text copyright © 2024 by Wendy Webb
All rights reserved.

Published by Lake Union Publishing, Seattle

www.apub.com

Amazon, the Amazon logo, and Lake Union Publishing are trademarks of Amazon.com, Inc., or its affiliates.

ISBN-13: 9781662517419 (paperback)
ISBN-13: 9781662517426 (digital)

Cover design by Faceout Studio, Amanda Hudson
Cover images: © Teresa Rico, © Nail Holden / ArcAngel; © ranasu / Getty; © maggee / Shutterstock

Printed in the United States of America

For my dad, whose greatest pleasure in life was sitting with his family around the dining room table, sharing a meal and telling stories. This one's for you, Pop. We miss you every day.

PROLOGUE

The women walked through the ancient village's labyrinthine stone streets at sunset, the mother carrying a set of her child's clothes. A solemn ritual, handed down by generations of women before them. It was the only way, their grandmothers had said, to break a curse. People had long since abandoned these old ways, these outdated beliefs. They had no place in this modern age. Or did they?

Little Alessandro was delirious with fever, mumbling strange and otherworldly words . . . if they were words at all. It had to be done.

Even the priest agreed, silently, with a quick, tense nod. He couldn't be seen endorsing such pagan foolishness outright, it was blasphemy, although he himself knew the truth of it in his heart of hearts. This was the work of a witch. No doubt. Nobody would say it, or even hint at it. But it began all the same, as the mother had walked out the door of her home and onto the street, a small bundle of clothes in her arms. Cradling it, as she would a baby.

As she walked, the women of the village joined her, emerging from their houses one by one, and together they made their way through the tunneled streets until they reached the piazza. In front of the fountain, all the women said a silent prayer, an incantation, to themselves—*please let my own child escape this curse*—as the mother set a torch to the clothes and lit them on fire. The women stood in a circle around the burning bundle, watching the flames engulf it.

And there. It was done. The curse, broken. Now Alessandro would be well. They all believed it, hoped it was true. All except one. Fiora had taken her place among them, joined the women on this walk, if only for show. For how it would look if she had not.

Across town, in the back room of their home, a makeshift shop that sold local honey, soaps, and oils, Violetta was filling a glass bottle with the honey she had infused with lavender from her garden earlier in the day. Her mother, Fiora, tended the bees, as Fiora's mother before her had done, in hives that seemed to be as old as the mountains surrounding their village. The lavender scent calmed and soothed. This honey would work the same magic.

Violetta was startled out of her thoughts by Fiora, who had burst through the door, her face a mask of concern. Even fear. *What in the world . . . ?*

"What is it?" Violetta asked.

"They're burning Alessandro's clothes in the piazza," her mother said.

Violetta set the bottle of honey on the counter. "Not that again."

Fiora held her daughter's gaze. "I think it's time you left this place. Long since time."

Leave Santo Stefano? It was unthinkable. Violetta had lived in this hill town most of her life. To leave it would be like leaving herself. And Giovanni was here, the man who had been her first and best friend and now was her husband. Her great love.

"Why would you even say such a thing?" she asked her mother. "Gio and I won't leave Santo Stefano. You. Auntie."

"You know they are going to come looking for us if that little boy dies."

"Looking for us? Oh, Mama." Violetta waved a hand. "It's the 1900s now. People don't believe those old tales anymore."

Fiora wagged a finger at her daughter. She remembered, in a flash, leaving Rome with her sister Florencia all those years ago. The memory stung, deep in her heart.

"These people aren't as modern as you think. I want you safe, away from here. We've overstayed our welcome."

"What about you? I'm not going without you. Or Auntie."

"We can handle them. We have, for much of our lives. It's you they're looking at now, Violetta. The prettiest girl in the village, married to the most handsome of men. The most eligible man here in town. People talk. I've seen how they look at you. You, who has more artistry with the old ways than I ever had. Than even my mother ever had. There is more magic swirling around you than there has been with any woman in our family."

Violetta didn't know quite how to respond to this. But then she winced, remembering something inconvenient. "I did give Alessandro a sweet a few days ago when he came with his mother to buy some of my soap."

Fiora threw up her hands. "There, you see? That is all it will take."

A knock at the door silenced mother and daughter.

The moment seemed to stop in time, stretching backward through the generations of their family. The knock was written into their bones. Their very cells. Neither woman breathed. Fiora reached for her daughter's hand.

"Go to the barn," she whispered. "And then, use everything in your power to get away. Hurry."

The knock came again. Louder this time.

CHAPTER 1

Cassandra

Looking back on it now, I can pinpoint the exact moment the witches of Santo Stefano whispered into my ear, telling me it was time. It was as though these women wrapped a thread of curiosity around me and pulled me into their story, a mystery that would send me on an adventure to find them. No, to find me.

It all began with a lunch with my cousin, Maria. Food plus family always produced a cauldron of drama in my world, and that day was no different.

Maria and I were at our usual table at the Flamingo, my favorite restaurant in Wharton, a small tourist town on the shores of Lake Superior where Maria and I had grown up. Both of us had lived much of our adult lives elsewhere—me in Minneapolis, her in Chicago—but we had been drawn back to this strange, magical place of our youth in recent years. The comfort of being where one's roots were planted was much needed by both of us, it seemed, though neither of us had said it out loud.

Even before we both—separately—moved back to Wharton, Maria and I had been trying to get together more often, pulling our family ties tighter after both of our mothers, Luisa (hers) and Carlotta (mine), had passed away.

Our once-large family was dwindling, with the passings of not only our mothers but my dad and brother, one after the other. Maria's father had moved into the assisted-living facility in Salmon Bay—a larger town about thirty miles from Wharton—the previous October. And our kids were out of the house, too. My son, Henry, and Maria's twins, Gia and Tamara, were all spreading their wings in colleges in different parts of the country.

Life was . . . different. Smaller. Lonelier. As though the edges were constricting inward.

Holidays now were quiet adult affairs, not the raucous, loud celebrations of the past filled with our parents, grandparents, friends, kids, all around a long table. Back then, we'd had no idea it would all end one day. As it all does.

And it wasn't just our blood family that was dwindling. It was our chosen families, too. Husbands, namely.

Maria's divorce had been finalized the year before. I was holding my own beating heart in my hands after discovering my husband's stunning betrayal months earlier. I still couldn't quite believe it, the reality of life not being what I had thought it was.

I think that's the reason I was so affected by what she revealed to me on that day, at that lunch. It was about family, the most important thing to me, the thing that kept slipping through my fingers, as if I were holding sand.

"You are not going to believe this," Maria said, putting her fork on the table with an air of finality.

"What?" I asked her, taking a bite of my salad.

She narrowed her eyes and leaned in, confiding. "You know I'm doing ancestry research."

I nodded. "Yes, so you mentioned."

"Get ready for your world to be rocked. I think. I'm not sure. I wanted to show it to you—what I found—to get your thoughts on it."

I wasn't sure I wanted my world to be rocked. I'd had enough rocking recently to last a lifetime.

I was about to say so, but I saw something in my cousin's face. A hesitancy. As though she wasn't quite sure if she should say what she was about to say. Her eyes caught mine and wouldn't let go.

"What is it, Mimi?" I asked her.

"It's about our family," she began, tripping over her words. "Well, of course it's about our family; I just said I was doing ancestry research." She laughed then, a pitch higher than her usual laugh. Strained.

I didn't quite know what to say. Maria had become interested—obsessed—with researching our ancestry recently, wanting to learn more about our relatives' births, deaths, and what lay between. I supposed it was her way of extending the branches of our family tree, given all the "pruning" that had happened in recent years.

She took a sip of her wine. "Promise me you won't get upset."

I held her gaze for a moment. "I can't promise that. And now you're scaring me. This sounds bad."

She nodded. "It's not bad, exactly. Just weird. I'm not sure."

"What, are we related to Mussolini or something?"

Another nervous laugh. "No, no, nothing like that."

"Just tell me, Mimi. It's in the past. Whatever it is, we can handle it."

She took a deep breath, reached down into her bag, and pulled out her tablet. She placed it on the table between us and fired it up, scrolling to a popular ancestry website.

She showed it to me, but I wasn't sure what I was seeing. There was our family tree, with "leaves" representing our parents—our mothers, Carlotta and Luisa, were twin sisters—and our individual families branching out from them. My brother Marco and me—his photo made my heart squeeze with grief—and his wife and kids. There were John and Henry. Maria and her ex-husband, Rob, and their twins.

Above all of us, Nonna (our grandma Gia) and her husband Marco, my brother's namesake, the grandfather I barely remembered.

Above them, our great-grandmother, Violetta Moretti.

I squinted at the leaf. "This isn't complete," I said. "Where's her husband? Giovanni?"

"Well, that's where it gets weird. It's what I wanted to show you. I can't figure this out. Our family is from around Portofino, right?"

Yes, that was right. Our grandma Gia had told us the story many times—how she had been born in Portofino and come to the United States as a baby with her mother and father, Violetta and Giovanni.

Their great love story was legendary, with epic tales about them told over and over again at our family's dinner table.

Violetta and Giovanni had grown up together in a small village, married, and come to the United States with their young child, Gia, before the First World War, following family members who had touted the wonderful lives they were carving out for themselves in this country.

Giovanni had passed away young, during the influenza epidemic of 1918, and Violetta had to make her way on her own. She eventually came to Wharton and opened up a boardinghouse and a shop where she sold local honey and other crafts to support herself and Gia. She never married again, so great was her grief for the love of her life. I could recite this story from almost the moment I'd learned to talk.

"Right. And?"

"I don't know. It looks like . . ." She shrugged. "It doesn't make any sense."

I tapped the leaf with our grandmother's photo on it. I leaned in and squinted as a new screen popped up. An old, yellowed document that seemed weathered and torn on one side. It was a form, filled in with heavy black ink, written in a beautiful old-style script.

Certificate of Live Birth

Name: Gia Fiora Moretti

Sex: Female

Date: January 22, 1912

City: New York

County: New York

Mother's Name: Violetta Moretti

Father: Illegitimate

I stared at the screen for a moment, taking in what I was seeing. Then, I turned my gaze to Maria.

"What is this?"

She set her wineglass on the table with an air of finality. "That's what I wanted to ask you. What do you think? I mean, obviously it's Nonna's birth certificate. But—"

"But it says she was born in the United States. In New York? So, why—"

"I know! Why would she have told us—everyone—she was born in Portofino?"

I looked back down at the screen.

"It doesn't make any sense," I said.

"That's the thing," Maria said, leaning closer to me. "She was born here. Why would she tell people she was born in Italy? Just say you're born here. It's a weird thing to lie about."

"And—illegitimate? Why isn't Giovanni's name on the birth certificate?"

Maria waved her hand in the air. "This is what I'm telling you," she said. "We were always told he and Violetta came here together, with Nonna as a baby, and he died in the flu epidemic, right?"

"Right."

"But this document, Nonna's birth certificate, says different."

My mind was running in different directions at once. There had to be an explanation.

"Maybe he died before the epidemic in 1918," I said. "Sometime before she was born."

Maria shook her head. "In those days, they put the father's name on the birth certificate, even if he had already died before the child was born. I think they still do, actually."

I took a sip of wine and considered this. "Have you dug any deeper? Like, did you find any death records?"

"No!" Maria said. "That's the thing. I couldn't find a record of Giovanni anywhere."

"No record? What do you mean?"

Maria leaned in even closer, as though divulging a secret. "Nothing. No birth certificate. No death certificate. No obituary. It's like . . ."—she lowered her voice—"he didn't exist."

I looked at her for a long second. "That's crazy. Didn't exist? They came through Ellis Island—did you check those records?"

"Nothing. No record of them coming through Ellis."

"But . . . Nonna told us that story a thousand times, about how Violetta turned the head of one of the intake workers there, who took a shine to her."

Maria nodded. "That's what I remember, too. But with no record, it occurred to me that maybe I was remembering the story wrong and they came into this country elsewhere, like from Canada? But since you remember it was Ellis Island, too . . ."

"And with this birth certificate from New York . . ."

We were talking in circles. I felt tears stinging at the backs of my eyes, and I took a deep breath to try to keep them at bay. It was silly, getting so upset about something that had happened so long ago. What did it matter now? But I had had enough of my life's rock-solid foundation crumbling beneath me lately. I didn't need this, too. Still, Maria was raising questions that should have answers. Easy answers.

"So, you could find no record of either of them coming through Ellis Island," I repeated, more for my own clarity than anything else. As if saying it again would bring a different answer.

Maria shook her head. "None."

"Maybe you had the date wrong?"

"You don't need the exact date to search those records. You can search by last name."

We sat in silence for a moment, staring at the tablet, as though it somehow held more information than we had already seen.

"But admittedly," Maria went on, "I'm not the greatest at this research. Or any online research. It's not my thing. It's more of your thing." She winced. "Would you have any time to dig into it? Do you even want to?"

I looked into her expectant eyes. It *was* my thing. I had spent most of my career as an investigative journalist for a newspaper in Minneapolis—if anyone in my family knew how to dig deep, research, and uncover hidden truths, it was me. I had always had a "nose" for it—somehow, I just knew where the truth lay buried. The irony wasn't lost on me, either. I had spent a career dredging up lies and secrets but had failed to see them right under my own roof.

"I'll see what I can find out," I said. "I'll poke around later and see if I can come up with any more information."

Maria smiled. "I had a feeling you might. I emailed you my log-in and password for the ancestry site before I left the house to meet you today."

I shook my head and chuckled. "Am I really that predictable?"

My cousin reached across the table, took my hand, and squeezed it. "You're not predictable. You're curious. And you loved Nonna, maybe more than any of us. You had a special bond with her."

Maria was right about that, but it surprised me to hear her say it. Nonna and I did have a special bond. Some of my fondest memories were of sitting beside her in the greenhouse in our backyard, watching as she made soaps and oils and honey infused with herbs and flower petals. She even had a hive, where she tended the bees for the honey, as her mother had. She tried teaching that art to Maria and me. Mimi didn't have the temperament for it—the bees were agitated by her—but I took to it. I loved the peacefulness of the whole process, how you had to step out of your world and into another, almost like being underwater.

My grandmother would tell me stories as she worked, half in Italian, half in English, about her mother and father and their lives in the old country and then, later, here in America. Since her father had died when she was so young—not more than a baby, she had told me—he had almost mythical status in her mind. The most dashing man in the county. A smile that could melt hearts but with eyes only for her mother. Their shelter in a storm.

But, in the face of what Maria was telling me, was it just that? A myth?

"I knew you'd want to get to the bottom of it for us, Cass," Maria had said. "For Nonna."

But, as I drove back to the house, I wasn't at all sure my grandmother would've wanted me to "get to the bottom" of anything. She had told us one story about her life, a story that wasn't lining up with what Maria could find in official records. Was it up to me to unearth what my grandmother had been trying to hide—if indeed she was trying to hide something?

I heard Nonna's voice, low and soft, in my ear. *Non svegliare il can che dorme.*

How many times had she said that to me over the years when I was fretting about something? *Let sleeping dogs lie.*

CHAPTER 2

Cassandra

I decided to do a quick online search after all. Give a reporter a mystery, and she won't be able to let it go . . . even if those dogs should really be left sleeping.

Sitting in the kitchen booth with my laptop, I navigated to the ancestry website, entered Maria's log-in and password, and watched as my family tree whirred to life. There was the sturdy trunk. There were the leaves.

How hard could it be to find public records? I imagined I'd call Maria within an hour with an explanation for why Giovanni's name wasn't on Nonna's birth certificate and where, exactly, they had entered the country. And as to her theory that he didn't exist? That was just crazy.

But after hours of searching, I had come up with exactly nothing. It was as though that side of my family didn't exist before Violetta, and at that, the only official record I could find of her at all was her daughter's birth certificate and the obituary that had run in the Wharton newspaper when she had died.

> Violetta Moretti, longtime owner of Violetta's Inn and
> Sundry Shop in Wharton, passed away on June 26, 1985,

surrounded by her loving family. Violetta is survived by her daughter Gia (Marco) Canavale; granddaughters Carlotta (Stuart) Anderson and Luisa (Thomas) Larson; great-grandchildren Maria, Cassandra, and Marco; and countless friends in Wharton. Violetta was preceded in death by her mother and beloved husband, Giovanni Moretti. She was 95 years old.

Nothing new there. My great-grandmother Violetta had passed when I was a girl. But I was old enough to remember her as being breathtakingly beautiful, right to the end. I always pictured her in her yard, wearing her floppy hat, crisp white shirt, and slacks, whispering to the bees in the hive. It wasn't just the bees that loved her. Animals did, too—she was constantly taking in strays. Guests at the inn would commonly find a cat curled up in their bed or a dog sleeping by the fireplace.

I closed my laptop, took a sip of my tea, and considered what we did know.

The birth certificate told us that Nonna, Gia Moretti Canavale, was born in New York. Not in Italy, as she had always told us. That was a fact. It meant either she was lying about her origins . . . or Violetta had told her the story of her Italian birth for some reason.

I turned this possibility over and over in my mind. I could imagine that in those days, 1912, women fudged the dates of their pregnancies and births for many reasons, usually having to do with their marital status. Adultery was another reason. Or a widow having become pregnant long after her husband had died. All would spell real trouble for women and were good reasons for playing a little loose with those dates.

But this didn't seem like that, did it? The fact that Violetta had kept the father's name off the birth certificate was puzzling. Where was Giovanni in 1912, when Violetta was in New York giving birth? If he had already died, she would've put his name on the birth certificate to save Gia from illegitimacy, wouldn't she?

Or maybe she was so new in the United States, she didn't know about birth certificates, legitimacy, and the importance of documents. Maybe she hadn't understood English well enough when asked about the baby's father, or the nurse recording the birth didn't understand Violetta well enough when she had said . . . what? *He is not here. He has passed away.* Something like that. And maybe the nurse misinterpreted.

Or . . . maybe she had come to this country alone and run into trouble somehow. Was assaulted aboard the ship—it happened more than we were ever told, I learned—or fell into a relationship that ultimately did not work out when they arrived in this new land, but she had found herself pregnant.

I took another sip of my tea.

Maybe the vast expanse of the internet wasn't enough. Oh, it held data and facts and figures; it could unearth secrets of many kinds. But not all kinds. The kinds that stayed hidden for generations, that weren't documented anywhere except in the hearts of the grieving, the lonely, the betrayed. Or the guilty.

I slipped out of the booth and padded across the living room to what had once been my grandmother's room. I stood at the closed door for a moment. Nobody had been allowed in her room when she was alive, unless they were invited. I had been invited many times for biscotti and hot chocolate, for bedtime stories, for tales of family woven with a thread that had been spun in Italy and tied off in Wharton.

"Nonna, please forgive me," I said aloud, and opened the door.

Her room was just as I remembered it. I knew it would be. My mother had told me, when Nonna died more than a decade ago, she wasn't planning to change the room in any way.

"Her spirit is too strong," my mother had said. "I want to keep this place just as it is, for her to return to."

And so we had closed up the room just as Nonna had left it. It seemed a fitting, respectful way to honor the great lady. None of us had wanted to go through her things. Dispose of a lifetime of her possessions. As far as her spirit returning—none of us had seen any evidence of that. Yet. It didn't mean she wouldn't come. Or hadn't.

The red floral duvet still covered the perfectly made bed; the matching curtains still hung on the windows, now dusty. A woven rug, in reds and blues and creams, still sat on the floor. I knew my mother had cleaned this room regularly after Nonna died. After my mom passed, there was nobody to do it. Except me. I felt a twinge in the pit of my stomach. I should have been better about coming to Wharton. Tending to my family home.

My gaze was drawn to the painting that hung on the wall. A wildflower meadow, sheep grazing here and there, a large white dog on guard of his flock, with one of Italy's famed hill towns in the background. I had always loved that painting. Nonna had told me it was a depiction of the village where her mother had been born, and I had spent countless hours as a child imagining myself there, running through that meadow, playing with that dog, petting those sheep.

The vanity dressing table that had once belonged to her mother still stood against one wall with its curved mirror, its tufted bench seat ready, waiting for a Moretti woman to sit and look at her reflection once again.

I pulled it out and sank down onto it now, gazing at myself in this mirror that had reflected four generations of dark-haired, dark-eyed women in my family, women who had gazed at their own image after births, deaths, griefs and triumphs, or simple ordinary days filled with the silent beauty and sorrow of life. Now I did the same.

I looked into my own eyes as if for the first time. I didn't see any of the strength I associated with the women of my family—my great-grandmother making her way alone in a new land; my nonna Gia raising a family, starting a greenhouse, and supporting herself after my grandfather passed; my mother forging a career in business. Instead, I saw the loneliness of betrayal. The blindness of trust. The loss of not knowing what came next. And a woman whose husband had been carrying on an affair. For years.

I found out about it on an otherwise ordinary Saturday.

Isn't that always the way? People go about their business—enjoying a twirl of last night's pasta for breakfast, curling up on the sunny screened-in porch with the morning paper and a cup of coffee, scrolling through social media to smile at the perfect lives one's friends liked to project to the world with a photo and funny caption—not knowing heartbreak is lurking, the obliterator of worlds is coming. What blissful ignorance lies in the moment before a life is shattered.

My shattering came in the form of a private message on social media in response to a photo I had posted of my husband and me.

Hi, the message read. I'm just curious how you know John.

Looking back on it, I'm sure I felt a tingling, a surge of electricity shoot through me when I read those words. It was something I had felt often throughout my life, a sort of odd pinprick. My grandmother had called it *chiaroveggenza*, or "second sight." Sometimes, I heeded it. More often, though, I shrugged it off. Not that day. Alarm bells rang in my head, big-time.

I had looked at the sender's screen name. A woman. I didn't know her.

John? He's my husband, I wrote back. Why?

Those few words. Enough to open a floodgate. Or stop a heart from beating.

You're married to John Striker? The man in the photo with you?

Striker? She obviously had the wrong person.

No, I wrote back. I'm married to John Graves. That's who is in the photo. I don't know anyone named John Striker.

And then, the deluge.

This woman—Julie was her name—was referring to a photo of my husband and me that I had posted on social media of our twenty-fifth anniversary trip to Saint Lucia. There we were, smiling at each other in the crystal-blue water, my legs wrapped around his waist. We had stolen back up to our room right after that photo was taken and made love for the rest of the afternoon.

But now this Julie was telling me things about the man in the photo that I couldn't quite understand.

John is my friend's boyfriend of two years. When I saw this photo, I had to contact you because if he's cheating on her, I guess she needs to know it. I wanted to be sure before going to her.

Cheating on *her*?

I've been married to this man for twenty-five years, I wrote. You must be mistaken. You've got the wrong guy.

No reply for a moment. Maybe that was the end of it? It wasn't. I'm so sorry, but I don't think so.

And then the photos came. She sent a half dozen shots of my husband with her friend, a gorgeous woman who was about half my age. Half his age. Blonde. Thin. Perfectly made up and decked out in designer clothes. She had one of those Hollywood faces—lips plumped just the right amount, suspiciously high cheekbones. Zero wrinkles on her forehead. She was stunning. And everything that I wasn't.

What's her name? I could barely type the words.

Cynthia.

Second sight, indeed. I had never seen this coming.

I thought we were in it to win it, John and me. We had it all. We were best friends. We made each other laugh every day and rolled like thunder under the covers at night. Even after twenty-five years. Sure, we had arguments from time to time like any couple does, but we usually ended up laughing by the end of it.

I just sat there in our screened-in porch, not knowing what else to do after seeing my husband in photos with this other woman, until he came home. Only an hour or so had passed, but it seemed like an eternity. It was, in fact, a lifetime.

"Oh, there you are," he had said, finding me on the porch. "What do you think about dinner? Do you want to go out? I have a hankering for a chicken sandwich."

I wanted nothing more than to go out to that dinner. I wanted nothing more than to not know what I knew. All I had to do was push myself to my feet, smile and kiss him as I always did when he came home, and pretend. I could put this genie back in the bottle by acting like it didn't exist.

But I didn't.

I said the first thing that came to my mind. "Are you leaving me, John?"

"Leaving you? To go where? What are you talking about?"

"I know."

There was silence then. Just for a second, an instant that went back and forth in time through our entire life together. From the beginning of our relationship all the way to the end of it.

A silence that encompassed every happy moment, every stolen kiss, every bit of laughter we had ever shared . . . and every tough time, too. All the times I had cried in his arms, all the frustration he had ever expressed to me and me alone, every grief-filled hour we had stood strong together as our parents left this earth, one by one. All the "for better and for worse" that decades together dishes out, the gift of true partnership.

But it also encompassed every evening he had claimed to be working late. Every trip he had taken for work and manufactured a reason to not take me. Every weekend he had gone golfing with the boys while I never suspected a thing.

I knew it was all true.

"Know what?" he said weakly, knowing damn well what.

I turned the phone over and over in my hand. A tear escaped my eye, and I whisked it away. "A woman reached out to me today."

He shook his head. "What woman?" I could see the life drain from his eyes. His face flushed.

"Someone named Julie. The best friend of the woman you've been seeing for two years."

Again, shaking his head. "Cass," he said, smiling slightly. "That's crazy. *Seeing?* I mean, come on. That's insane."

I held out my phone. "She sent pictures."

He stared at my phone as though it were on fire. His face, which had reddened, was now ashen.

He pulled out a chair from the table where we had enjoyed dinner together so many nights, the breeze wafting around us, and sat down, hard. He ran a hand through his hair.

We sat in silence for a moment, both of us realizing this was a watershed. A point in time we could never undo.

"I'm going to Wharton," I said finally. I hadn't planned to say it, or to do it, but something was speaking through me at that moment. It was exactly what I needed to do.

I got to my feet and walked past him and into the main part of the house. The home we had made for ourselves. Where we had raised our son. Our shelter from the storm. Only now it was storming inside. Black, heavy clouds hung low in the rooms. Rain poured down, soaking the floors and the furniture. Fat raindrops tinkled off the crystal decanters on the sideboard. Lightning sizzled and hit the kitchen wall. Thunder shook the foundations.

Somehow, I made my way up to our bedroom through the wind and the rain, lightning striking the stairs as I stepped, and packed an overnight bag. I stared at it for a moment and then dug out my big suitcase and started throwing more clothes into it.

It's not like it is in the movies, with love turning into strength and determination as women stalk out of their houses . . . or stay to burn their husband's clothes in a bonfire and rise like a phoenix from those ashes while an anthem about survival plays in the background.

No, it's the quiet desperation of knowing the person you loved most in the world did the impossible. It's the little voice telling you that you might be the cause of it. Everything inside you wants it not to be true. Somehow, it will be revealed to be a big mistake because, really, how could the impossible happen?

When I looked at John from across the room, he seemed very far away. Almost blurry, in the distance, as I thought all this. He was still the sweet, funny, wickedly intelligent, optimistic man with the deepest voice I had ever heard, the broadest shoulders I had ever seen, and a smile so bright it would make the sun itself hang its head in shame.

I dragged my big suitcase down the stairs and out to the car. He followed me, and I knew he was standing on the edge of the driveway, on the edge of our lives, watching me pull away from our home. But I couldn't bear to look at my husband in the rearview mirror.

I shook that memory out of my head and got to my feet. It was not the time. I was in Nonna's room to find something, anything, to explain this current mystery, not to lament over my life, now in shambles. I cleared my throat and scanned the room.

"I should just get to it," I said aloud, to Nonna, if to nobody else.

And so I got to it. I looked under the bed—nothing except a couple of dusty shoeboxes containing only shoes. I opened her closet and, faced with her familiar dresses and blouses, felt the urge to gather them into my arms and hold them close. I looked on the shelves—the hatboxes contained hats, the plastic storage tubs contained clothes.

Frustrated, I sat back down on the vanity bench with a thud. "You were an old Italian woman. You're telling me you didn't have a secret stash of *something*?" I chuckled at the thought of it.

But then my eyes were drawn to her jewelry box. A metal affair with intricate swirls carved into its lid, not typical of the delicate jewelry boxes usually associated with women of a certain age. This, instead, looked like it was built to withstand a fire.

What better place to store secrets?

I took a deep breath and opened the lid. My grandmother didn't have much jewelry . . . only a few pairs of no-nonsense earrings, a necklace or two, and—my heart squeezed—the bracelet I had given her many years before she died. A few brooches. A well-used strand of rosary beads. They all sat on the black velvet bottom of the box. But then I had a thought. Was it really the bottom? That was an awfully sturdy box for a few pieces of jewelry. I ran my fingers around the edges, and sure enough, it was removable.

I lifted it up, careful not to disturb the jewelry atop it, and saw that it was, indeed, a false bottom. Below it, a small latch.

I clicked it open and lifted it up.

Inside was a stack of black-and-white photographs that sat on an envelope.

I took a deep breath and picked up the photos, careful to touch only the outside edges.

The first showed a beautiful young woman with long, dark, wavy hair, leaning against a heavy wooden door on a stone house. The door was rounded on the top and had a leaded-glass window. She was wearing a simple white dress tied at the waist with a sash. Her hair was blowing in an unseen breeze, and she was laughing. I could see the twinkle in her eyes. My great-grandmother Violetta.

But it was the second photo that caused me to gasp. It was the same young woman, with a man, sitting on a stone wall. He was blazingly handsome, with curly, dark hair. His arm was around her, lovingly, protectively. Behind them, a meadow, where sheep were grazing. At their feet, a big, shaggy white dog.

My eyes glanced up at the painting on Nonna's wall and back down to the photo. Was it the same place? It had to be.

I turned the photo over and saw the words that would send me on a journey across the sea.

Violetta Rossi and Giovanni Moretti, Santo Stefano, April 1910.
So he did exist. Here was the proof. But . . . Santo Stefano? I had never heard of that town. My grandmother had said the painting on her wall depicted her mother's birthplace, and the photo certainly resembled the painting. It was the same place, I was sure of it. But . . . Rossi? I hadn't heard that name in any connection with my family.

The other photo showed her with an older woman—her mother?—inside what looked to be a shop of some kind. Glass bottles sat on wooden shelves; candles burned, illuminating the room. A wooden sign hung on the wall. IL MIELE DI ROSSI. "Rossi's Honey."

I thought about that for a moment, but then it made perfect sense. Violetta had sold "sundries" out of her boardinghouse, and my grandma Gia had run a greenhouse for years, selling flowers, plants, vegetables, herbs . . . and honey. The bees. A skill passed down? It had to be.

I set the photos aside, picked up the envelope, and removed the paper folded inside, careful not to rip or otherwise damage it. At first, I didn't quite understand what I was seeing. I squinted at the years-worn script.

Comune di Santo Stefano

Abruzzo

Italia

Atto di Morte

1911, 07 Ottobre

Violetta Moretti

Causa della morte: Stregoneria

I blinked a couple of times. My Italian was pretty rusty—almost nonexistent, actually, except for the words my grandmother had taught me. But I knew I was looking at a death certificate for Violetta, dated before my grandmother was born.

And the cause of death was listed as . . . witchcraft?

CHAPTER 3

Cassandra

"Can you come over here? To the house?" I was on the phone with my cousin Maria. "I know it's late, but I found something that you really should see."

"Late? It's seven thirty. You're turning into your mother."

This made me chuckle. She was so right.

Maria went on. "What is it? Can't you tell me now?"

"No, I want you to look at something. If you think we had a mystery before . . ."

"Oh no." I heard her take a breath. "I'll be right there. Should I bring some wine?"

I smiled. "Well, that's a silly question."

"I know. What was I thinking. Red?"

"I've got some biscotti."

And she hung up.

Wharton's not a big place, so in under ten minutes, I heard Maria rapping on the kitchen door. Her family home was just a few blocks from mine, and she had been staying there of late, just as I had been staying in mine.

I opened the door and, after a quick hug and kiss on the cheek, she whooshed in, carrying two bottles of Italian red from Montepulciano.

Our family always had it on holidays. I smiled and raised my eyebrows. "Two?"

She shrugged. "I thought we might need them."

I motioned to the booth in the kitchen, where I had set up two stemless wineglasses, a plate of biscotti, and the box I had found in Nonna's room.

We slipped into the booth, and she poured the rich red into the glasses. She and I dipped our biscotti into our wine, as our family always did after a meal, and took a bite before saying anything. That was the way of it in our family. Before saying anything important, we eat a little something.

It seemed ritualistic, what we were doing. Drinking the wine. Dipping the biscotti. Just as our family had always done. Almost as if we were consecrating the moment.

"Okay, so what's this?" she said, pointing her biscotti at the box. "It's what you wanted me to see?"

I nodded and finished my bite. "I found it in Nonna's room."

Maria raised her eyebrows and grinned. "You had the nerve to go in there?"

This brought a smile to my face, too.

I opened the box, drew out the photos, and set them in front of her. "Look who I found."

She squinted at the photo of Violetta and Giovanni, then turned it around and read the writing on the back. She shook her head and smiled.

"There's the proof right there," she said, her voice almost a whisper. I could tell she was in the photograph with them, our great-grandparents. "There you are, sir."

"It doesn't explain why we can't find any records of him, but a Giovanni Moretti certainly existed in our great-grandmother's life."

She nodded and gazed back down into the photo. "Holy cats, he was handsome," she said. "And her! Stunning." She turned her eyes to me. "Cass, you look just like her."

I waved my hand as if to whisk away the compliment. "Oh, I do not," I said. I could feel my face reddening.

"Yes, you do," she said, flapping the photo in the air. "You have the same face. If you wore your hair like that, you'd be a dead ringer for Violetta."

She fished a small mirror out of her purse and held it up to my face, along with the photograph. I looked from my reflection to that of my great-grandmother and back again. Maria was right. I could see the resemblance to the young Violetta. I hadn't when she was alive.

"Maybe a little," I said.

"Yeah, yeah," she said, smiling. "You know, I'll bet that's why Nonna took such a shine to you. You reminded her of her mother."

"I don't know if she took a shine—"

Maria shook her head. "Don't be silly. You were her favorite. We all knew it."

Memories threatened to flood back. Listening to Nonna's stories. I'd have loved nothing more than to sit with my cousin and reminisce about our grandmother and our mothers, but I had one more piece of information to show her. I pulled the death certificate out of the envelope and laid it on the table.

As she read it, the expression on her face went from expectant to concerned to confused, almost in an instant.

"What does this mean?" she asked.

I shrugged. "I have no idea. We know for a fact Violetta didn't die in October of 1911, because Nonna wasn't born until 1912."

"And we both knew her, for goodness' sake. She had a whole life here in Wharton. She didn't die in Italy as a young woman. She died here. As a very old woman." Maria set her wineglass on the table, as if punctuating her statement.

I let out a sigh. "What do you make of the cause of death?"

Maria squinted at the certificate. "*Strega . . . ,*" she said, as if turning the word over in her mind. "Does that mean what I think it means?"

"Yes, it does. 'Witch.' My Italian isn't what it should be, but I think this says Violetta died of witchcraft."

We sat in silence for a moment, each dunking biscotti into our wine.

"I can't even begin to make sense of that," she said finally. "It's ridiculous. One, she didn't die there. Two, if she did, it sure as hell wasn't because of witchcraft."

"And what does it mean, anyway? Witchcraft. That a witch put a curse on her? Which, okay, c'mon. Or that she was one?"

Maria shook her head. "This was modern day," she said. "The 1900s. It's not like it was the Middle Ages. They didn't persecute witches in 1911." Then, a short pause. "Did they?"

"No. Of course not." But I wasn't so sure. It sounded unlikely, but I really didn't know. Certainly not in large cities, but in small towns?

"None of it makes any sense," I said.

As I said it, the truth of it, the enormity of that statement wrapped itself around me.

It wasn't just this mystery about the women in my family. Nothing made sense in my life. That was the real problem.

Me living in the house where I grew up instead of the one where I had raised my own son. It was crazy. I was a grown woman with a family of my own, but there I was, staying in my old childhood room.

My parents were gone—how could two such powerful presences, people who filled up a room when they walked into it, just not exist anymore? How could everyone but me who had populated this house over the years—Nonna, Marco, my parents, even our dogs—have just disappeared?

How could everything in my childhood have vanished with time? All the joy and the bustle and the laughter in this house? Gone.

And how could my husband have—my throat seized up at the thought of it. How could John have been with another woman? How crazy and unbelievable was that?

It felt like I had no control over anything in my life anymore. That things were just happening *to* me, not *because* of me, not *by* me. Just happening around me while I watched as my whole world burned.

Nothing makes sense.

A tear slipped from my eye and I brushed it away.

All at once, I knew that there was one thing I could do. One thing I could control.

Before I could say the words, Maria broke my train of thought. "We may be as far as we can go with this. I mean, we know Violetta didn't die in Italy in 1911. We know she lived here in Wharton. So did Nonna. So did our mothers. So do we. Maybe that's all we need to know."

"But this witch thing," I said. "And the weird death and birth certificates. And Giovanni! I feel like there's too much here, we're too far in, to just let this go now."

Maria smiled at me. "Ever the reporter with a story."

And there it was. She had just tied up my crazy idea in a nice, big bow.

"I think there may be a way we could get some more answers," I said. "Not everything is online."

Maria furrowed her brow. "What do you mean? You're not thinking—"

I grinned at her. "I *am* thinking. What if I went to this Santo Stefano? There would have to be town records. Church records."

My cousin looked at me for a long time. "You want to go to Italy to find out what happened to our great-grandmother."

"I do. I think. And what you said about a story? I could probably convince my editor to let me investigate this and write a feature about it. Everybody is doing this ancestry thing right now. It might be a hot topic to cover."

"The paper won't pay for it, though, right?"

"Oh, Lord no," I said, chuckling. "But I think I may have a way around that, too."

We sat there for a moment, both running the idea through our minds. "I wish I could go with you," she said.

I raised my eyebrows. "Can you?" The idea of doing this with Maria sounded wonderful to me.

She shook her head. "I don't have much time off left this year, and I'm using it to go see the twins at school next month."

So, it would just be me, then. Trying to unearth our family history on my own. I felt a shiver go up my spine. Anticipation mixed with . . . what? A little fear? Did I really want to do this alone?

"Frankly, I could use a getaway," I said, surprising even myself.

She reached over the table, took hold of my hand, and squeezed. "Yes, you could, honey. And some time in Italy? How bad could that be? Even if you don't find anything, come up totally empty handed, who cares? You're in Italy."

I smiled at her. It sounded . . . real. Like it could actually happen.

"I think you should go," she said.

I shrugged. "I do, too. I think. But . . . alone? I'm not sure."

"What, alone? You'll be in Italy. Nobody is ever alone there. Certainly not our family."

Maria refilled our wineglasses and held hers aloft.

"If you're really doing this, then *buon viaggio*, Cassandra!"

Clink

"To Violetta and Giovanni."

Clink

"*La famiglia!*"

Clink

❧

Later that night, after Maria had gone and I had cleaned up the kitchen, I started researching flights to Italy . . . and winced at the price tag. If I wanted to go now, which I did, it would cost more than a few Roman coins in a fountain.

I had always chuckled to myself when characters on television shows or movies or in books needed to go somewhere immediately and just waltzed onto a flight at the last minute, oblivious to the cost. Never a mention of sticker shock. In the real world, it didn't work that way. Even an economy seat would cost more than I was comfortable shelling out on a moment's notice. I couldn't afford it on my budget.

I picked up my phone and hit John's number on speed dial.

After we had exchanged a few strained pleasantries, I got down to the reason I had called. "I'd like to use some of your frequent-flier miles for a trip I'm thinking of taking," I said.

He was quiet for a moment. "What trip?"

I explained the whole thing to him. An abbreviated version. I told him I was looking into a family mystery involving my grandmother and her mother.

"I may be able to write about it for the paper," I added. "An ancestry research angle."

"We always wanted to go to Italy together," he said finally. I could hear the regret in his voice.

It had been a dream of ours to go to Venice. Florence. Siena. Rome. Somehow, with the business of raising a son and building our careers, we hadn't ever made it happen. We said we'd do it when we were empty nesters and had time. Funny how that had worked out. Or, more appropriately, hadn't. We were now empty nesters. Only I wasn't sure we even had a nest anymore.

"I'll text you my frequent-flier number," he said. "You go. You deserve it. First class. I've got so many points, I don't know what to do with them all. And get yourself a fancy hotel room in Rome for a few nights when you get there. You deserve that, too, Cassie. And a whole lot more."

His voice was so soft, so kind then. It brought me to tears, wishing. Wishing this debacle between us had never happened. Wishing he was a better man. Even wishing I didn't know what he had done. Wishing that woman had never contacted me. I wanted my old life back so much—but it was just my heartbreak talking. My mind knew the life I wanted back so badly, the life I thought we had, wasn't real. At least for the two years before our split. And maybe long before that.

"And use our Mastercard for everything," John went on. "I'll pay the bill."

I knew that was his guilt talking. But I'd take it.

The next few days were a flurry of activity. John had always used to joke that I was a travel agent at heart, and I had to admit I enjoyed prepping for the trip.

First, I had a couple of phone calls to make.

My editor was astonished I'd actually be taking some time off—I had so much PTO accumulated it had stopped accruing—but was generally supportive of the story angle I'd be pursuing as long as I knew the paper wasn't paying for the trip.

My son, Henry, was a bit more taken aback. Even more taken aback than when I had told him his father and I were separating. I hadn't given him any specifics—I didn't believe, and still don't, that kids, no matter how old, should know the gory details behind a parental breakup—but my gut told me he had an inkling of the reason why I was relocating to Wharton for a while.

But the news of my trip came as a surprise.

"What do you mean, Italy?" he said. "By yourself?"

"Yeah," I said. "Your aunt Maria and I have uncovered somewhat of a mystery about Nonna and her mother, Violetta, and I just feel like I want to go over there and see if I can find out anything more."

He was silent for a moment. Then: "I think it's a great idea, Mom."

That was unexpected. "You do?"

"I do. Go, and have the time of your life. Eat pasta at every meal. Hell, drink wine at every meal. Even breakfast. You deserve it, Mama." His voice had cracked a little at the use of his childhood name for me.

Kids know more, see more, understand more than you think they do.

That handled, I spent some time researching Santo Stefano online and was entranced by the cobblestone roads and buildings of the same stone, the mysterious tunnels and archways, and the friendly central piazza where people gathered. It looked to me like something out of *Game of Thrones*, or Middle-Earth, but certainly not of modern times. It was as though time itself had no effect on the place.

I found the one and only hotel in town, which they called an *albergo diffuso*, which translates roughly to a dispersed hotel. I learned that it wasn't a hotel proper, not as we think of them. Instead, it had a main office, and the rooms were separate units dispersed throughout the village. Some were rooms in what had been the main castle that the town had been built around, and others were scattered here and there in what had once been private dwellings.

The owner of the place had apparently come in and bought several empty buildings, along with the castle itself, in the 1970s, when the town had more or less dwindled into disrepair. It had sparked a renaissance of tourism, with people wanting the experience of being pulled out of time, seeing what it was like to live back in the Middle Ages.

I composed an email asking about availability, took a deep breath, and hit Send.

A response came a few hours later. Ciao! Yes! We'll be happy to have you. What are the exact dates?

I was really doing this.

I reserved one of the units for a month, with an option to stay longer, not knowing exactly how much time I would need.

Then, I booked my flight—first class, thank you—and a stay in Rome to manage the jet lag and, frankly, to eat my way through the Eternal City. I reserved a rental car that I would pick up back at the Rome airport when I was ready to head to Santo Stefano—I knew better than to try to drive out of Rome proper.

Next, I called my cell provider and ordered international coverage for a month and found international health insurance just in case something happened over there. I made sure my passport was in order and even ran to the mall in Salmon Bay to get some new outfits to wear. I couldn't possibly be swanning around Italy in my old mom jeans and T-shirts.

I was all set. It was really happening.

I had never traveled anywhere by myself. Not even an overnight at a nearby spa. But something inside me told me it was time for a solo adventure. A time for a new beginning. A time to shake off my sadness—I had been moping around for months—head back to my roots, and dive into my family's past, to uncover our history. And maybe rediscover myself in the process.

I could almost hear my grandmother saying it.

Buon viaggio, Cassandra. Buon viaggio.

CHAPTER 4

Cassandra

I had never taken a first-class international flight. Was it worth the money? On John's dime, absolutely. I was surprised to find I had my own little pod to myself on the plane, with a large flat-screen television, a seat that folded all the way down into a bed, a gift bag of slippers, fancy headphones, even a toothbrush and toothpaste, in addition to a full-fledged duvet and real pillow. Champagne and chocolates even before the plane took off. *I could get used to this,* I thought. I must admit to quite enjoying the pampering. I was usually the one making sure everyone else was comfortable.

On the way, I brushed up on my Italian, did a bit more research into the region where I'd be spending most of my time, and figured out what I was going to see and do in Rome before I headed to Santo Stefano. Then, after watching a movie, I settled in with my slippers, pillow, and blanket and caught a few winks.

I had a jumbled dream with Nonna, Violetta, my mom, and two women I didn't know, all talking at once around my parents' kitchen table. They were speaking in Italian, but, as happens in dreams, I could understand what they were saying.

"Cassandra is coming to find you," Nonna said.

"It's so tangled and complicated," Violetta said.

"She's a good girl. She'll get all of this straightened out."

I woke up with just a few minutes to spare as we touched down. Da Vinci–Fiumicino Airport was busy and bustling—everyone was dressed snappier than I was, even the toddlers—but I didn't worry much about that as I found my way to the baggage claim. Once I had collected my suitcase, I saw a young man in a black suit holding a sign.

Signora Cassandra Graves

My heart swelled, just a little. A bit of familiarity so far from home. I smiled and raised my hand, and the driver came over and scooped up my bags.

"Benvenuti a Roma!" he said, flashing a killer smile.

I settled into the back of the car. Maybe we'd pass by some of Rome's famous landmarks on the way to the hotel. I was looking forward to a leisurely drive.

It was anything but. I had heard about Roman drivers, but nothing could've prepared me for the amusement park roller coaster of a ride that was our "leisurely drive" to the hotel. Tailgating closer than I'd thought was physically possible, we weaved in and out of speeding traffic on the highway like we were on our way to a hospital with someone giving birth in the back seat.

Once in the city, the ride turned into the likes of a video game, with the car racing down ancient roads no wider than one car length (yet there was two-way traffic), careening into tiny alleyways to avoid stoplights, up and down hills (we were airborne several times), and we even backed up a full city block into oncoming traffic on a one-way street at one point. When the car screeched to a stop in front of my hotel, I let out a breath I hadn't realized I had been holding most of the way.

Benvenuti a Roma, indeed.

My hotel, with a soaking tub on my own private balcony overlooking the city, more than soothed my frazzled, travel-weary nerves.

After a meal of the best *cacio e pepe* I'd ever eaten in my life, even though my grandmother had often made this rustic, simple dish of pasta with black pepper, pecorino cheese, and a bit of pasta water (sorry, Nonna), I slipped into the steaming tub with a glass of cold white Italian wine and gazed out past the vined terrace on my balcony to the twinkling lights of the city below.

I wished I had someone to toast with, to clink glasses and marvel at the fact we were actually in Rome, the Eternal City. Referred to as *Imperium sine fine* by the ancient poet Virgil in *The Aeneid*, it meant "the empire with no end," signifying the belief that even if the Roman Empire fell—which it eventually did—the city would still stand. Which it had.

As I soaked in the tub and sipped the delicious trebbiano, looking out over this incredible city, I reflected on this belief. It could be said to describe the resilient heart of the Italian people and, I hoped, my own heart as well.

No matter what comes, the ups and downs of life, the triumphs and the tragedies, the heartbreak and the happiness, the heart still stands. My heart would still stand. Even alone.

~ ❧ ~

The next day I was in full-on tourist mode. I had made reservations for the Vatican and Colosseum tours, so after a breakfast of pastries, cheese, and salami and the most velvety, satisfying cappuccino I had ever had (this would become a familiar refrain when eating or drinking anything in Italy), I pulled on my all-too American sneakers, jeans, and a crisp white shirt—and wound a floral scarf around my neck for a little Italian flair—and headed out to see a couple of the wonders of the world.

My tour group at the Vatican crept its way from room to room in the museum to the highlight of the tour, the Sistine Chapel. It was smaller than I had imagined it would be, but the ceiling and walls were worthy of the silent reverence that fell upon us as we entered the space.

Shoulder-to-shoulder tourists, all looking up with their jaws dropped, in stunned silence at the miracle that is Michelangelo's masterpiece. Nobody said, or whispered, anything. Nobody took photos. Nobody breathed. If evidence of divine inspiration is anywhere on this earth, it is in that room.

I reached for John's hand too many times to count.

After a lunch of pasta carbonara—one of the dishes Rome is known for that nearly brought me to tears with its utter cheesy, salty, velvety deliciousness—I walked down the long street between the Palatine and Capitoline Hills, past the Roman Forum, and all the way to the Colosseum.

Climbing up the seemingly endless steps, I stood overlooking the interior and said a silent prayer for those who had perished there, and also for those who had cheered it on. Both of those groups needed help, it seemed to me.

That night, as I soaked in the tub again, I thought about my game plan. From the airport, where I would pick up my rental car, it was a little more than two hours to Santo Stefano, highway driving all the way.

My phone ringing startled me out of my plannings. I had the phone perched on the ledge of the soaking tub, next to a couple of candles that were flickering in the dark Roman night.

"*Ciao, bella.*" It was Maria, her voice sounding so close. My heart squeezed a little. As wonderful and awe inspiring as all of this was, it would have been better if I had had her to share it with.

"Hey," I said, my voice catching.

"Well? What do you think? How was your first day?"

"It's unbelievable," I said. "Everything I imagined it would be, and more."

"Our ancestral homeland," she said. "You did the Vatican and Colosseum today?"

"I got my steps in, I'll say that," I said, enjoying the warm water soothing my aching feet. I was secretly glad I had worn sensible shoes.

"When in Rome," Maria said.

"And ate my full body weight in pasta carbonara," I said, taking a sip of wine. "So I was glad for all the walking. And you never told me how many ancient, crumbling steps there are in the Colosseum. I kept imagining people in togas and sandals trying to climb up to the top."

She was quiet for a moment. "Are you sure you're okay, though? All by yourself?"

She knew me so well. "It's fine. If a little lonely here."

"What, you haven't found some beautiful Italian guy to take your mind off things?"

That hadn't even occurred to me, frankly, although the city was indeed full of handsome men who were better dressed than I'd ever be. I'd certainly noticed that.

"Not yet," I said, looking down at my bare left hand. I had taken my wedding ring off when I moved into the house in Wharton. It didn't seem to signify much anymore.

"I'm sure it'll be better once you get to the village," Maria went on. "Rome is full of tourists and really busy all the time. But where you're going, it's a smaller town with a slower pace. And people know you're coming, right?"

She was right about that. I had spoken on the phone with Lorenzo, the man who ran the hotel where I'd be staying.

"One person, at least," I said.

"I wonder if Nonna and Violetta know you're there," Maria said, her voice soft. "And our moms."

Evoking our family's names there, in that place where our heritage ran deep, was a powerful incantation. It made me think about my dream on the plane. Maybe they did know I was coming.

Later, as I crawled into bed, snuggled down, and pulled the fluffy duvet up to my chin, I thought about why I was in Italy in the first place. Yes, being the awed tourist in Rome had been a fun day. A necessary day. You don't come to Italy without seeing Rome, at least once. There was too much world history, ancient history, to not experience it for yourself.

But I was here to delve into my own history. Maria's. Her children's. My son's. And it was time I got to it.

Early the next morning, I packed up and took a taxi to the Roma Termini train station, a big, bustling affair with more than two dozen gates, confused tourists walking every which way. I boarded a train to the airport, where I'd pick up my rental car.

Keys in hand, I found the car I had reserved . . . and was astonished when I saw the size of it. I figured I could kick it over onto its side if necessary.

Okay, I told myself. Everyone in Italy had a little car like this, didn't they? I settled into the peashooter, popped the key into the ignition, set my water bottle into the holder between the seats . . . and noticed the stick shift. To my horror, I realized the car had a manual transmission—something I hadn't driven in many years. The last thing I wanted was to be relearning how to shift on an Italian freeway.

Minor glitch, I told myself. I'd just switch it out for another vehicle with an automatic transmission. Maybe I could find a bigger car while I was at it.

I slipped out of the car and went back to the rental office, where the same young man who had given me the keys was on the phone, speaking in rapid-fire Italian. He smiled at me and put up a finger, telling me without words he'd be right with me.

"Everything fine? With the auto?" His English was shaky at best.

"No," I said, fishing my phone out of my purse and hitting the Translator app. *"L'auto ha un cambio manuale."*

He furrowed his brow. Was the translator not accurate? But I went on, asking if he had a car with an automatic transmission.

"Hai delle auto con cambio automatico?"

He nodded, and I was flooded with relief. The feeling was short-lived.

"No," he said in English. "Only manual. Is okay? You can drive?"

I had owned a stick-shift car in college, so way back when, in the far reaches of my memory, I had once been proficient at driving a stick. But it had been decades.

"Is okay," I said, managing a smile. "I can drive."

Back in the car, I groaned aloud and put my head down on the steering wheel. I don't know if it was the jet lag or the loneliness of traipsing around the Vatican and Colosseum all by myself when I had dreamed for so many years about seeing those wonders of the world with my husband, or even the stark slap in the face of soaking in a romantic hot tub on my Roman balcony without John *or anyone* to share it with—but I lost it. I dissolved into tears. Right there in the parking garage.

It was one thing to live alone in my childhood home, where I was the mistress of everything. Every rock, every tree, every store, every person in Wharton enveloped me with not just familiar memories of the past but a feeling of belonging in the present and a definite home for the future.

In Italy, everything was new and unfamiliar. If I had had a partner to share the experience with, discovering all the newness might have been a fun adventure. But at that moment, I just felt alone. Small and alone and confused and incapable. Had John been with me, he would've slipped behind the wheel of this impossibly tiny car, and we would've taken off with no problems whatsoever. Probably laughed about the smallness of the car in relation to our big SUV at home.

But there I was, by myself, having to reach back decades to the last time I had driven a manual transmission car and realizing I was about to head out onto the Indy 500 that is an Italian freeway in a vehicle I wasn't exactly sure how to drive. It felt like too much.

My last straw was apparently a tiny tin-can car with a manual transmission in the parking garage of an Italian airport.

All the grief and anger I had been carrying around, suppressing as I went about my day-to-day life, came out of me. How was I here, in this car, without a partner to help me? How had I gotten to this point in my life? How did *my* husband, who was the other half of *my* perfect marriage, decide it was a *good idea* to get involved with another woman, leaving me alone here to have to figure everything out by myself and drive this car with a stick shift on this trip I was in the middle of *alone*? What had I been thinking?

In the end, when I didn't have any more tears to cry, I realized there was no choice but for me to just get on with it. I was here. And I— alone—had to put on my big-girl pants and make this work.

Tantrum over, I took a few deep breaths to calm down and considered my options. I knew there was no train to Santo Stefano. It was a hill town accessible only by car. I had researched that before I left the States. There was a train going to a city nearer to Santo Stefano than I was in Rome, but that journey required changing trains several times and took a full day. Driving from Rome would take only two hours. That's why I had decided, before I left Wharton, that I would make the trip by car.

Okay, I told myself. *If I'm going, I need to drive there. Right now. You can do this, Cassandra.*

Praying I had enough muscle memory of driving a stick to get me through this without killing myself or others, I blew my nose, took a sip of water, pushed in the clutch, started the car, and put that baby in reverse. I took a few practice laps inside the garage before unleashing myself onto the actual roadway.

After a few halting stops and starts, I remembered the fluid magic motion of easing up on the clutch just enough with one foot and giving it enough gas with the other to put a car into first gear. It was coming back to me. I cleared my throat, gripped the steering wheel with one hand and the gearshift with the other. I was as ready as I would ever be.

After about twenty harrowing minutes of driving, the Roman traffic eased up, the highways emptied out, and I was able to unclench my body, stop white-knuckling the steering wheel, and actually enjoy the scenery of rolling hills covered with pines, dramatic gorges over rivers, and towns perched atop what looked like mountains.

The farther I got from Rome, however, the more clouds rolled in, obscuring the dramatic views. The closer I got to Santo Stefano, the foggier it became, with sleet hitting my windshield in bursts.

But as I turned onto the mountain road that would lead me to my home for the coming month, I knew I had made it. I'd pushed through the loneliness and grief and frustration and fear, and I had done what I set out to do.

CHAPTER 5

Cassandra

The village was shrouded in fog, as though a weary cloud had sighed and settled in. I snaked my way up the winding single-lane mountain road—limestone-covered hills on one side, a sheer drop on the other—silently regretting this whole idea and hoping nothing, animal or human, would choose that moment to dart out into my path.

As the lonely road thankfully straightened out and gave way to houses and a storefront or two and finally what looked like a parking lot, I pulled to a stop and pried my hands off the steering wheel, my heart beating hard and fast.

You're here. You can do this.

I took a deep breath, opened the door, and slipped out of the car, squinting at my phone, which, oddly enough, still had service. I hadn't expected that. Not here.

I looked around. I had received instructions on how, exactly, to find the house where I'd be staying. It was part of the only hotel in this medieval town. But once I got there, everything looked the same. Heavy wooden doors and ancient windows peered out of thick limestone walls, every house just like the other, all connected in one long row of stone that snaked its way into the fog and disappeared. And now it was raining softly, the drops taken by an unwelcoming wind and swirling through the air.

The manager of the hotel had suggested I go right to the unit when I arrived instead of meeting him in the main office. Much easier that way, he had said. He had given me directions, but how many meters from the village parking lot to the front door? And . . . exactly how far was a meter? Was it about the same as a foot? My knowledge of the metric system was more than a bit . . . American.

Taking a few steps, I saw the house numbers were haphazard at best, 20 above one door, 37 above the next. I could see no street signs. Was I in the right place?

Yes, there was the post office that was noted on my directions, shuttered tight on such a day. And there was a restaurant I had seen in photos, but its strands of tiny lights wrapped around the curved archway of a door that had looked so inviting in photographs were now dark and silent, signaling that it, too, was closed.

I saw no other person as I walked down the ancient cobblestone streets, just a stray cat here and there before they flitted away, up stone steps that disappeared into the fog.

Dubbed one of the prettiest towns in Italy, Santo Stefano stood suspended out of time. It was a perfectly preserved medieval hill town complete with an ancient castle, although its tower was obscured by the fog when I arrived. I'd see it another day, I told myself.

The cobblestone streets, stone houses, archways, and tiny passageways with shops tucked into small corners were much the same as eight hundred years before, when the powerful Medici family had built up this place to access the heavenly wool from Apennine mountain sheep that grazed on the rocky hillside and the unique lentils that grew in the region.

Back in those days, Santo Stefano was a bustling merchant center, located on a trade route between the Adriatic and Rome. Drawn by the Medicis, traders came from all corners of the region and even the world, and soon the locals began selling other things—clothing and blankets, local honey (deemed the sweetest in the region), soaps, olive oils, wine. There were ebbs and flows over the years, the centuries, and a time of near total abandonment, but now the town was experiencing a renaissance.

In the summer months, Santo Stefano was teeming with tourists, many from other countries but mostly Italians themselves, who came to walk in the footsteps of their ancestors on the ancient streets, drink some delicious Abruzzo *vino*, and relax in the piazza in the center of town while stray cats approached shyly, then skittered away. That's what the guidebooks said, anyway.

But I wasn't thinking about any of that. I was thinking only about finding the house where I'd be staying and closing its door behind me. I wanted a cozy fire and bit of dinner and maybe a glass of wine. Certainly a glass of wine, after the drive I'd just had. People tell you about driving in Italy, but until you experience it, you never really know.

I buttoned up my jacket and shivered, the dampness seeping its way into my bones.

I walked up the empty street and through an archway, the sound of my footsteps disintegrating, seeping into the stones as I walked. Was I the only person in this entire village?

Then, finally, an open door. I hurried toward it and saw a man standing next to the hearth, lighting a fire.

He was tall and olive skinned, with dark hair and eyes, maybe forty years old, and wearing a puffy down jacket and a bright-blue scarf wrapped around his neck. When he saw me, his face lit up in a smile.

"Cassie Graves?"

Relief washed over me. I recognized him from the Zoom call we had had weeks ago. He was the manager of this place. I was where I was supposed to be. "Yes, it's me!" I said. "You're Lorenzo."

"Come in, come in, Cassie Graves," Lorenzo said, his Italian accent making music of the words. "Call me Renzo. All my friends do."

"Renzo," I said, passing through the ancient arched doorway. As I did so, I entered the past.

"*Benvenuto a casa!*" Renzo said, opening his arms wide. "Welcome home."

"*Grazie,*" I said, a bit of hesitancy faltering the word. I didn't know more than a few phrases in Italian but was determined to make the effort.

I had seen photos of this house—"dwelling" might be a better word—but they did not prepare me for the reality of this place.

The enormous arched wooden door looked like something you might find in a medieval church. Two shutters opened to reveal a pair of leaded-glass paned windows. A heavy black wrought-iron latch-and-lock arrangement assured me I'd be safe inside.

The main living area consisted of one large room with heavy, strong stucco walls and an arched ceiling, all of which were patterned with stones, almost as if the cobblestone had spilled into this room from the streets, run up the wall, and covered the ceiling. A huge wrought-iron light fixture hung from the ceiling, and two or three more were perched as sconces on the walls.

The queen-size bed, its iron headboard against one wall, was flanked by two small alcoves hewn out of the stone and stucco, both lit by lamps within. The deep yellow duvet covering the bed was fluffy and looked cozy. Pillows embroidered with a tapestry pattern in reds and blues and yellows completed the look.

On the opposite wall, a flat-screen television seemed oddly out of place. Or rather, out of time. But I was glad for it. The kitchen area consisted mainly of a terra-cotta-tiled countertop, a deep sink and a faucet, and a range unit with four burners.

"Let me show you how it works," Renzo said, pressing a black button on the range top. "It's tricky." I heard the hiss of gas and watched as he turned and pressed down on one of the dials. He held both the button and the dial down for a moment until the gas caught fire and flickered. He turned off the burner and smiled at me, a little sheepishly, I thought. "This button first, then the dial, then *whoosh*."

"Got it," I said.

He crossed the room and opened another heavy wooden door to reveal dishes and glasses and mugs for tea, silverware and utensils and pots and pans. Spices. Olive oil. Everything I might need.

A little fridge stood next to it, a half-size version of what looked to me like a fridge from the 1950s. Stark white with rounded edges and a silver handle to open it. I did and found a container of half-and-half, two bottles of wine, some yogurt, cheese, sliced deli meats. On top of the fridge sat a loaf of bread.

I turned and smiled at Renzo. "*Grazie!* This is so kind. You didn't have to do this."

"*Prego, prego,*" he said, using the common, all-purpose Italian word for "you're welcome" or "please" or "come in" or many other polite things. He smiled back at me. "I wanted to have a little something here for you when you arrived. Not everyone remembers to stop at the market down the hill in town before they make the drive up. There's a little deli up here that sells the basics, but no grocery store."

I hadn't stopped at the market, although now that I thought of it, I remembered he had said something about that in one of the emails we had exchanged. I hoped there was toilet paper, but of course there would be. This was part of the only hotel in town.

In the center of the room, a small wooden table, well used and scrubbed until it shone, was flanked by two chairs.

At the back of the room sat an enormous stone hearth, where the fire was already blazing. He showed me how to work a flue with a lever coming out of the wall. "Open," he said, and then pulled the lever down. "Closed." He pushed up the lever to open it again.

Next to the fireplace, a heavy wooden armoire and an overstuffed armchair with an ottoman.

Renzo led me through an archway to the left of the hearth, where I found a bathroom with what looked to be brand-new fixtures. It was stocked with a new toothbrush, toothpaste, and soap. And, much to my relief, a package of toilet paper. A vertical heater that looked something like a ladder stood tall against one wall, radiating warmth.

"Now, come see the masterpiece," he said, grinning and raising his eyebrows. Just past the bathroom, we entered a round stone room, almost like a cavern . . . if the cavern were in a high-end spa. There was a glass shower with a rainwater showerhead, and a huge, deep, free-standing whirlpool tub, flanked with alcoves that were lit from within. A stack of white, fluffy towels sat next to it.

I took a quick breath. "This is incredible." I was imagining how good it would feel to slip into that tub for a long soak.

"*Grazie mille!* We just finished it last week. My guys were determined to get it done before you arrived."

Excellent timing, I thought, knowing I'd use the tub often.

"How was the drive up the hill?" he asked as we made our way back to the main room.

I winced, remembering the twists and turns, the steep drops with no guardrails, the fog. It had been one of those experiences in which you think you absolutely cannot continue for another second, realize that you must, and so you do, with white-hot fear running through your veins.

Renzo let out a deep laugh. "That bad?"

"The fog made it more than a little . . . challenging."

He raised his eyebrows. "I'm used to that old road by now," he said. "I drive it nearly every day. But . . . being careful is wise. You never know what's out there, in the fog."

I shivered at the thought of it.

He looked around and frowned. "Your suitcase? You have one, no?"

"It's back in the car," I said. "I wanted to find where I was supposed to be before dragging it along the cobblestone."

He held out his hand. "Keys? I'll get it for you."

Was he seriously offering to get my suitcase? "Oh, no! You don't have to—"

He closed and opened his hand, beckoning for the keys. "Of course!"

I fished the keys out of my jacket pocket and tossed them to him, very glad to not have to go out of my cozy cave and back into the gloom. A few moments later, he was back, laden with my heavy suitcase and carry-on bag.

Thanking him, I took the smaller bag as he set my larger one by the bed.

"Nessun problema!" he said. He clapped his hands together. "Now, do you need anything else before I go?"

I thought about the emptiness of the town. *Another living soul would be nice,* I thought. "Do you think there's someplace open for dinner? It seemed like everything was closed when I got here."

He nodded and took his phone from his pocket, dialed, and put it to his ear. He began speaking in rapid Italian that I had no hope of understanding. Not the words, anyway. He shook his head and slipped his phone back into his pocket.

"No?"

"I'm sorry," he said. "Everything will be open tomorrow. The weather will be nicer, and you can explore the village. Did you see the stairs as you came from the parking lot?"

"I did," I said, remembering the wide stone steps that ascended into the fog.

"Up, up, up," he said, gesturing with one hand, "and you'll be in the piazza. Restaurants, shops. The hotel office is up there, too. Everything sort of fans out from the piazza, little streets and alleyways going every which way. La Oliva will be open for coffee and breakfast in the morning. It's a good place to start the day."

"I'll do that," I said as Renzo gathered up his things.

"For tonight," he said, crossing the room to the pantry and opening its door, "you might want to try this." He pulled out a small bag of what looked like soup mix and held it out to me, smiling.

I took it from him and saw that it was lentils, spices, and other dried ingredients.

"These lentils, very special to this region. Mix with water, simmer for a while. Quite good!"

It sounded perfect. "Just the thing for a night like this," I said.

We said our goodbyes then, and Renzo went out into the blustery night. He shut the door with a thud behind him. I locked it and turned around, leaning back against it. I took a deep breath.

Okay. I'm here. Now what?

"Now what" was dinner. I filled up a pot with water, per the soup mix package directions, and after several attempts managed to light the stove. Renzo was right—it was tricky. When the water came to a boil, I emptied the soup contents into the pot and stirred, turning down the flame to low. A savory, herby fragrance wafted through the air. It made me wonder when I had last eaten.

The soup had to simmer for about twenty minutes, so I busied myself unpacking. I opened the armoire to find it had a rod on one side and drawers on the other. I hung my shirts and sweaters and tucked away my panties, a couple of pairs of jeans, and my yoga pants in the drawers, lining up my shoes on the floor of the armoire. Then I transferred my makeup and other toiletries to the bathroom and laid out the necklaces and earrings I had brought with me in one of the little alcoves by the bed. I slid my computer and various cords onto the countertop, stashed my suitcase next to the armoire, and I was set.

I grabbed the loaf of bread on top of the little fridge, found a wooden cutting board, and sliced a few pieces, along with some hard cheese. I opened some wine and poured myself a glass. When the soup was done, I ladled some into a bowl and settled down at the table. My first dinner in Santo Stefano. It wasn't exactly pasta carbonara, but it tasted delicious.

As I dunked a piece of bread into the steaming soup, watching the flames dance in the fireplace, I brushed a tear from my cheek. I was surprised, a bit, that I could even conjure one up. I guessed being "cried out" wasn't a real thing after all.

The human heart has an immense capacity for sadness. But how much was too much? When would my weary heart simply sigh and lie down, giving in to the weight of it all? I don't know if a heart breaks so much as deflates when the sadness overpowers it. No strength to beat anymore.

I shook my head—*don't start*—and turned my thoughts to what had brought me to this tiny village, halfway across the world from my home.

I was here to find my family. And, maybe, a witch.

CHAPTER 6

Fiora

Nobody in Santo Stefano could remember exactly when the Rossi sisters came to the village, only that they had come on a day when the wind was stealing through the streets and alleyways and tunnels like a cat on the prowl. The whispers around town said the sisters hailed from Triora—people called it Italy's version of the infamous Massachusetts town of Salem—but that speculation came later, much later.

It was as if they had always been there. But, of course, that was not the case.

As the story went, the two beautiful, raven-haired sisters, Fiora and Florencia, baby Violetta, their patient donkey Giuseppe, who never so much as complained, and the big, white dog Freddo walked into town on that windy day and went directly to the office of the mayor to lay claim to a house they said was rightfully theirs.

The house, in the center of town just off the piazza, had belonged to their grandfather, they said, and they had produced a deed to prove it.

Everyone knew the house had been empty for a decade or more, since the death of Leonardo Leone, an old man of ill humor whose wife had passed a decade before that.

"Leonardo," the mayor had said, rubbing his chin, looking from the will to the sisters and back again. "He lived alone after his wife died. But had a daughter, as I recall."

"She ran off," someone piped up. "With a boy from Verona."

And that was good enough for the mayor, who was just happy to see the house occupied again, it being in the center of town. Not good to have it empty, right there, where traders from all corners of Europe and beyond had been conducting their business for hundreds of years.

Many of those traders and buyers and residents from ancient times were still there, roaming the alleyways of Santo Stefano, some looking like wisps of shadow, others casting a chill wind as they passed by, while others were like the flesh-and-blood versions of themselves until they would fade into the ether on foggy nights.

The Rossi sisters saw this immediately upon stepping foot in Santo Stefano, but it didn't stop them from settling there.

They knew how to keep them away. A broom above the door. Salt sprinkled on the windowsills. Charms to ward off evil spirits. They knew you could never be too careful. Never think those old folktales of demons and spirits and faeries weren't true. The Rossi sisters knew strangeness could lurk around every ordinary corner.

That handled, they turned the front room of the house into a shop, where they sold the soaps and oils and herbs they had brought with them from wherever they had come.

Soon, Fiora and Florencia constructed beehives in the wildflower field by the lake and eventually began selling honey in their shop as well.

They would throw open the heavy wooden front door to their house and receive the women of the village, who would come for the honey and the spicy-smelling soaps and fragrant oils.

"Drip some of this in your bath tonight," Fiora had said to the mayor's wife. "It will help soothe that sore knee of yours."

And she did. And it did. And soon the women of the village were coming to the Rossi sisters for more than just the fragrant soaps.

One afternoon, Fiora was labeling jars of honey when a woman entered the shop. She was young and blonde and was wearing a dress with a smart blue-and-white pattern. Angelina Martinelli, Fiora knew. Married to one of the most gifted stonemasons in town. She had seen Angelina at the market and in the piazza, but they had never formally met.

She nodded at Fiora and began browsing around, running her fingers along the shelves of honey and soaps and candles as though she was looking for something in particular.

"Can I help you find something, Signora Martinelli?" Fiora asked, wiping her hands on her apron.

"Oh, you know me?"

Fiora smiled. "Of course. I also know your husband does fine work."

Angelina nodded, eyeing up Fiora, seeming to weigh something in her mind. "Snoring," she said finally.

Fiora wrinkled her nose. "Excuse me?"

"My husband snores," Angelina confided. "It's keeping me up at night. I'm wondering—do you have anything for that?"

Fiora knew just the thing. "I do," she said, pushing herself up to her feet and making her way through the room to the pantry, where several dozen glass jars sat on wooden shelves. She pulled out a jar containing small seeds. She held it aloft. "Cardamom. It's difficult to find here. We bought this from traders in Venice, who had come from the far east."

She sprinkled some of the seeds into a sauté pan and heated them up for a moment, shaking the pan so the seeds wouldn't burn to the bottom. Their fragrance soon filled the room.

Angelina sniffed the air. "It smells . . ."

Fiora smiled. "Mysterious? It does. I think so, too. It's hard to describe. Citrusy, but also like the forest."

Angelina nodded. "That's it! You bought it from traders, you say?"

"Yes," Fiora said. "It's used widely in Scandinavia in baking—breads and cookies and the like. But it also works for snoring."

She cooled the seeds in the air for a moment, then poured them into a stone bowl and ground them into a powder with a pestle made of the same stone.

She opened a jar of honey and poured the powdered seeds into it, whispering a few words that Angelina could not hear. She added a spoon or two of olive oil, mixed it up, and set the spoon on the table with an air of finality.

"Put a spoonful or two in your husband's tea at night—"

"He's not much of a tea drinker, I'm afraid," Angelina said.

Fiora shrugged. "You can dissolve it in hot water as well. Does he know he snores and you'd like it to stop?"

Angelina smiled, tucking a stray tendril of blonde hair behind her ear. "We laugh about it. But yes, I've complained enough."

"He sounds like a good man," Fiora said. "You ask him to try some tea before bed, with this in it."

Fiora screwed the lid onto the jar and held it out to Angelina. "It's also good for sore throats. Colds. And coughs. Anything with the nose and the airways. But always dissolve it in hot water and drink it as a tea."

Angelina took the jar and tucked it into her bag. "Thank you," she said. "I'll do that. And I'll be back."

Fiora laughed as the woman was leaving the shop. "It's also an aphrodisiac. Be advised!"

She looked over her shoulder and smiled. "Oh, no, that's the last thing he needs. Thanks for the warning."

A short while later, Florencia came through the back door, Violetta at her heels. The girl was carrying a basket of wildflowers.

"We were out on the hills, picking all of these," Florencia said, waving a hand at the basket. She pulled out a chair from the table and sank into it. "The fields are filled with flowers. I really like this place. Do you?"

It had been several months since the day of their arrival, and the sisters hadn't yet talked about their intentions to stay. Or go.

Fiora had had her doubts in the beginning, but now? "I like it, too," she said. "The people are good here. Kind."

"The bees are happy," Florencia added.

"Violetta, too," Fiora said.

Neither sister mentioned that Leonardo Leone hadn't actually been their grandfather, and that his daughter, who really had run off with a boy from Verona—Eduardo Rossi—to escape the old man's cruelty, had forged the will and given them the house, to which she had vowed she would never return. The gift was in exchange for services rendered and heartbreak endured . . . which neither sister felt the need to discuss. The sisters adopted the surname Rossi at the same time. Their parents had taught them the art of reinvention. It proved useful time and time again.

Neither sister mentioned how it stung to tell the townspeople the Rossis were their parents when they loved their own mother and father so fiercely and missed them so terribly. And neither sister mentioned how they had come to acquire Giuseppe and Freddo. The pair had simply shown up outside the inn where they had been staying the night. Freddo hopped into the coach the sisters and Violetta would take on the last leg of their journey, and Giuseppe followed behind.

It was the doing of their mother and grandmother. Protection for their beloved twins and Violetta, whom they loved most of all. Freddo would stand between the girls and the world, and Giuseppe would help them all make their way through it. It was their last gift, as they and the girls parted ways.

Fiora shook those thoughts of the past out of her head as she crossed the room to the desk on the opposite wall from the pantry, opened the drawer, and pulled out the well-worn leather-bound book. Flipping through the pages until she reached an empty one, she dipped her pen into the inkwell on the desk and began to write.

Angelina Martinelli. 17 October 1893. Honey, roasted cardamom seeds, olive oil. For husband snoring. Will also help with il raffreddore he gets every autumn.

How she knew Angelina's husband came down with a very nasty seasonal cold every autumn that settled in his lungs and worried Angelina every year, Fiora could not say. How she knew many things, she could not say. She had long since stopped concerning herself about that. Many of the women in her family had had what their mother and grandmother used to call *chiaroveggenza*, the second sight. Their father called it "the shine."

The girls' father was a Black Creole American from Louisiana by the name of Constant Broussard, who had traveled to Rome with a famous American scholar, long before the slaves in his home country were freed. Long before the war to free them started, long before the first drop of blood was spilled.

Constant was the son of a free woman of color of Creole descent. That's how it was in the Louisiana bayous back then, African and Haitian and French and Spanish and Native American and some whites all mixed together in a melting pot, just like their language. Nobody was sure who was what, and in the place Constant had lived, nobody much cared. Traditions mixed together, too, with voodoo and magic and Christianity and this old way and that old way, all stirred up in a cauldron of mysticism and magic and miracles.

Constant was highly educated, not unusual for Creoles at that time, because his family owned property, and so gifted was he in school that he caught the attention of a professor, also a man of color, who had need of an assistant during his travels abroad. That is how Constant found himself reclining on the banks of the Tiber River, which flowed through the center of Rome, on a sunny summer afternoon, when the most beautiful woman he had ever seen spoke to him. It is said that Rosa bewitched him right then and there, but in later years, people weren't sure who had done the bewitching.

Rosa had been on her way to tend to her bees—the hives were in a nearby meadow—when she noticed this enormous, dark man wearing what looked to be an expensive suit lying on the grass, legs crossed at the ankles, arms bent so the back of his head rested on his hands. His hat was positioned over his eyes and a book lay, opened, on his chest. His mouth was curled into a slight smile. *Serenity personified,* thought Rosa.

She stood there for a moment, gazing at him, until he stirred, removed his hat, and opened his eyes. When he did, he saw a raven-haired woman in a red-and-white dress, standing there with the light behind her creating a sort of halo around her. He scrambled up and leaned on his elbows. A literal vision of loveliness.

"Can I help you?" he asked her, in broken Italian. Rosa had never heard a voice like his. So low and velvety. Almost like music.

Rosa smiled. "I don't need any help," she said. "And by the looks of it, neither do you. You seem very comfortable there."

Constant smiled back at her. "I was reading and the sun was so warm and the riverbank so comfortable, I thought I might take a nap."

"I'm sorry to have disturbed you," Rosa said, her confident smile a bit more shy now. When he held her gaze, she could feel it all over her body.

"You did not disturb," he said, getting to his feet and extending his hand. "I'm Constant Broussard."

"I'm Rosa," she said, taking his hand, noticing hers was almost swallowed up by his.

He brought it to his lips, and Rosa took a breath. She knew it was very forward—they had not been properly introduced; he was an utter stranger to her. He might have been dangerous, for all she knew. Except . . . she knew he wasn't dangerous. And she knew he wouldn't be a stranger for long. She knew he would be her husband one day. One day soon. She knew she would lie next to him and rest her head on his strong, broad shoulder, burying her face into his neck to inhale the scent of him.

She also had the feeling he knew something of her. She was right about that. The Creole women in the Broussard family carried the shine, nurtured by generations in the bayous of Louisiana, traditions passed down with stories told and told again, and rituals performed again and again around the fires on moonlit nights.

Constant had a bit of it himself, but being a man, it wasn't too strong. Much later, after he and Rosa married and the girls came along, he used to love to say his darling twin daughters, Fiora and Florencia, carried a double dose of it.

Whatever it was, Fiora thought to herself as she sat with her daughter and sister in their new home in Santo Stefano, it was just second nature to her. It helped her in her healings . . . even if it couldn't help what might come of them.

As she looked across the room at her young daughter Violetta, just three years old, Fiora saw her father's shine and her mother's *chiaroveggenza* as clearly as her jet-black hair and unsettlingly beautiful violet-colored eyes.

She set her pen on the table and, seeing that the ink was already dry, closed the book and put a hand on top of it.

"Yes," she said to Florencia. "This is a good place. Let's stay awhile."

CHAPTER 7

Cassandra

My eyes fluttered open. I found I was lying on my back, arms at my sides, bound. I tried to break free, pushing against whatever was binding me to open my arms, but I couldn't move. I was trapped, immobile, like a spider's prey.

The moon shone through the window, casting a faint light onto my bed. I looked down and, sure enough, I saw whisper-thin white filaments wrapped around me, tight. It was a spiderweb.

I tried again to wrestle free, but a thought hit me then: How big would a spider have to be to catch a human in its web?

And where was it now?

At this, I broke the gossamer chains and leapt out of bed, hurrying to the light switch that I knew would illuminate the room. I flipped it just in time to see an enormous black spider, the size of a small dog, perched on the ceiling above the bed. I watched as it scurried off and . . . disappeared.

What?

I glanced at my phone, which was plugged into one of the outlets in an alcove by the bed. Not yet 3:00 a.m. After taking a sip of water, I climbed onto my bed and stood up, examining the ceiling where the spider had vanished. Was there a crack or a fissure? Someplace for a spider, even one of that size, to hide?

I didn't see anything. The ceiling was smooth. No cracks. No hiding places.

I flapped my duvet, looking for the remnants of a web. Nothing. Not one thread. It must have been a dream, then.

But . . . my eyes were open. I had jumped out of bed, turned on the light, and then saw the spider. I was fully awake. I didn't dream it or see it in my sleep somehow. Or did I?

My nerves were on fire. I had no idea what had just happened, and I didn't like it. I walked from room to room, turning on every light in the house, looking everywhere for a nook or cranny a spider could scurry into.

There was nothing.

When I had talked to Renzo on the phone before leaving the States, he told me this house had recently been renovated. It had been, of all things, a barn where the owner kept a couple of donkeys a century ago and had been revamped recently to be part of the hotel. Stonemasons had meticulously restored the walls and ceiling. New tile had been laid on the floor, above a system of hot-water pipes that would heat the place in the winter. The bathroom had been added, Jacuzzi built. It looked like a high-end spa room . . . if that spa had existed in the Middle Ages.

Still, spiders could find their way in most anywhere. Couldn't they?

I put a couple of logs on the fire and poked them a bit until they began to burn. Then I grabbed my laptop, settled into the chair by the hearth, and began to search for "Spiders in Italy." If I had a giant spider in this place, best to know exactly what it was.

There were several spiders that called this region of Italy home, including a few poisonous ones. But none anywhere near as large as what I had seen. Or thought I had seen. Even if I had been exaggerating or my eyes had been playing tricks on me, there weren't any spiders in Italy that were any bigger than a garden-variety tarantula. And most were just normal spider-size spiders. Nothing to worry about. Certainly nothing so big it could encase a human in a web.

That was the stuff out of fairy tales and fantasy and horror.

Was it a dream, then? I crept back into bed and lay down, pulling the duvet up under my chin. I'd ask Lorenzo about it tomorrow.

I must've fallen back asleep, because I found myself opening my eyes to morning. It was just after 7:00 a.m. The fire had gone out, and the overhead lights were out, too. Had I shut them off before curling into bed? I wasn't sure.

I slipped out from under the covers and padded over to the door, where I opened the shutters to find it was a bright, blue day. I unlocked the heavy wrought-iron latch and pulled open the door to a whoosh of chilly—but not cold—air. Fresh. Crisp. This was mountain air.

I don't know why, but it filled my heart with possibilities. Excitement. I couldn't wait to see what this little town had to offer me.

But first, coffee.

I opened the pantry and found a heavy silver coffee maker with one chamber sitting on top of another—*An espresso maker,* I thought. It looked complicated. I noticed a French press, also silver. Thank goodness. That was more my speed. I filled the kettle with water and, after a few tries, got the stove lit.

While the water was boiling, I hopped into leggings and a sweatshirt, washed my face and brushed my teeth, and stared at my reflection for a moment. That was me, on my first morning in Santo Stefano.

I found the coffee grinder and gave some beans a quick whir, spooned them into the French press, and poured the boiling water over the beans. I grabbed a mug and splashed some milk into a little creamer pitcher, put the whole thing on a tray, and carried it outside to the bench next to my front door.

I settled in and enjoyed my first glorious sips of the rich brew as I took in my view for the first time.

The sky was impossibly blue, not at all like the foggy gloom of the previous day. Santo Stefano was a hill town like so many others in Italy, but this one was surrounded by the Apennine Mountains. Not the Alps, which many tourists mistake them for, but to my untrained eye they looked just as I imagined the Alps to be. High, craggy, breathtaking peaks covered with snow. I could see them in the near distance, right from where I sat on the bench outside my own front door.

I made my way to the stone wall across from my door and peered over it to find rolling hills covered in low grasses, shrubs, and rocks— the same sort of white rocks that lined the cobblestone streets and the walls and ceiling of my little hovel. Limestone? I didn't know. I supposed it didn't much matter what they were called, what names we had given them. By any name, they were beautiful and strong and evocative of the town itself and the hills that surrounded it.

I looked up and down my street and saw that all the houses were connected, sort of akin to a block of row houses you might find in New York City or other urban areas. Only this was one long stone wall with doors and windows at regular intervals. There were stone steps that led down a flight to more of the same. I saw flowerpots here and there, many with cheerful red and yellow blooms.

As I sipped my coffee, a calico cat stole onto the street from a nearby stairway. It padded closer to me, investigating this new interloper, and wound its way around the legs of the bench where I had been sitting. My first visitor.

"Buongiorno," I said to the cat. He (or she) curled up under the bench and sighed.

I didn't see any of my neighbors that first morning. Instead, I simply enjoyed my coffee with my calico companion and marveled at the view I was lucky enough to see right out my front door.

Later, French press and mug washed, bed made, I showered, dried my hair, dressed in jeans and a light sweater, and set out for my first day in the village where my great-grandmother had lived.

What had Lorenzo said? Find the stone staircase and go up, up, up? I did find it, just a few doors down from my own. The wide stone steps did indeed go up, up, up to a landing and another street like mine, and more steps leading up, until finally I reached the top. I was not used to this much exertion in the mountain air—that's what I told myself . . . it certainly couldn't have been the fact that I hadn't worked out for months. I leaned against the wall and caught my breath.

I saw that a piazza opened up before me. Several buildings were clustered around a main square, with alleyways and tunnels fanning out in all directions like spokes of a wheel. A gaggle of small tables sat along one of the buildings.

Another looked like a town hall or official building of some kind. There was a restaurant, not yet open for the day, and a taverna, and several shops. No people yet, but I did notice several more calico cats and others that were black and white. *They must be families of feral cats,* I thought, belonging to no one and everyone in the village. Water bowls sat here and there by the doors of various shops.

"Cassie Graves!"

It was Lorenzo, rounding a corner.

"Buongiorno!" I said to him.

"You found your way up, up, up!" he said, gesturing over to the stairs. "A much nicer day than yesterday, no?"

"Gorgeous! And that view right outside my door!"

"I know," he said. "It is breathtaking, isn't it? I knew you'd enjoy that. How was your first night? You were comfortable?"

"More than comfortable," I said. "It was heavenly. That Jacuzzi . . ."

"Oh yes," he said, nodding. "You're the first to use it. As I said, we just got the place finished. Everything work just fine?"

"Yes, it did," I said. "It was perfect."

"And sleep? How was the bed? Did you sleep well?"

I didn't know whether to tell him about the spider dream . . . or whatever it had been. Now, in the bright, beautiful day, it seemed like a strange and nightmarish vision too fantastic to bring up.

"I slept great, except . . ."

He leaned in closer. "Except what? Not the bed, I hope? You're the first who has slept on it. Is it not comfortable for you?"

"No, the bed is great," I said. "I had this weird dream in the middle of the night and didn't sleep much after that."

He nodded, frowning. "That is not surprising. First night in a new place." Then, he gestured to one of the alleyways. "I told you about this deli—La Oliva. They're open now. Come, let's get a cappuccino and I'll introduce you to the owner. Luna. She is always talking about dreams. Maybe she can tell you what yours means."

I followed him out of the piazza and down a tiny stone alleyway, where four stone steps led up to an open door. **LA OLIVA** said the hand-painted sign above it, featuring birds and olives and vines. We walked up the steps and through the open door.

"Luna!" Lorenzo called.

A woman I presumed to be Luna popped her head out of the back room. "*Buongiorno*, Renzo!" she said, her voice musical and lovely.

"Luna, this is Cassie," he said, putting an arm around my shoulder. "She is staying in *la suite dell'asino*."

I gave Lorenzo a mock scowl. "Did you just call it the donkey suite?"

He laughed, and so did Luna. "You know it had been a donkey barn, back in the day."

"Donkeys are kind," Luna said as she made us, unbidden, two cappuccinos. "I love them. And it's wonderful to meet you, Cassie. Renzo tells me you're staying awhile."

She handed a cup to me and one to Renzo. *"Grazie,"* I said, taking a sip. "Yes, I'll be here doing some research into my family history."

Luna raised her eyebrows. "Oh? You have family from Santo Stefano?"

"My great-grandmother was raised here," I said. "She came to the United States around 1912 when she was a young woman, but I don't know much about her life here before that. We—my cousin and I—tried to research it online but hit a dead end. That's why I came. I could still have family here, for all I know."

"What is the family name?" Luna asked.

"Moretti. There's also a Rossi that we found on a document, but we're not sure that's accurate."

"Rossi?" Luna frowned. "You might have quite a search on your hands if you're looking for a Rossi."

"It's a very common name," Renzo explained. "Like Smith in the United States. There's a Rossi around every corner in Italy. It would be hard to narrow it down."

"Any here in Santo Stefano?" I asked.

"I don't think so," Renzo said. "Not any of the permanent residents, that is. Now Moretti . . . that sounds more familiar."

"We went to school with some Morettis," Luna piped up. "But they left town long ago."

I sighed. I didn't really expect to have this mystery solved in one conversation at a coffee shop, but it certainly would've been nice.

"I think she should start at the church," Renzo said. "They have records going way back."

"The town hall, too," Luna added, and then turned to me. "If you'd like, I can make some calls about those Morettis. My mother may know where they ended up."

"Oh, I can't ask you to do that," I began. But Luna put up her hand.

"It's no trouble at all. I need to call her anyway. It's been too long."

"Thank you," I said. "That's very kind."

Renzo waved his hand. "Kind? She's just nosy. Wants to know your business, this one." An amused look passed between them, and I could see the love in their eyes. It wrapped itself all around them then. These two were a couple. Or wanted to be. I wasn't quite sure how I knew that, but I knew it for certain.

Renzo glanced down at his watch. "I need to get back to the office," he said. "I have some guests checking out this morning." He turned to me. "You go enjoy your coffee in the piazza and then explore the town. Get lost in our tunnels and alleyways, I always tell guests. All you need to do is look to the sky—you'll see the castle tower from wherever you are and be able to find your way."

"I'll do that," I said.

"And stop into La Lenticchia for lunch. I'm going right by there and I'll tell him you'll be coming. You'll love the view. And the food."

After saying ciao to Renzo and thanking Luna again—I wasn't sure how much to thank people or how much to protest when they offered to go out of their way—I did take my coffee (she gave me another cup on the house) to the piazza and settled myself at a table in the sun.

Only then did I realize I hadn't told her anything about my dream about the spider. *Oh well,* I thought. *Maybe that's for the best.* It was such a beautiful day, that dream was fading with every ray of sunshine that hit my face.

I fished my phone out of my purse and looked at the time. Nearly ten o'clock. I wanted to talk with Maria but did a quick calculation of the time change and realized it was three in the morning back in Wharton. So I sent her a text message instead, letting her know I had arrived in Santo Stefano safe and sound. I sent a similar one to Henry—love you, honey!—and, after thinking about it for a moment, sent another one to John. We may have been separated, but I knew he'd want to know I was safe.

To my surprise, I got a message back from him right away.

Who's this?

I scowled at my phone.

What do you mean, who's this? Who do you think it is?

Well, I see your name—Cass—but I'm wondering who you are. John is sleeping.

I stared at the phone in my hand, as though it were about to morph into a spider. Or already had. I could feel the heat rising from my neck to my ears. It was crystal clear to me exactly what was going on.

This wasn't the woman my husband had been cheating on me with. She—Cynthia—knew my name, or I imagined she did, after her friend contacted me. This was someone else. Someone who didn't know John had a wife. It wasn't just one woman he was cheating on me with, then.

I wasn't going to respond, but then I thought, *No. I'm not taking the high road this time.*

My name is Cassandra Graves. Yes, that Graves. Whoever YOU are, tell John his WIFE arrived safely in Italy. And that he can go to hell.

CHAPTER 8

Fiora

Violetta loved the animals and they loved her, Fiora used to say. She saw it very early on in her daughter, even before the girl could walk. The neighborhood cats would curl around her, rubbing their soft fur against her baby skin, letting her hold their tails. Dogs, too. And birds. Any living creature, really. They all gravitated to her, and she to them.

As she grew older, Violetta's imagination had grown as deep as her love for animals, so when she came home from the wildflower fields with stories of seeing a pure-white donkey with blue eyes, at first Fiora smiled and encouraged the girl, thinking—hoping—it might have been a figment of her imagination.

But when the talk continued, Florencia sat her sister down one evening when Violetta was in bed.

"I don't like this white donkey business," Florencia said, setting a cup of tea in front of her sister, along with one for herself.

"Have you ever seen it?"

"No," Florencia said. "And I've followed her to the meadow a number of times. But that doesn't mean—"

Fiora shook her head and took a sip. "I know what it means as well as you do," she said. "I was hoping it was an imaginary friend. Or even a ghost."

Florencia sniffed. "This town is surely full enough of those."

"Everywhere you look."

"But this donkey . . ."

"It means protection," said Fiora. "But why does Violetta need to be protected? We're right here."

Florencia chuckled. "I pity anyone—living or dead—who tries to harm that child with you by her side."

Fiora reached over and took her sister's hand. "And you."

The sisters didn't know they would all need protection one day.

⚜

That summer, Violetta spent much of her time outdoors, even on the rainiest of days, picking flowers and plants and braiding them into garlands for her hair. She would run down the gravel road to the small lake on the edge of town and sit on the bank, singing to herself.

Fiora never worried about her daughter playing out of doors, not in those days, not in that place. Very shortly after the sisters and Violetta arrived in town, all the townsfolk knew them, and with their growing business, they had become a fixture in Santo Stefano. A part of them, just as though they had always been there. People looked out for Violetta, but nobody asked about her father, or where the sisters had come from . . . which was just as well.

The Rossi sisters taught Violetta about the plants and flowers that grew naturally in the region, and those they were cultivating as well. It was a love of the land and the plants and everything of the earth they had inherited from their mother Rosa and their grandmother Isabella, and also from their father's line, whose "shine" was darker, more mysterious, and even more powerful than their own.

"Lavender soothes and calms," Fiora said to Violetta as the two sat together by the lakeside in Santo Stefano. She held one of the light-purple flowers to her daughter's nose.

"It smells like dreams," Violetta said.

Fiora nodded. She had never heard anyone say it like that before, but it was the truth.

"It also smells like safety," she said. "Lavender can ward off evil of all kinds."

Violetta wrinkled her nose at her mother, and Fiora ran a hand through her daughter's hair and let it rest on her cheek. *She has no concept of evil,* Fiora thought. *Please let it stay that way, just a little longer.*

"If someone is worrying, or nervous, or having trouble sleeping, we mix a little lavender in with the honey harvested during the full moon," Fiora said, braiding a chain of clover for Violetta's hair. "We tell them, 'Put a spoonful in your tea tonight.'"

"And it helps?"

"It helps."

"But how do you know they're worried?"

Fiora smiled at her daughter. "We just know. So will you."

Fiora knew this, too, was true. But she felt the need for a little lavender herself as her daughter grew older.

The summer Violetta turned five years old, she returned home one evening with a snow-white donkey following behind her, the one she had told her mother about.

As she walked through town, people poked their heads out of their windows, then opened their doors, then came out into the street to see it.

Fiora caught sight of her daughter as she walked under the archway near their home, white donkey following close behind. She beckoned Florencia, who watched, hands on her hips, as the girl and her donkey neared.

"All right. This is happening," Florencia said.

"Yes, it is," Fiora said.

By this time, Violetta and her companion had reached their front door.

"Her name is Bianca," Violetta announced.

"Fitting," Fiora said. "Why has she come?"

"She was tired of being alone," Violetta said, petting the donkey's muzzle. "She wants to stand by my side. And I thought Giuseppe might like some company, too."

And so, Violetta, Fiora, and Florencia led Bianca around the corner and down the steps to Giuseppe's barn, a big, sweet-smelling room filled with enough hay for him to have a comfortable place to sleep and a window where he could look outside and smell the fresh air whenever he wished to.

He nodded in greeting.

"You will be responsible for feeding them and making sure they have water," Fiora said. "And for taking them out into the fields every day so they can wander and play and roam and do what donkeys do."

"And for getting them back in at night," Florencia added, wagging a finger at her niece. "Giuseppe likes to sleep indoors."

Freddo, their enormous white dog, of the breed that protected sheep in the nearby mountains, jumped to his feet and immediately ushered Bianca into the barn. She allowed herself to be herded and took her place, standing next to Giuseppe.

"I think I'll stay and talk with them awhile," Violetta said. "If that's all right with you, Mama and Auntie."

Fiora stroked Bianca's white fur. "Welcome, Bianca," she said. Then she turned to her daughter. "We'll be upstairs. I'm in the middle of infusing some honey, and you know it does not like to wait."

As the sisters made their way from the barn back up to the main house, Florencia took her twin's arm. She didn't need to say anything, but she did.

"The way Freddo took to her," Florencia said. "A good sign."

"Yes," Fiora said.

Florencia sighed then, a sigh of contentment. All would be well. Or so she believed. Fiora wasn't so sure. She had thought the town itself was their protection. Why did they need more?

As Fiora sat with Violetta that night, brushing her hair before bedtime, she thought of her mother and father, and the tales they would tell in the old days. Before.

Fiora let her mind drift back to so many starry nights as they sat around the fireplace, when Constant would tell his girls dark and entrancing stories about the women in his family. Stories of his mother, Cecile, whose cooking—some say it was otherworldly good—regularly brought the poor folk in town to their back door in the evenings. Cecile was a landowner, a very controversial state of affairs that came about when her wealthy husband passed away—not that anyone could, or would, dare do anything about it. Because she had been given that gift, she always gave what she could to those less fortunate.

His mother was tenderhearted, Constant would say, but not faint of heart, for Cecile had fought for the rights of her family and others in their small community, not with her fists but with the magic she brewed into her gumbos and stews and soups, magic that could help people . . . and hinder them. If they needed hindering, Constant would say with a grin, raising his eyebrows.

The girls knew so many stories of their grandmother Cecile that they felt like they knew her, too, but they outright knew Rosa's family—her stern father, Geno, who was none too pleased about his daughter marrying an American and a Creole at that, and, while he didn't banish Rosa after she married Constant against his wishes, he didn't have much to do with the young couple. Or his wife. Although he couldn't keep a twinkle out of his eye when the twins came along.

But Rosa's mother, Isabella, who had always known her daughter would encounter a dark and handsome stranger on the banks of the Tiber and build a life with him, was very much the doting grand-mother to Fiora and Florencia and sprinkled love all around them—into their tea, into their soups, onto the meat she roasted in her ovens, into the sauces for her pasta—every day as they sat with her in the family kitchen.

Isabella was the one who first taught the girls the ways of nature, how they could work with it, talk to it, ask it to use its bounty to heal and help and, like Constant's mother Cecile, to harm. If harm is what was needed.

Isabella whispered spells and incantations to her granddaughters, verses she recited from a leather-bound book, a volume that seemed to the girls to be very old. Ancient, they suspected.

The girls loved to lie on their bed and get lost in the book's cover. It was etched with curlicues and symbols, drawings of the sun, the moon, and the stars, faces of people with knowing eyes, animals with wise smiles, even frightening images of cauldrons ablaze. The images seemed to change, day by day. The girls never knew what they were going to find. One day, they saw their grandmother's face, and their mother's.

Soon, they noticed images that looked like them—the girls themselves—appeared on the book's cover, in a corner, on the back. Their small images were peering out from behind their mother's skirts.

Isabella had smiled. "I've been wondering when it would happen. The book belongs to you two now."

The girls didn't look upon these happenings around their home as unusual or dark or mysterious but simply how their mother and grandmother moved through the world and, especially, through their kitchen. Fiora and Florencia learned the spells and the magic from the book as other girls learned family recipes for favorite dishes from cookbooks passed down from mother to daughter. It was simply how they lived. A pinch of this in the red sauce will open a man's heart. A pinch of that in evening tea will usher in good fortune in the morning.

This was about the time Fiora's eyes began to change. They had been dark brown since birth, like Florencia's, but little by little, the iris faded and morphed in color, first to light brown and then to a strange sort of ashen gray, which frankly had worried Rosa and Isabella. Then, they turned to hazel and one day, Fiora awoke with eyes as stormy and green as the sky when the weather is threatening.

Isabella and Rosa didn't know what to make of it, and neither did the sisters. But Constant noted that his mother had the same sort of stormy eyes.

"She is reaching out, all the way from Louisiana," he said, kneeling down and holding his daughter's chin gently with one hand and gazing into those eyes. He looked up at his wife. "It's the mark of power, in her line. Strength. That old magic runs deep in these girls, both of them. But in Fiora especially. The eyes tell the tale."

Florencia jutted out her bottom lip.

"Don't pay that no mind," Constant said to her. "The shine has to pick one to shine more brightly on, when there are twin souls. That's just how it works. Your turn will come in other ways, in your own time. Don't you worry, now."

Florencia wasn't so sure about that. But one thing her father said was right: she and her sister were twin souls. Florencia knew that if it was happening to Fiora, it was happening to her too, eyes or no eyes.

"He is right," Isabella said, echoing her granddaughter's thoughts. "All of the women in our line have the gift, but it comes differently to each one. We don't know what your gifts will be yet, but you surely will have them. For me, it's cooking, as it was for my grandmother. My mother, she worked with oils and soaps, scenting them with herbs for different occasions. For your mother, it's the bees."

Rosa did have a way with the bees; everyone knew it. She tended their hives in the meadow not far from their home, near the Tiber where she had first seen Constant. It had been love at first sight for Rosa, and for Constant, but she made up her mind about the man when, many days later, she walked with him to the hives and the bees went calm as he came near to them. It seemed to Rosa that they sensed him and stopped their work, just for a few moments, to take in his aura of strength and serenity and peace.

That's where Constant had kissed her for the first time, there among the hives on the banks of the Tiber, not far from the old sycamore tree where he had been reclining on that fateful afternoon.

Constant had taken her in his arms, the strongest arms Rosa had ever seen, and had whispered his intentions into her ear.

"I want to make you my wife," he said, in that low and velvety voice Rosa had already come to love. "If you'll have me."

And that was that. Objections from her father, and from people who lived nearby—an American? A Black man?—meant nothing to Rosa, who felt that Constant's cappuccino skin was not any darker than her own olive skin. Two parts of the same meal, from the same pot, on the same table. The same nourishment, the same love. Anything else, to her, was foolishness. And she let people know it.

They—the neighbors in the family's corner of the city—had already realized Rosa, like her mother, was not to be trifled with. So they didn't. Not at first. Not because of her husband. Not at first.

One afternoon when the girls were growing into young women, Rosa called them to her side in the kitchen as she was stirring the red sauce that had been simmering for much of the day, filling the house with the aroma they loved best.

As they were stirring and tasting alongside their mother, Rosa grew serious.

"I have something important to tell you," she said, leading them to the table and sitting them down. "You will be out of this house, out of my sight, more and more now. But you must never talk of our kitchen, our special recipes, and our ways."

But Fiora and Florencia already knew this. Their mother didn't have to tell them, just as Isabella hadn't needed to tell Rosa. It was something that was born inside them, the instinct to keep the old ways to themselves.

They had heard whispers about persecution and trials and death and all manner of horrible things, not just throughout Europe but in America, too. Even that new, progressive, modern place had a dark history.

It never made any sort of sense to the girls—it was just the ways of women.

CHAPTER 9

Cassandra

My eyes filled with hot, angry tears as I tucked my phone back into my purse and set it on the ground with a thud. I didn't know why I was so upset. I knew the man had been cheating—that was part of the reason I had come over to Italy in the first place. Yes, I had wanted to dig into this family mystery, but the bigger part of it, the part I hadn't said out loud but I suspected Maria knew, too, was that I wanted a break. A change in scenery. A change in perspective.

It's good to get away when the weight of the world is bearing down. My mother had always said that to me. To remind yourself that the weight of "the world" is just your immediate reality.

"There's a whole, big world out there, Cassie," my mother would say. "It's filled with people who know nothing of this drama that is consuming you. You think this problem is so huge, but when you look at it like that, it's really small. Can you see that?"

I did see that. Don't sweat the small stuff, certainly. But even the big stuff—death, divorce, illness, catastrophe—could be softened, even slightly, by giving oneself a little breathing room and perspective. Just being in Santo Stefano, in this town where the very streets ran through my family's veins, reminded me that John's choice to betray his marriage—me—did not mean the end of everything. It meant the end of life as I knew it, yes. But there was still life out there, wasn't there? A whole world filled with people and possibility.

Still, as I sat in the piazza that morning, seething because of a text from a woman who was lying in bed at that very moment with my sleeping (cheating dog of a) husband, I felt very much alone.

As if reading my thoughts, one of the town's feral calico cats padded around the corner and joined me, curling around my feet and swishing its tail before lying down in the sun just out of my reach. It brought a slight smile to my face. Not so alone after all.

I finished my coffee and pushed back from the table. Time to shake it off and get on with the day. I walked around the corner to take the cup back to Luna at La Oliva.

I found her on the phone speaking in rapid-fire Italian. When she saw me come through the door, she raised one finger, as if to say *Wait a moment.* She was nodding, keeping eye contact with me all the while. After she hung up, she smiled at me.

"That was my mother," she said. "There are some Morettis living nearby." Luna pointed out her window to the mountains. "She said they had lived here in Santo Stefano years ago. She's going to call them to see if they'd be willing to talk with you. I'm sure they will."

"That's amazing!" I said.

"Yes," Luna said. "These could be your people! Who knows? My mother is going to call me back once she's talked with them. This afternoon sometime. Stop back after lunch and maybe I'll have good news for you."

Could it be as easy as that? I was a little skeptical, but it was something to go on.

Luna smiled at me. "You Americans," she said. "You love to research your family history. Here, it's not so much a mystery. They live down the hall." She laughed then. A big, hearty laugh. "Maybe it's better your way! With my relatives, at least."

But then her smile faded, just a bit, and she looked at me a little closer. "Is something wrong?" she asked, leaning against the deli counter that stood between us.

"Why would you say that?"

"It's your eyes," she said. "They don't have the laughter they did when you were here earlier with Renzo."

Was I really so transparent that even someone I had just met could see what I was trying to hide? I sighed. "It's my husband," I said. "Or former husband. We've been separated for a while now."

She shook her head. "Men! He shouldn't be bothering you, if you are not together."

No, I thought. *He shouldn't. In more ways than one.*

"They bother us enough when they are in our houses and we have to deal with them. But if he's out of the house"—she waved a hand—"let him be somebody else's problem."

I nodded. "Right. I have other things to think about today."

I turned to go then, but something made me turn back around. I wasn't at all sure I should bring it up, or what I'd say if I did. But Renzo had said Luna liked to talk about dreams. Should I tell her about mine?

"Luna, can I ask you something strange?"

"If it's about husbands, I won't know the answer," she said, laughing. "I didn't do so well myself in that regard."

"Not husbands," I said, grasping for any kind of words that made sense. "This is going to sound odd, but . . . are there any big spiders here in Santo Stefano?"

She furrowed her brow at me. "Spiders? Well, of course, we have spiders, but . . ."

"I'm not talking about regular spiders. I'm talking about really big ones." I held out my hands to simulate the size of the spider I had seen, or thought I had seen, that morning. "Like, this big."

Luna scowled at the very thought of it. "No," she said. "Not at all. Not anything like that. Why?"

"It's just that . . ." The expression on her face made me wonder if I should continue. I had just made a new friend in her, or hoped I had. Should I come out as a crazy lady right away?

"It's just that," I repeated, "when I was sleeping, last night, I had this rather unusual dream and—"

"About a spider?" She lowered her voice and leaned closer, over the deli counter.

"Yes," I said.

She narrowed her eyes at me. "I like to interpret dreams. Did Renzo tell you that?"

"He did say something about it," I admitted, wincing. "That's why I brought it up."

She slid out from around the counter and closed the door to the deli, turning the CLOSED sign around. "Let's go into the back room for a minute," she said to me, waving her hand toward the door. "They can wait."

She led me around the deli counter and through a small doorway, which opened into a wide room with a stone fireplace on one wall and four large windows on the other. A round table sat in the middle of the room covered with a red-and-blue floral tablecloth, and there were two armchairs on either side of the fireplace.

Photos and paintings in frames covered the walls, which were a dark red. Candles sat here and there.

A doorway on the far side of the room led to a hallway—I suspected many of the buildings in Santo Stefano were rooms within rooms within passageways like this.

"This is lovely," I said, looking around. "Is this your home?"

Luna smiled and nodded. "Such as it is," she said. "Most of the people who run the various shops and businesses in town live in them. It's how the town was set up, back when it was a major trading center for the region. One big room that held whatever it was you were selling or trading, and rooms to live in, in the back."

She gestured to the chairs on either side of the fire. "Let's sit. And then you can tell me about this spider."

After settling into the chair, I began—even though as I said the words, I felt a little silly.

"Like I said, this is going to sound really weird," I said.

She made a tsking noise and waved a hand. "No matter what you tell me, I have heard worse. You can believe me on that." She smiled and her warm eyes shone.

So I took a deep breath and told her that I had dreamed I had awoken within a spiderweb, or more exactly, was encased in one.

"I tried to get free of it, to move my arms. But I couldn't. It was like this spider had spent a good deal of time spinning a web around me. Almost like a cocoon, in a way."

She nodded. "Okay. That's pretty easy," she said, as though hearing about a giant spider was nothing new to her. "Especially since you told me about your husband. Typically, when people dream about being in a spiderweb, it's because they're trapped in a situation and don't feel like they can break free of it. It's often about a relationship. But it can be a job, too, or any number of things that we feel caught in. But usually, it's the husband or wife. And since you talked about your husband . . ." She frowned slightly and shrugged, as I had seen many Italians do.

That made perfect sense. I was feeling exactly that when it came to John. And, looking back on it, over the past two years at least, I was stuck in a situation that I really didn't even know I was stuck in. But that's not all there was to it.

"That fits, if we're talking about my husband," I said. "But there's more to the dream. And this is where it gets really weird."

"Okay," she said. "What is it? Again, I've heard weird. Don't worry."

"I'm not quite sure how to explain this, but it wasn't like a regular dream. That is, I dreamed that I woke up in a spiderweb. I was in my bed in the hotel room. And I woke up in the bed, where I really was, in the spiderweb—so, it was like I was in a dream but not in a dream, if that makes any sense. I'm not explaining it very well. I mean, obviously I wasn't really in the web, right? But when I realized I was stuck, I thought—if I'm encased in this web, a fully grown person, how big does that spider have to be to have woven this web around me while I was sleeping? I was having trouble breathing, too. I took several deep breaths. That's when I looked up and saw it, on the ceiling."

"Yes, but as real as it seemed, it still was a dream, right?"

I shook my head. "That's the thing. I don't know. I broke free from the web, jumped out of bed, and ran to the light switch, which is by the front door. I stood there—wide awake—and turned on the overhead light. I saw a spider, a huge spider, on the ceiling and watched as it crept into a crevasse in the ceiling. I was wide awake, Luna. Standing by the door."

Luna furrowed her brow. "So, you—"

"Yes! I watched it crawl away. I was going to tell Renzo in the morning to move me to another room and have him get somebody in there to take care of that spider. Except . . ."

She nodded. "Except there was no crack. No crevasse. No place for something that big to go."

I shrugged and turned both my palms up. "Exactly. I actually stood on my bed and examined the ceiling. There was nothing. I don't know how to explain it. But it happened. I mean, the part about me being in a spiderweb had to be a dream, right? But when I got out of bed, I was wide awake and I stayed awake. After I inspected the ceiling, I sat in the chair by the fire and researched all of the different kinds of spiders in Italy."

Luna chuckled. "I would've done the same thing. You must've been terrified."

I had been. She was right.

Luna pushed herself to her feet and crossed the room to the window. She was silent for a moment, gazing out at the mountains in the distance.

My skin began to crawl. "How could something like that happen?"

She turned back to look at me. "More things happen than you can imagine. Strange things. Otherworldly things."

I waited for her to go on. Instead, she held one finger up in the air and disappeared down the hallway. A moment later she returned, holding something in her hand. And then she dangled a necklace in front of me. It was a small red horn on a gold chain.

I held her gaze. "I may not have been born here, but I know what that is."

She nodded. "*Cornicello.* I think you should wear it while you're here. All the time."

A chill ran up my spine. "It's for good luck, right?"

"For good luck, yes. And to ward off evil."

She draped it around my neck and clasped it. I fingered the pendant and felt a tingle of electricity.

"Why do I need to ward off evil, Luna?" I asked, my voice wavering. "The spider?"

She pulled her chair close to me and sank into it, resting a hand on my knee. "You are in a very ancient place," she said. "Nearly one thousand years of living has happened here. Right here. In these buildings. Births, deaths, business, commerce, trade, happiness, tragedy, love, hate—it all happened here, where we are sitting right now."

I nodded, understanding.

"The old ways are very close to our hearts here," she said. "Not that we believe it all, but . . ."

"Better safe than sorry?"

She smiled. "Exactly right. So now I'll tell you about a folktale we have here in Abruzzo," she said slowly, as if measuring her words. "The Pantafica. It is a shape-shifting witch, or evil being, who comes to people, especially women, at night. During the dream time. It takes many forms and . . . paralyzes them and takes their breath."

What? I didn't know quite how to respond. That sounded exactly like what had happened to me. But . . . it was a folktale, right?

"It's a folktale?"

Luna nodded. "Folktales get their start somewhere."

It felt familiar, this deference to old tales and legend. In Wharton, people felt the same about Lake Superior. In native lore, the lake is the Great Spirit—at turns kind and benevolent or vengeful and rage filled.

It gives peace, restores the soul. Even in the modern day, Lake Superior is not to be trifled with, ignored, or insulted in any way.

I leaned back in my chair and sighed. "So, you don't think I'm crazy."

She smiled and shook her head. "Crazy? This is Italy. We've all seen a lot of stranger things than this. No. You saw what you saw, there's no doubt in my mind. Was it the Pantafica? I don't know. Whether it was that or a dream, the larger question is, why?"

She crossed her arms and leaned back against the window frame, the sunlight shining in around her, bathing her in a halo.

I shrugged. "I'm here doing family research," I offered. "Could that be why?"

She smiled, rather sadly, I thought. "It depends on what there is to dig up."

A chill ran through me then as I thought of Violetta's death certificate. Witchcraft.

Before I had a chance to mention that to Luna, she pushed herself out of her chair and slipped out of the room and came back with a small, old-fashioned-looking wooden broom. "One more thing to deal with the Pantafica," she said, holding the broom out to me. "You've probably noticed most everyone has a broom like this over their front door."

I had noticed it above many of the doorways in town. I thought it was a cute decoration.

She handed the broom to me. "It wards off evil spirits."

I stared at the broom like it was on fire. "Really?"

Luna let out a laugh. "You can never be too careful. It's just a folktale. But humor me. Put it by your front door. And wear the necklace, even at night. Especially at night."

"Okay, I'll do that. But . . . what if it was just a dream? You interpret dreams. What do you make of it?"

"Dream or evil spirit, it's all wrapped up in the 'why.' As I said, spiders, specifically being in a spider's web, can mean you are stuck in a situation and need to break free from it. If that were all there was to it, I'd go with that as an explanation. Your husband . . ." She let the rest of her thought trail off.

I realized I was still tied to John and had been thinking of him the whole time I had been here. In my hotel in Rome. At the Vatican. In the rental car. Everywhere. Was I still stuck? Was that what this was about?

"Or—"

"Or what?"

"It can mean they're here to warn you."

A shiver ran through me. Why would I need a warning? I had come to Italy to get away from the situation I was "stuck" in. This was supposed to be a fun diversion, a vacation. An excuse to eat pasta and drink wine every day. Yet something about the way my skin was crawling made me think Luna might have a point.

"Warn me about what?"

"That you are about to walk into a trap. Or are already in one."

CHAPTER 10

Cassandra

Later, after I had said my goodbyes to Luna with the promise of coming back to the shop that afternoon to hear news from her mother about the Morettis in the neighboring village, I walked aimlessly around town for a bit, down alleyways, around tight corners, running my palm along stones that were cool to the touch.

Luna was right. These narrow streets and alleys were eight hundred years old. The passage of time was not evident in these passageways—they looked much as they must have back then, if the guidebooks were correct. Many generations of people had walked these same streets, my own great-grandmother Violetta among them. I wondered if she felt the same sense of awe at the age of the place.

I could almost see it as it was then, a bustling center of trade and commerce, with people from all over Europe—all over the globe—converging there to sell spices and silks and all manner of strange and exotic things the villagers had never seen, or even imagined. It must have seemed a bit like magic to them, having their piazza and streets and shops filled with travelers who didn't look like them, dressed in clothes that were foreign to them, speaking languages they had never heard.

How cosmopolitan it must've been at one time in this sleepy little village. When the wealthy and powerful family built the castle to safeguard and store the fine wool and unique lentils of the region, they truly brought the world to Santo Stefano's doorstep.

How many of those souls were still walking the alleyways?

As I strolled, imagining those long-ago encounters, it was almost as if I had stepped back into that time. Nobody was on the streets. No light flickered. No cell phone towers loomed. No airplanes flew overhead. No evidence I was in modern times at all.

It occurred to me then that I was walking the same streets as my ancestors walked. Violetta, her mother, the dashing Giovanni. It felt as though I could turn a corner and bump into one of them, hurrying home from the piazza where they had sold or bought the exotic things that were exchanged there.

Pulling me out of my time traveling, Luna's comments snaked back into my mind. I couldn't shake what she had said. "A trap" sounded rather melodramatic, I thought, didn't it? What sort of trap? I was here researching my family history, not trying to decipher the Dead Sea Scrolls or uncover the truth about whether the mob had hired Lee Harvey Oswald to assassinate Kennedy. What sort of trap might be lying in wait for me here? How could me researching my family history possibly threaten someone—something—enough to set a trap for me?

Or was it simpler—and yet, darker—than that? I was a woman traveling alone. Was the spider trying to tell me to be on guard, lest I walk into the trap of the wrong man at the wrong time in the wrong place? It was, naturally, a concern.

It was the folktale that nagged at me. I fingered the amulet around my neck. It felt warm. I was glad for its protection—a tale though it might be.

With all of that running through my mind, I noticed one of the shops was open. I poked my head inside. It was filled with yarn creations—hot pads, scarves, mittens, sweaters. The wool was dyed in deep blacks and reds and yellows. Along with stark white.

I picked up a jet-black scarf as I spoke to the woman sitting by the cash register. "Did you . . . *lavorare a maglia?*" I was trying, in my broken Italian, to ask if she had knitted it.

Apparently used to dealing with tourists who had only a slight grasp of the language, she smiled and nodded. "Wool is from our sheep. *Pecora.* The best in the world."

She pushed herself to her feet, took the scarf from my hands, and wound it around my neck. It was incredibly soft. Softer than any wool I had ever felt. "It suits you," she said, showing me to a mirror. She was right. It did look nice with my skin color and stormy eyes.

"I'll take it," I said, reaching into my purse.

After leaving the shop, I made some time to run down to my room and position Luna's broomstick next to my door. Sure, it was just an old tale. But better safe than sorry.

I had just enough time to get back to the restaurant Renzo had recommended. I was sitting at a table by the window—as Renzo had told me, the view of the mountains from this restaurant was amazing— enjoying my lunch of prosciutto, mozzarella, basil, and tomato piled on a baguette, with a small salad and a glass of white wine, when he breezed through the door. He scanned the restaurant for a moment before his eyes settled on me. He lifted up a hand in a wave and smiled.

"Yes, yes, here you are," he said, joining me at my table and pulling out a chair, unbidden, to take a seat. "How do you like the restaurant? Good for lunch?"

"It's great!" I said, smiling. I rather enjoyed how he just sat down like that. The way a friend might. "Thanks for the recommendation."

He scowled at my plate. "A sandwich? You're in Italy, Cassie Graves. Eat a noodle."

I laughed. "I have eaten my full body weight in pasta every day since I got here."

He wagged a finger at me. "See that you continue it," he said, smiling through his mock scowl. "Now, what I came for: I have some news for you."

"Oh?" I asked. "I want to hear it, but before we get into that, do you want lunch?"

Renzo raised his eyebrows at the server, who clearly knew him.

"Are you bothering this lady?" the server said to Renzo, a laugh in his voice. "Miss, would you like me to ask this strange man to leave you alone?"

I laughed, too. "No, I think he's okay," I said.

"I am okay enough to be ordering food from you," Renzo said to the server. "A paying customer."

"We'll see about that when the bill comes. What would you like today? The usual?"

"I'll have what she's having," Renzo said, winking at me, "and two tiramisus."

I smirked at him. "Two?"

"One for me, one for you."

So much for not gaining weight on the trip, I thought. But . . . when in Santo Stefano . . .

He placed his palms on the table with a sense of finality. "Now! The news."

I took a bite of my sandwich. "Good news, I hope."

He nodded, narrowing his eyes. "You mentioned a Rossi in your family tree, from here, right?"

"That's right," I said. "That's the information I have, but . . . I just found out about them. The Rossis. I was always told about the Morettis—that was my great-grandmother's last name, her married name. But I saw a photo of her here in Santo Stefano. Her name was written on the back. Violetta Rossi. So Rossi must've been her family name. And then there was another photo, of her in the doorway to a shop, with a sign above it that said 'Il Miele di Rossi.'"

Renzo nodded and rubbed his chin. "A honey shop. The plot thickens, as you say."

"Yes," I said, my eyes expectant. "But thickens to what?"

"That is in line with the news I've uncovered for you!" he said. "I can't believe you brought that up. I spoke to my grandparents and they said, yes, there had been Rossis here in Santo Stefano. And—get this now—there was a shop with that name! That's why they remember the Rossis. Because of the shop. My grandmother remembers hearing stories about the place. She said they sold local honey, and oils and soaps and those kinds of lady things."

Lady things. It made me smile. But my nerves started to tingle all the same. "It must be the same shop," I said. "I don't know much else about it, but I do know my great-grandmother Violetta had what was called a 'sundry' shop in the town where I grew up, where she lived after leaving Italy. She sold those kinds of things. Honey. Soaps. Oils."

"It would make sense, then. Opening up a shop like that, if her family had one here."

"Is it still here?" My nerves tingled.

"There is a shop that sells local honey," Renzo said, nodding. "It's just off the piazza. But the name of the owner is not Rossi. Or Moretti. It's Caruso. They're relatively new here. Only a generation or so."

He laughed at this. I did, too, understanding that in small towns, new people were "new" for generations.

"But this is what I'm thinking," Renzo continued. "I think it's the same shop. I mean, how many honey shops could there have been? It had to have changed hands somewhere along the way."

We looked at each other for a moment. "But you're not in Santo Stefano just for the honey," he said finally. "You want to know why your people left this village."

He was right about that. I wondered how he knew.

Just then, the server arrived with his sandwich. "Extra basil. Just like you like it."

"*Grazie mille, amico mio,*" Renzo said. "Cassie, this is Leonardo. He owns the place. Leo, my friend Cassie Graves."

Leo bowed slightly. "Miss Graves."

"The sandwich and salad were delicious. That dressing . . ."

Leo smiled. "My mother's recipe. Very simple. Olive oil, lemon, garlic. Oregano. But the key is using lemons from my family's property. The best in the world. We get them shipped in."

"Shipped in," Renzo said, rolling his eyes. "His cousin loads a couple of crates into his old truck and drives up here every week."

I laughed. "However you get the lemons, the dressing is delicious," I said. "Please give your mother my compliments."

After Leo had left the table, clearing my plate as he went, we turned back to our conversation.

"People left Santo Stefano for all different types of reasons," Renzo said. "Today, the town is bustling again. Busy. People are making a living. Like me, with the hotel and other properties I manage. People and their shops. Shepherds with the wool. But a few decades ago, it was, how do you say it? A ghost town. Before tourism, there was nothing here for a long time."

"That's what I've heard," I said. "Young people left to find more opportunity in the bigger cities."

He nodded. "My own grandparents didn't go far, just to the town down the road. But yes, many people did leave for new lives in Rome or Florence or Verona or any number of places. Milan. America, too. And then, the war. Both world wars."

"Yes," I said, drawing out the word. All of what he said was true, and very viable. Of course younger people left the small towns in Italy back then. The same thing had happened all across the United States. Young people wanted opportunity and choices and the chance for their own slice of a dream. Oftentimes, it took them away from the towns where they were born, their roots, their foundations.

But my people had left this place well before either of the world wars. Before Santo Stefano fell into disrepair.

And there was something else hanging in the air—something big that I hadn't mentioned to Renzo, or to anyone other than my cousin. Violetta's death certificate, signed in Santo Stefano. Cause of death: witchcraft.

Why didn't I mention it? First, I didn't even know if it was legitimate. Obviously it wasn't true—I had known my great-grandmother, so she certainly lived an entire lifetime longer than the death date on the certificate, 1912—but even though that was a fabrication, I didn't know why. There was something legitimate behind it, some grain of horrible truth, that had caused her—or someone—to fabricate it and then for Nonna to keep it. I couldn't put my finger on what it was, or why.

I had a feeling it held the key to the whole mystery. Yet I couldn't bring myself to broach the subject with Renzo.

The whole thing was ugly. Death from witchcraft could mean Violetta had been persecuted as a witch. Here. In this town.

Witch persecution, as barbaric as it was, was relatively common in the Middle Ages and later than that, all over Europe and in the "new world," too. The story of the Salem witch trials was well known in the United States, but Italy had its own version, in a town called Triora during the late-1500s, when women were rounded up and accused of witchcraft after bad weather led to famine—obviously the work of a coven of witches.

But that sort of witch hysteria died out long ago, hundreds of years earlier. The death certificate was dated 1912—a long time ago, yes, but thoroughly modern times. The *Titanic* sank in that same year featuring the newest technology of its day, a luxury liner with captains of industry aboard. I highly doubted anyone in those first-class cabins was persecuting women for witchcraft. Nor anyone in steerage, either.

Yet . . . that certificate said different. Or so it seemed. It might be a dark chapter in the town's history, embarrassing and even shaming for Renzo, whose ancestors had lived here at that time. The people of this village now, in modern day, wouldn't take too kindly to that sort of ugly history being dredged up, either. I didn't feel as though I could talk to him about it.

Maybe Luna? I hadn't mentioned it to her earlier. But I was thinking maybe I should.

Renzo and I talked about other things for the rest of our lunch—Luna and her shop, and even world events.

"Is there a way I can search the city archives for records of families who have lived here?" I asked him after we paid the bill and walked out the door, waving our thanks to Leo.

Renzo nodded. "You can start at the city hall—it's right off the piazza. You can't miss it. But now that I think about it, they're going to send you down into town, to the main library for the region. That's where all the old records are kept. On film. You'll probably have to pay to search them."

We went our separate ways then. I stopped in the piazza and leaned against the stone wall, where I found a strong signal for my phone. I punched in the search engine and looked up the address of the library in the bigger city, just down the hill from Santo Stefano. Apparently, I was going for a drive.

But before that, I had a stop to make in town.

CHAPTER 11

Cassandra

The shop sat a few doors down from the piazza. Its wooden sign above the door had a hand-drawn bee pollinating a flower. I pushed open the door and was greeted with the clang of a deep, sonorous chime.

I took a quick breath when I caught sight of the shelves. Short, squat glass jars of honey with handwritten labels lined the shelves, along with slim, elegant bottles of what I assumed was olive oil, rough-hewn soaps tied with twine, and other goods. Candles were everywhere, some in deep-purple stained-glass holders, other pillar candles in a dark cream color standing on their own.

The effect of all those candles flickering reminded me of an alcove in a church. Or what an apothecary might have looked like when this town was new.

"Benvenuta."

A man was standing in the doorway leading to the back room, leaning against the stone wall. I hadn't noticed him when I came in.

"Hi," I said. "What a beautiful shop you have."

"Thank you," he said, smiling. "We make everything ourselves."

That's when I noticed this man. Really noticed him. Something about the moment, his image right then and there, made me bookmark it in my mind.

I put him at about my age, maybe a few years younger. Or was he older? It was hard to tell. He had a look that was altogether ancient and modern at the same time. His dark hair was closely cropped, but curly. His skin was a dark olive. He was wearing a black T-shirt tucked into jeans—his broad shoulders seemed to strain the material. He had a goatee tinged with gray. And his smile was electric.

I held his gaze for a moment . . . as my mind went blank. I tried to think of something to say, but for the first time I could remember, I was tongue-tied. To my horror, I felt heat rising at the back of my neck. I fervently hoped it wouldn't extend to my face.

"Please, feel free to look around," he said. "If you have any questions, don't hesitate to ask."

So I started browsing, grateful for the cool breeze that was wafting in from the heavy leaded-glass windows. I found various varieties of honeys on the shelves—infused with lavender and rosemary and lemons. And many more. I ran my fingers along the jars, noting the old-fashioned script on the labels, as though they had been written with a quill pen.

Was this the type of shop my ancestors had operated? Was this the very shop? I could almost see my great-grandmother here, pouring honey into the small jars, popping in a sprig of rosemary, and sealing it with wax.

"Would you like some tea?" the man asked me, his voice jolting me out of my imaginings.

"That would be lovely," I said. As he disappeared around the corner, I cringed, thinking, *Lovely? What am I, in a Jane Austen novel? Lovely.* I chuckled to myself. *Get it together, Cassie.*

He reappeared carrying a tray with two earthenware mugs, a teapot, and a box of tea bags.

"It's cinnamon," he said, pouring the steaming water into the mugs. "I hope that's all right."

I smiled. "Sounds great!"

"The real purpose of us serving tea is to get people to try the honey," he said, grinning and gesturing to several jars that sat on the counter.

"Clever tactic," I said, reaching for a mug. "Which variety do you recommend for this tea? The honey, I mean."

"That's my mother's specialty, recommending different types of honey, but if I were to be asked, I'd say the plain. Nothing added to it so it enhances but doesn't overpower."

"Plain it is," I said, taking a spoonful out of the jar and drizzling it into my mug. I took a sip. "Delicious!"

We looked at each other then, both smiling slightly. Not saying anything. Truthfully, I forgot why I was there.

"You're the American staying in Renzo's new room," he said finally.

"I am," I said as I took a sip of the tea. It was spicy and sweet and incredibly hot. "Word travels fast here, I see."

"With lightning speed," he said. "We are a small town. Visitors tend to stand out. But actually, Renzo was in here earlier and let me know you'd probably come by. He said you're staying awhile."

Why didn't this surprise me? "He's everywhere," I said.

"At all times," the man said, laughing. "Anything happens in this town, Renzo is there like magic."

"I'm Cassie Graves," I said to him. "And Renzo is right, I'm planning on staying awhile. I'm researching my family history."

"Dante Caruso," he said.

"Nice to meet you, Dante," I said.

"So," he said, sipping his tea. "Your people. They came from Santo Stefano?"

"They did," I said. "But I just found out about it. Rossi is the family name, or was then. They owned a shop a lot like this one, right here in this village. They sold honey."

Dante frowned. "When was this?"

"More than one hundred years ago," I said. "My great-grandparents immigrated to America in 1912, or thereabouts. But I don't know anything about . . . well, anything else. They may have had family who stayed here after they came to America. I'm almost sure they did."

"Rossi, you said?"

"Yes," I said. "And Moretti. My great-grandmother Violetta Rossi married a Giovanni Moretti. Or so we were told. I don't have much information on him. Nothing, actually, except an old photo. So I'm going to start looking there, with their last names, to see if I can find out more."

Dante rubbed his chin. "I know my grandparents bought this shop, the house, and the beehives when they moved here from Cortina—that's how the story goes. I'm not really sure about the particulars. Like, who they bought it from. Or exactly when."

"That's how it is in my family, too," I said, nodding. "Lots of stories, tales, remembrances of the past. Not too much documentation, though."

Dante laughed. "The oral tradition could have used a little ink, right?" He smiled and leaned against the counter. "How are you coming along with this research of yours?"

"I haven't really even started," I said, wincing. "I was planning to head down to the library in town later today to search through old records."

"I'll be happy to ask my mother about the people who we bought this shop from," he said. "It's likely it was your people. It just makes sense, doesn't it? It's not like there were a lot of folks coming and going from this town in those days. Nor a lot of shops that sold honey."

He was right. A twinge of excitement sizzled through me. Could my ancestors have once owned the shop where I was now standing?

He furrowed his brow and continued. "You know about the bees?"

Obviously, since the shop sold honey, there would be some sort of pipeline to bees, but beyond that, I wasn't sure what he was referring to. "Bees? No," I said. "I mean, yes, I know they sold honey. What about the bees, though?"

"When my family bought the shop, it came with a colony of bees," he said, gesturing out the window. "For the honey. The hives are in the meadow by the lake. It's one of the oldest colonies anyone around here can remember. The honey is rather legendary. We ship it all over the world."

Again, that familiar tingle.

"Of course . . ." he began, and then broke into a smile. "I'm going to reveal what a—how do you say it? Nerd I am right now, with what I'm about to say."

I smiled back at him. "I like a good nerd."

"We ship the honey all over the world, but the whole thing about honey is—"

"Local," I finished his thought.

He clapped his hands together. "Exactly! Local honey is so healthy for people who live there because the bees collect pollen from local flowers. So the honey is helpful for allergies to that local pollen. For someone in America, my honey isn't going to be as healthy or beneficial."

I knew that. It's why people in Wharton loved the honey Violetta sold.

"I think I know what you're thinking," Dante said. "Your ancestors started that colony. Or at least tended to it. If they had a shop to sell local honey, it's a near certainty they did. You can see the hives from the window."

I crossed the room to the window and scanned the meadow until I saw several tall and narrow wooden boxes. The hives. There was that tingle again. It felt like electricity shooting through my veins.

As I gazed at the hives, the image of them began to sway and shimmer. And then a woman with long, dark hair came into view. Had she been there before? Maybe she had been crouching down and then stood up? I squinted, somehow thinking that might help me see better. Or at least stop the shimmering.

Dante joined me at the window. I took my eyes off the hives to smile at him, looked back, and the woman was gone. And so was the shimmering.

"Of course, those are the new hives," he said, fully breaking the spell of whatever had just happened. "My grandparents built them a couple of decades ago, if I'm not mistaken. You need to switch it up for the bees every now and then, my grandmother used to say."

As I looked into the face of this impossibly handsome man, I realized that his ancestors may well have known mine. May well have purchased the shop we were now standing in from them.

"I'd love to talk with your grandparents," I said. "If they're still in the area. Anything they could tell me about my ancestors, the Rossis, would be so helpful."

He smiled and shook his head. "My parents live down in town," he said, "with my grandmother. They take care of her. She's not too well these days and does not travel, not even up here to Santo Stefano. My grandfather has been gone for several years now."

I didn't want to push or pry, but I felt that this—something, whatever it was—was so close to me. Actual, living people who had known my ancestors. Maybe they could clear up this mystery once and for all or at the very least answer some questions.

The chime on the door rousted me out of my imaginings as Renzo breezed into the shop.

Dante grinned at me. "Didn't I tell you about him?" he said, nodding in Renzo's direction. "He's everywhere."

Renzo held up his hand. "I keep my ear to the ground, my friend. It's my job to know what's going on in town."

"Remind me not to do anything illegal with you on the prowl."

Renzo snorted. "Someone dies of a bee sting and I'll know who's to blame."

I couldn't help but smile. This village was so friendly, I thought. Everyone teasing each other, with an undercurrent of love. Or at least affection. It reminded me a little of Wharton. For the first time, I wondered if that friendliness, that vibe, is what had drawn Violetta to stay in the small town I called home.

Then, Renzo turned to me. "It's you I was hoping to find," he said. "Somehow, I thought you'd be in here. Luna is having a little dinner party tomorrow and hopes you'll come."

I raised my eyebrows, delighted. "I'd love to!"

"Good," he said, "because she's inviting her mother, who is bringing some people you might be related to."

My hand flew to my mouth. "The Morettis?"

Renzo nodded. "Yes, that's them. You seem excited!"

I shrugged but couldn't stop smiling. "I am! This is what I came for! To find my roots! They could be related to me, if it's the same Moretti family."

Renzo waved his hand, as if dismissing my doubts. "Oh, I'm sure it is. The families who live in these towns, the ties run deep. Even if the younger people move away, they are still tied here. And there aren't that many families, not that many names, you know? It's not like there are fifteen Moretti families, none related to each other."

Dante squinted at him. "I should call my parents," he said, rubbing his chin. "Maybe they can drive up, too. My great-grandparents bought this shop from people who were likely related to Cassie."

"The Rossis," I added.

Renzo clapped his hands together. "Okay! This is shaping up to be a nice group. I'll tell Luna. We'll talk tomorrow, but I'm sure she'll want you to come by seven o'clock."

"Can I bring anything?" I asked. "Bread? An appetizer?"

Renzo rolled his eyes. "You Americans," he said with a grin. "In Italy, we don't bring food. Just a small gift for Luna. Flowers. A candle. Like that. She'll have the menu planned and will be cooking all day." As he was leaving, he turned back around and winked at me. "You're in for a treat."

"The man appears and suddenly there's a dinner party," Dante said, shaking his head. "He's right, though. You're in for a treat. Have you been to dinner at an Italian's home since you've been here?"

"No," I said. "But it sounds like fun."

"Come hungry," he said, and grinned. As he did, I could see the little boy in him. How could someone so big, so muscular, look so adorable at the same time?

"I really should go," I said.

He grabbed a jar of honey infused with lavender and held it out to me. "On the house," he said.

"Really? I'll be happy to pay for it," I said.

"No, no," he said. "Call it a small welcome gift."

As I took the jar from his hand, our fingers touched, just for a second. I felt the heat rushing, once again, to my face. Butterflies in my stomach. What was I, fifteen years old? I hadn't had that feeling in a long time.

As I left the shop and was walking back down to my room, I stopped and leaned against the stone wall, which was waist high, and gazed down at the hives in the meadow. The woman with the dark hair was gone. If she had ever been there at all.

CHAPTER 12

Violetta

Word spread quickly about the strange white donkey that had followed Violetta home. First, their nearest neighbors came to peer into the barn, and over the course of the next few days, they began talking about it in the piazza. *A white donkey? Isn't that a sign of protection? A blessing from above? It's in the barn of the Rossi sisters. Yes, the ones who sell the honey. We heard the girl came upon it in the meadow, by the lake. And it followed her home.*

Soon, people from other parts of the village heard about it and started coming by. Even the priest who traveled among the nearby hill towns to hold church services paid a visit.

"Is it a miracle, Don Paolo?" one of the townspeople whispered to the priest.

"I wouldn't presume to say," Don Paolo said, scratching his beard. "That is for someone wiser than I am. But she certainly is a beauty, isn't she?"

He was right about that. Bianca was the most beautiful donkey anyone had ever seen, if there was such a thing, with her pure white hair, her blue eyes, and her contented gaze. But Fiora wasn't thinking about that. Not at all.

Fiora didn't much like all the attention. No good ever came from it, her mother used to say. Rosa and Constant and the girls had lived a small life, with very large abilities and gifts—and funds—but they went out of their way to not call attention to their family. And certainly didn't call attention to what they had. Too many prying eyes never spelled anything good. Fiora knew that on a deep level, for certain. Like she knew her own name.

But Florencia thought differently. Despite the fact she had lived the same life her sister had, learned the same lessons her parents tried to impart, saw what happened to their family, she looked upon Bianca's arrival into their lives as an opportunity.

Florencia had a head for business. She began bringing jars of honey, and bottles of oils, and the soaps that they made and sold upstairs in their shop down into the barn with Giuseppe and Bianca. That's where all the people came to see this white donkey. So it was like the sisters had two shops now, selling their crafts. Even Fiora had to admit it was a smart idea, to take advantage of the steady stream of people who came to see Bianca with their own eyes. Who wouldn't want to buy a souvenir of that? Some nice honey to take home? The sisters even began drawing the donkey on the labels for their goods.

Soon, sales had jumped so much that the sisters had trouble keeping up with the demand. Fortunately, Violetta had grown and was already helping her mother and aunt craft their wares, imbuing them with quietly whispered incantations and spells from their leather-bound book. Between the three Rossi women, they got it done.

"Bianca might not be a miracle," Florencia said to her sister one afternoon as she was counting the money from that day's sales, "but she has been a blessing."

One person in the village who was not especially taken with the white donkey was Giovanni Moretti, a boy about Violetta's age whose family lived in a set of grand rooms in the main castle.

Giovanni's father, Silvio, was the town's banker, and because of this, Silvio's wife, Sofia, wore extremely fine clothes, finer than any woman in

Santo Stefano. Silvio and Sofia each had their own reasons for disliking the Rossi sisters.

Sofia did not trust the sisters—despite the fact that she would secretly go to them with ailments and always receive just the thing to cure them—because they were, as many people said, the most beautiful women in the village. Her husband had a wandering eye.

But Silvio's eye wasn't wandering toward the Rossi sisters for the reason his wife suspected. He alone knew how much money the sisters had when they arrived in Santo Stefano and how successful they had become since then. For women to be so wealthy—it wasn't right. It wasn't seemly. How did they have a near fortune when they arrived in town? Why was everyone drawn to their damnable honey? It smacked of something sinister and dark and even—although Silvio wouldn't say it out loud—evil. Other men thought so, too. The mayor, for one. But nobody had any proof of anything. And ultimately, people thought it was none of their business. Silvio wasn't so sure.

The fact they were alone gnawed at him. No man in sight, for either of the sisters? No father for the young girl? Where was he? What was going on there? One thing was for sure, though. Their purported relation to the old Leonardo Leone, the man whose house they had taken possession of years ago when they first came to the village, was shaky at best. Frankly, Silvio didn't believe it was true. They probably didn't know the old man at all, and they certainly weren't his granddaughters, he thought. But what could anyone do about it? The sisters had produced the deed. How they had gotten their hands on that document, he did not know. Again, his theories went toward the dark side.

Silvio would think these thoughts to himself as he smiled at Florencia when she'd make her deposits. *There is something not right about them.*

So he was none too happy when word reached him that his son had been seen with Violetta in the meadow by the lake, walking alongside the patient donkey with the large white dog trailing behind.

"I don't want Giovanni anywhere near that Rossi girl," Silvio declared to his wife one evening after the boy had gone to bed.

Sofia squinted at her husband and wondered why. Something wasn't right there, she thought. Silently, she told herself to ignore her husband's wishes. She knew her son wasn't one to take that kind of directive well anyway. "Stay away from the girl" would fall on deaf ears. The boy had always been headstrong, if utterly charming, his mother thought with a small smile. But that wasn't why she wouldn't forbid him from seeing the girl.

She just didn't see the harm in Giovanni spending time with Violetta. Quite the contrary. Especially if they were in the barn with the donkeys or in the shop with the girl's mother and aunt. Her son could be Sofia's eyes and ears in that household. If Silvio was anywhere near either one of those women, Giovanni would see it.

So the next day when the boy announced he was going to see the white donkey, Sofia smiled.

"Have fun, *bambino*. Say hello to the donkey for me. And to the girl's mother and auntie. Tell them I'll come by for some honey later today."

"*Bambino?*" Giovanni frowned. "Mama, I'm not a baby anymore."

Sofia ruffled her son's hair and let her hand rest on his cheek. He was growing up, she knew. Just too fast. He was their youngest child. Soon he, too, would be gone with a family of his own. "No matter how old you are, you will always be my baby."

Giovanni wrapped his arms around his mother's waist and hugged her close, a kind of melancholy descending over him at hearing those words. He didn't know why, but it was the passage of time he was feeling. The end of childhood, the beginning of the next stage. There is always a frantic clinging to the stage one is leaving before embracing the next. As he hugged his mother that day, Giovanni felt it.

But as he ran down the cobbled streets, down the stairs, and through the alleyways to Violetta's house, he wasn't thinking about that, or the donkey or the aunt or the mama. He was thinking about the girl. His next stage.

"I prefer Giuseppe," he announced upon entering the barn that day, after finishing up with his tutors. The Morettis, like other wealthy families of the day, had tutors for their children. So young Gio learned about art and history and mathematics and science and all manner of things. Violetta didn't have a formal education—most girls didn't in those days, in that time—but she learned everything she needed to know at her mother's kitchen table from Fiora and Florencia.

Violetta was brushing Bianca as the dog Freddo looked on and Giuseppe patiently waited his turn.

"You don't think Bianca is beautiful, Gio?" she asked, her own face reddening a bit at the sight of the boy. "What's wrong with you?"

"Oh, she's beautiful," Gio said. "But Giuseppe is kinder. More patient. I think he's wiser."

Violetta considered this, nodding. He was right. Bianca, it seemed to her, was pure goodness. But a little naive. Giuseppe did have the wisdom.

Nobody knew it, but Violetta believed she had conjured Bianca up, called her to come and join their family out of . . . , well, she didn't know where. Wherever one calls to, prays to, asks politely. One day in the meadow, she had called. And Bianca had come. Shyly at first, stepping down from the hills, over the stones, watching Violetta and Giuseppe and Freddo for a bit, considering the bees, and then returning to wherever it was she'd come from. But as the days passed, she stayed longer and longer. Until the day she had decided they were her next stage and followed them home.

Violetta had several reasons for calling, or conjuring, Bianca. Most importantly, she thought Giuseppe was lonely at times. In fact, she knew it. She could feel it radiating off his sweet face. Oh, he knew how much she loved him. And how much Freddo loved him. And he loved them right back. But it wasn't the same as having one of his own kind to share his thoughts with, to stand beside in the barn when everyone else had gone to the main house, to sleep next to. To commiserate about the grasses and the flowers in the meadow. To gossip about the bees.

But Violetta also felt that her aunt and mother needed Bianca, too, as much if not more than Giuseppe did. The townspeople would think Bianca, a white donkey, was some sort of miracle. A blessing. A sign. And she was that, no doubt about it. Violetta knew that her household having this donkey meant one thing: protection. The townspeople would see that they—she and her mother and her aunt—had been blessed with this good omen. And therefore, the townspeople would believe they were good and deserving and worthy.

If she had been asked to articulate why she thought her mama and auntie needed that sort of protection or shield, she would not have been able to say why. She just knew it was true. And it was.

She turned her eyes to Gio. "Do you want to brush Giuseppe, then, if you prefer him? He likes to look handsome before we go outside for the day."

"You know I like to brush him."

Gio got to work. As he brushed the donkey's bristly coat, he found the rhythm of it to be a sort of meditation. Although he didn't know that word. Or the concept. He just knew that the repetitive motion, coupled with Giuseppe's patient and kind aura, brought Gio a sense of peace. He exhaled with every stroke of the brush.

Or maybe it was being with Violetta that gave him the peace. He shyly glanced at her over Giuseppe's back. Her beautiful hair. Her startling eyes. All he wanted was to be near her. They had known each other since they were very young children, but now, something felt different.

He wondered if she felt it, too. But he didn't have to wonder. Violetta had always known Gio was the one who would stand beside her, sleep next to her, commiserate about all manner of things, gossip about the bees.

She knew Gio was her only love. She knew they would marry and have a child one day, a daughter named Gia, who would have a granddaughter who would come back to this village, long after everyone

Violetta knew was in the ether, looking down and watching. Sending protection. Sending warnings. That was all crystal clear to Violetta. But the rest was murky. She couldn't see any more of their future, but she convinced herself that was because she wasn't supposed to see it.

That was true. She couldn't have known what was coming. She would have changed everything if she had.

But that day, as their little band—Giuseppe, Bianca, Freddo, Violetta, and Gio—set off for the meadow, Gio cast his gaze up to the hills and then to the mountains beyond. What an incredibly blue sky—had it always been so blue? What a beautiful scene before them, snowcapped, rugged peaks ringing a peaceful meadow by the lake where turtles sunned themselves on the flat stones by the shore. And Violetta. The most wonderful girl in the world. He looked into the face of this girl, whom he loved so much, and thought: Could life get any better than this? Gio didn't think it could.

Violetta had brought a blanket and a basket with cheeses and meats and bread for her and Gio, carrots for the donkeys, and a bone for Freddo. As she set up their little outpost, doled out the treats to the animals—the donkeys swished their tails in thanks, and Freddo turned in a few quick circles to signify his delight—and settled in next to Gio with a book she had tucked into her basket, she looked into the face of the boy sitting next to her and thought: Could life get any better than this? Violetta didn't think it could.

CHAPTER 13

Cassandra

On my way from Dante's shop, I stopped by the city hall in the piazza. Renzo had said they wouldn't have records dating back as far as I needed to go, but I was right there so I popped inside anyway.

The ancient building, marked with the Medici crest above the door, felt damp and cool inside, even on this warm day. Walking down the marble hallways to the main office, I half expected to encounter a scribe behind a big wooden desk, his work lit by a candle. But instead, when I pushed open the office door, I saw a regular woman in a smart blue dress, sitting at a desk that looked like it had been stamped out in the 1970s.

I had inputted a question into my phone's translation app and read it to the woman: "I'm looking for town records from around 1911. Maybe earlier. Do you have anything like that here?"

She shook her head and answered in English. "No, not from that far back. The library down in town has those archives."

I wasn't surprised, but I thought I'd check just in case. Truthfully, I was none too excited about getting behind the wheel again.

The last time I had been in my little peashooter of a car, I had been white-knuckling it up the mountain road in the fog. With the bright sunshine of the day, I felt like the drive was going to be immeasurably easier. That's what I told myself, anyway, as I headed out to the parking lot. It was only around two o'clock. Plenty of time to get down to town, do some research, and get back up before night fell.

I put it in gear and set off, hugging the edge of the winding mountain road as I crept along, not daring to go faster than second gear would allow.

I noticed a flock of sheep grazing on the mountainside, a peaceful sight . . . until I rounded a corner and saw a huge white dog standing in the middle of the road. I slammed on my brakes without engaging the clutch, and it killed the engine.

The air seemed to electrify just then as I held the dog's gaze. He was looking right at me. Not in a menacing way. In a familiar way. I could've sworn he was smiling. We sat there for a long moment, both looking at each other, and then he bounded off onto the hillside after a wayward sheep.

Par for the course in this mountainous region, I said to myself, and started the car once again.

Finally off the mountain—mere miles seemed like a lifetime—I used my phone's navigation to find the main library in town—*biblioteca*—and made my way inside, armed with the trusty translator on my phone.

But I wasn't any more successful than I had been at the city hall in Santo Stefano. Thanks to a helpful librarian, I did manage to find some town records from Santo Stefano on microfilm, but—as if it hadn't occurred to me before—they were all in Italian. Many of the original records had been handwritten, and all of them were faded. I scanned through the documents, not knowing quite what I was looking for. So I settled on names. Rossi and Moretti. I found very few entries for Rossi, and many for Moretti. But even with the translator on my phone, I couldn't find anything very helpful.

So in the end, I left without getting what I had come for. Walking outside and down the street to the piazza, I noticed a gelato shop. I might not have found anything more about my family, but I could at least get some gelato.

Taking my cone to a park across the street, I sat and watched the bustle of life go by. So different from Santo Stefano. So cosmopolitan. So modern.

As I thought about it, I figured not finding any records was not a setback, not really. I had Violetta's "death" certificate, which certainly didn't tell me anything. But I was having dinner the following night with some people who, potentially, could. The other guests at Luna's dinner party might be able to relate some stories. Oral history.

If Dante's family was able to join us, they just might be able to shed some light on the Rossi side of mine. It was too bad his grandmother was in ill health—I'd have loved to talk directly with the woman whose parents had purchased the shop from my relatives. I did a quick calculation of the years—all I knew was that my great-grandmother Violetta was in the States by 1912. So Dante's grandmother couldn't possibly have purchased the shop and the bees from her. It would have had to be Dante's great-grandparents who bought it.

Although . . . it was only Violetta and Giovanni who came to America. Maybe her relatives kept the shop in Santo Stefano, lived here for years after that. If that was the case, Dante's grandparents may well have done the transaction. Would that mean I still had Rossi relatives somewhere in the area? That was a distinct possibility.

And then, there would be people from the other side of my family, the Giovanni Moretti side. These were likely direct relatives of his and, by extension, mine.

Although . . . I didn't have any proof Giovanni was actually my nonna Gia's father. Only what she and Violetta had told me. Gia's birth certificate said different. *Illegitimate.* I shook my head at the thought of it. That had to be some sort of mistake.

The ringing of my phone startled me out of my thoughts. The cell signal came and went in this village, and I never knew when I'd be able to make or take a call. I fished my phone out of my purse and saw it was Maria. It was morning back in Wharton.

"Hi!" I said. "I'm sitting in a park in town, eating a gelato." I snapped a quick photo and sent it to her.

"By contrast, I am sitting at my kitchen table having my first cup of coffee after cleaning up the dog's vomit that I found when I got up this morning. Which of us is having the better day?"

"I wish you were here!" I said, chuckling.

"I do, too," she said. "How's it going?"

"A strange set of circumstances happened today," I began. "Now that I'm going to say it all out loud, it seems really weird."

Maria was silent for a moment. "What is it?"

"So . . . I met the owner of a deli here in town. Luna is her name. Really great woman. I think she and Renzo are together."

Maria laughed. "You're in town five seconds and you already have the gossip."

"Right? Anyway, I told her I was researching our family tree, and she told me she knows some Morettis who live in the next town. Renzo is all but sure we're related to them. Like he said, around here, there aren't that many families with the same name that are *not* related to each other."

"Get out!"

"I know! And get this. Luna is having a dinner party tomorrow, and they're coming. So I just might be meeting our relatives."

"Are you kidding me?"

"It gets weirder," I said. "After lunch, I was wandering around town and I came upon—get this—a honey shop."

"Like the one in that photo of Violetta that you found?"

"Not like it. I think it *is* it."

"I can't stand it! This cannot be happening. For real."

"I know, but there's more. The guy who owns the shop, Dante, said his great-grandparents bought it from the Rossis. Dante and his parents are also coming to dinner."

"So at this one dinner, you are going to potentially learn about both sides of our mothers' family. The Rossis and the Morettis."

"Yes! It seems too fantastic to be true. Yet there we are. Tomorrow, I'll be sitting at a table with people who can tell me all kinds of things we don't know about Nonna's mother and potentially other relatives."

"I cannot get over the fact that you made this happen in one day."

Something about what she said stopped me short. I didn't make anything happen, other than coming to Italy in the first place. All of this simply happened *to* me. It was like I had opened one door and it all came tumbling down at me. I knew that feeling all too well. I had come to Italy partially to get away from that, and I had walked right into it again.

"And what about this *Dante*?" she asked, drawing out his name so it had several more syllables.

I felt the back of my neck heating up. "He's really handsome, Mimi," I said, thinking about his dark hair.

She clicked her tongue. "Available?"

"I don't know," I said. "He kept saying 'we' this and 'we' that, so I'm wondering if there's a wife involved."

"And he's coming to dinner, you said?"

"He is. And bringing his parents, if they can make it up from town."

"Hmm," she said, her voice singsongy and teasing. "So let me get this straight. At the dinner table, you will have the Morettis, who may or may not be related to us. The handsome owner of the shop Violetta and her family ran in that town a century ago. He may or may not have a wife—and you're hoping not. His parents, who may or may not have known Violetta's people. And Renzo and Luna, who may or may not be an item. Is that about right?"

I laughed out loud. "When you say it like that, it sounds pretty weird. But that's exactly what's going to happen."

"In one day, you conjured all of this up," Maria said. "Oh, my dear Cassie. What tangled webs you're weaving in Santo Stefano."

I took a breath. My whole body went cold. What had she just said? I fingered the amulet around my neck.

Shake it off, Cassie. It's just a coincidence.

We talked for a few more minutes until Maria had to get going and start her day. After dropping my phone back into my purse, I sat there a while longer, taking in the view, trying not to think about webs and dreams and spiders. A chill wind blew around me then, as if it had swirled down from the snowcapped mountain peaks.

I rubbed my arms, realizing it had gotten downright cold as the sun had moved through the sky. I imagined that's how it was in these towns at this time of year, warm in the heat of the day and chilly as that day faded into night. I headed back to my car, imagining a long soak in the Jacuzzi with a glass of wine and a good book.

A few miles outside the center of town but not yet to the road up to Santo Stefano, I spotted the Oasi, a sort of "everything" store Renzo had told me about. I pulled in, figuring I'd need some provisions for the coming week. Inside, I saw the store carried groceries, wine, and the odd lawn chair, wrench, or bird feeder. I filled up my cart with produce and pasta, cheese and yogurt, bath salts and toilet paper.

As I was wandering the aisles, looking for anything else I needed, I noticed an old woman, dressed all in black, eyeing the deli case of meats and cheeses. She was tiny, maybe five feet tall, hair pulled back into a tight bun. She turned her eyes my way and I smiled at her, but she did not return it, giving me a glare that could have sunk a ship.

For reasons I didn't quite understand, my hand went up to the amulet around my neck. It felt warm, almost hot, to the touch. I shook my head, not knowing what the old bird might have to glare at me about—maybe she didn't like Americans?—and I hurried down the aisle, away from her.

But a few moments later, as I was loading a few bottles of wine into my cart, I felt the hair on the back of my neck stand up. A shiver ran through me.

I turned around and saw the old woman standing right behind me. She nodded. *"Strega,"* she whispered under her breath and walked on, disappearing around the corner into another aisle.

I knew what that word meant. *Witch? Me? What was that all about?* I went after her, pushing my cart around the corner, but there was no sign of her. I glanced up and down the aisles on my way to the register, but she was gone.

⁕

Back on the road, I found I was getting more used to traversing the mountain—no white-knuckling. It was easier going up than it was going down. I arrived back in the town and pulled into the parking lot and thought, *I'm home.* Funny, I had been there only a little more than one day, and I was already starting to feel like I belonged. I made my way to my room and pushed open the door, gingerly at first, hoping not to see a huge spider or its webs or anything of the kind. I exhaled when I saw there was, blissfully, nothing out of the ordinary. Just the small wooden table, my bed, the chair by the fire. All my familiar things. I shut the door behind me and latched it, realizing it felt good to be "home."

I set my bags on the counter, peeled off my jacket, and unwound my new black scarf. Groceries put away, I headed to the Jacuzzi room. I turned on the taps and flipped the lights on in their little stone alcoves, giving the room the glow of an apse in a church.

Then I lit the fire I had laid before leaving the house that morning, making sure the flue was open, and watched it blaze to life. Then I tapped the tunes app on my phone and filled the air with Renaissance-era music—lutes seemed like just the right ambiance—and poured a glass of wine. After undressing and grabbing my book out of its alcove by the bed, I padded back to the tub room for my blissful soak. I couldn't help stealing a glance up at the ceiling above the bed—no cracks, no places to hide, no spiders the size of Chihuahuas.

I exhaled. There were no webs woven here. That I knew of.

I was a few chapters into my relaxing soak when I noticed the lights in the tub room flickering. Slightly at first. And then they, and all the other lights, went dark with a loud pop. The jets stopped humming. The whole place would've been completely black if not for the glow of the fireplace in the main room.

Ugh. What a bother. I wondered if something was wrong with the wiring. Or if it was up to code. If Italy had the same kind of electrical codes we did in the States. Maybe I had had too many lights on at the same time, along with the jets, and it blew a fuse. Or something.

I slipped out of the tub, wrapped a towel around me, and headed into the main room, where my phone was plugged in. I had intended to call Renzo and let him know about the blown fuse, but I didn't get a chance to do it. Not right at that moment. Because as I stepped into the main room, I caught the scent of something musky. Earthy. A little sweet, almost like fresh hay. Not a bad odor, necessarily; it was just strange. It shouldn't have been there at all.

And that's when I heard it. Steps. It sounded like hoofbeats on cobblestone. Slow and rhythmic. *Clop. Clop. Clop.*

And then I saw the eyes. Bright, searing blue eyes. On the other side of the room, by the door. I was not alone in this place. But this was not a person. Not a human. Those eyes looked like the eyes of an animal. I heard it make a noise. A low sound, almost as though it were sighing.

I took a breath and could feel my heart pounding in my chest, in my whole body, as though it was pumping my blood furiously, at high speed. I grabbed my phone and, after my shaking hands fumbled with it for a moment that seemed to stretch on forever, I hit the flashlight feature and pointed it straight at those eyes.

A beam of light shone across the room, illuminating specs of dust that were floating in the air. For a millisecond, it caught the image of something, something big, but just then, just as quickly, the overhead lights flickered back on. The jets in the tub whirred to life. Whatever had been there—if anything had—was gone.

CHAPTER 14

Cassandra

I stood there for a moment, shivering in my towel, not knowing quite what to think. I pulled on my robe and sank into the armchair next to the fire. It was not a dream, that much I knew. The spider might have been conjured up by my overactive imagination somehow, but I had not been anything close to sleeping just now. I was immersed not only in a bath of deliciously warm water but in a captivating book, too.

I didn't want to think about the strangeness that had begun to swirl around me, the crazy coincidences that had happened since I arrived in Santo Stefano, and what I might (or might not) learn at the dinner the following evening. The spider. The odd specter of a figure by the hives. The creepy lady at the grocery store. I wanted to put it all out of my mind, and for a few blissful moments, I had. And now this.

I pushed myself up from the armchair and crept across the room to where I had seen . . . whatever it was. Nothing was there. Nothing out of the ordinary, that is. I had smelled hay, I thought, and a musky animal smell. But there was no odor like that now. All I smelled in the air was the scented water in the tub and the cozy aroma of the wood fire.

I unlatched the door and opened it. The sun had all but set, the pink sky bathing everything in a warm glow of twilight. I looked this way and that—the street was empty, save for a couple of calico cats padding down the lane. I didn't know what I expected to see—an animal running away?

I closed the door and leaned against it. I was still clutching my phone as though it were my only lifeline to civilization, which in a way I guess it was. I dialed Renzo.

"Hello, Cassie Graves," he said, his voice radiating warmth and familiarity. "What can I do for you?"

All at once, I wasn't at all sure what I was calling about. To hear a friendly voice?

"The power in my place just went out," I said finally. "It came back on after a minute or two, so everything's fine now. But I just thought you should know."

He made a clicking sound with his tongue. "Okay," he said, drawing out the word. "Not unusual here in Santo Stefano, for power to be glitchy, but we rewired your place when we did the renovation so . . ." He went silent for a moment, thinking. "Was everything on? Like, the TV and all of the lights and the tub and the heaters?"

"No," I said. "Just some lights and the tub."

"Hmmm," he said. "That's definitely not right, then. It shouldn't be doing that. I'll call my guys and have them come by tomorrow to check it out. But until then, make sure your phone is charged. And there are some candles in the pantry, so put them in the alcoves by the bed, just in case."

"I'll do that," I said. "Thanks, Renzo."

"No problem!" he said. *"Ciao, bella!"*

"Ciao," I said, but he had already hung up.

I looked around the empty room. It was just me. No strange animals with bright blue eyes. No spiders weaving webs around me. No traps.

I wasn't quite sure what to do then. After the spider incident and now this . . . was it safe to stay there? Was this place haunted? The thought seemed ridiculous in one way, but on the other hand, what else could explain these strange happenings? I could be going off the deep end—that was a distinct possibility. There was certainly enough stress in my life to manifest my own share of crazy.

I can't explain why, but despite these two odd occurrences, I didn't feel unsafe or threatened in that place. The vibe was still the same—warm, welcoming, cozy. Even familiar. I could probably ask Renzo if he could move me to another of the hotel's properties, but deep down, I really didn't want to do that. I liked my little room.

So I shook it off. What else could I do?

With that inviting tub of hot water beckoning, I slipped back into it. After I had read a couple more chapters, I remembered what Renzo had called this place earlier in the day. *La suite dell'asino*. Donkey suite? He had told me this had been a barn for donkeys back in the day.

Is that what had visited me? The smell of hay, the sound of hooves, the animal eyes . . . I chuckled to myself. There could be worse things to haunt me than an ass. Come to think of it, I had been married to one for a few decades. What could the ghost of a donkey do to me that a real, live ass hadn't already done?

❧

Out of the bath, I wasn't quite sure what to do with myself. It was just after six o'clock. Settle in for the night? Read some more? In the end, I pulled on jeans and a sweater and headed out for a walk.

The air was crisp and clear. Lights were twinkling in many of the windows I passed, people gathering with their families after the day of doing whatever they did. Many of the shops were closing or had closed for the night. I noticed Dante's door was shut, lights off. I wondered if he lived behind his shop, too, like Luna did. La Oliva was closed, too. The piazza, empty, but for a couple of calico cats.

I wandered down one of the alleyways and saw some lights twinkling in a window near the end. Above the open door, a sign that said **Il Caminetto**. I poked my head inside—a taverna, then. I hadn't seen it during my walk around town earlier in the day.

I took a few steps through the heavy wooden door and saw a bar made of dark wood with five leather stools in front of it. A black wrought-iron candle chandelier hung from the ceiling. Candles flickered on all the wooden tables.

My jaw dropped when I saw the enormous fireplace on one end of the room. It was massive enough for a person to walk into, the type that is basically an arched opening in the wall itself. Its stone hearth extended well past the opening, and the wooden mantel, set with a dozen candles, was the size of a tree. A black cauldron hung over the blazing fire.

A young man came walking into the room, wiping his hands on a towel.

"*Ciao!*" he said.

"*Ciao!* Are you open?"

He smiled. "Yes, yes, we're open," he said. "Take any table you like. Wine?"

"Please! Trebbiano, if you have it."

I settled in at a table by the window, facing that breathtaking fireplace. My thoughts were lost in the flames when the young man came with my wine—a bottle—and a wineglass.

"That fireplace. I've never seen anything like it."

He pulled out a chair and sank into it, pouring some wine for me.

"*Magnifico*, no?" he said, smiling. "This room, this place was the kitchen in the castle when it was first built. And for hundreds of years after that. This is where the meals for the Medicis and their guests—kings, queens, artists, popes, everyone—were prepared."

I imagined the ado and bustle that must've taken place in these rooms. Maybe Michelangelo had been here. Da Vinci. It was possible.

"Unreal. It feels like I walked into *Game of Thrones*."

He laughed. "Much less bloody here, I promise." He smiled at me for a moment. "You're Renzo's American."

Renzo's American, indeed. Word traveled fast.

"Yes, I'll be in town awhile," I said. "I'm Cassie."

"Very nice to meet you, Cassie," he said. "I'm Tony. Come in anytime. I like to practice my English."

"You don't need much practice! Your English is very good. I should be practicing my Italian . . . which is not very good."

"Allora, benvenuta, Cassie," he said slowly. *"Godetevi il vino."*

Of that, I got "welcome, Cassie" and "wine." I would have to work on it, I thought.

We chatted a bit then, partly in Italian, partly in English. He asked what I thought of the town, where I had been, what I had seen—the usual. But then he said something that made the hair on the back of my neck stand up.

"Have you noticed the other hill town near here, the one you can see from the piazza? It's Castel del Monte."

"I have," I said, nodding. I had seen it the day before and thought it looked like an interesting place to visit, ancient, like Santo Stefano.

"You should go," he said. "It's a lot like here. But there? Only witches. Lots of witches there."

I choked on a sip of my wine. "Really?"

Tony laughed. "Well, not *only* witches. But there is a famous witch festival there every summer. A big attraction. People come from all over the country. Everything witches there."

How could he have possibly known?

"An old lady at the Oasi called me a witch today," I said, not quite knowing why I blurted that out.

He laughed again. "Old ladies will do that," he said. But then his hand tapped at his throat. "I see you're protected."

He was referring to the necklace.

"Luna gave it to me," I said.

He raised his eyebrows. "Oh, Luna? Well, good then. You're fine."

He tapped the table and pushed his chair back. "You don't want to get the evil eye," he said, winking at me before he slipped back behind the bar.

I stared into the flames, thinking about witches and the creepy old lady and evil eyes and festivals. I was so lost in thought, I didn't hear Dante come in.

"Hello," he said, appearing next to my table. "I see you found the best place in town for a glass of wine."

Warmth ran through me at the sight of him. "I did," I said. "Care to join me . . . unless you're meeting someone?" I looked toward the door, wondering if I'd see a wife. Or someone.

He pulled out a chair. "It's just me. And I'd love to."

Tony brought an extra glass and a cutting board piled with sliced meats, cheeses, dried fruits, and nuts. "To snack on," he said. "And I'll open another bottle, just in case."

"Nice kid," Dante said after Tony had left. "His family has owned this place for a couple of generations."

As we sipped our wine and chatted about the day, I glanced down at his left hand. No wedding ring. A twinge of guilt slithered through me. Why should I care? I was a married woman. Or was I? John certainly had no doubt about whether he was married, considering yet another woman had been in his bed the night before.

It occurred to me that, despite everything, I had been hanging on to what we once had. To those memories of our lifetime together that I still held so dear. But as I sat across from this handsome Italian man, in this magical place, I realized that I could still have those memories, cherish them as part of my past. But I knew they wouldn't be part of my future. Nor would John. It was as though I could feel the cord cutting, the ties, unbinding. The vows, disintegrating.

I turned my attention to the man sitting in front of me. Would he be in my future? I didn't know. I had just met the guy. But I knew he was there, right then. I was a bit unsure about what to say, but I pulled out my timeworn tactic when I was at a loss for words: I asked him about himself.

"Have you lived here in Santo Stefano all of your life?"

"I grew up here," he said. "My parents ran the shop, as you know. My dad was also the town veterinarian—he was the one who was interested in the bees at first. Then my mom took that over. But I haven't lived here my whole life. I went to school in Rome and lived there until a few years ago. More opportunity than I'd find here. I'm afraid I was one of those young people who moved away, looking for a better life."

"What did you find? I know you run the shop now, but did you do something else before?"

He nodded, taking a sip of wine. "I'm a lawyer," he said. "I practiced in Rome for, what, twenty years."

That surprised me a little. Dante seemed so laid back and relaxed. My image of lawyers was quite the opposite. But it could be my image was wrong.

"What made you come back here?"

"Life, you know? My daughters grew up, and my wife and I divorced and . . . I don't know. I got tired of the *corsa sfrenata*. The rat race, as you say. My parents were getting older and couldn't really handle the shop anymore. They were ready for a quieter life. I guess I was, too."

It sounded familiar. Very familiar. Funny, we were an ocean apart, on different continents, in different worlds, speaking different languages, and having much the same experience in midlife.

"That's very close to what my life has been for the past few years," I said. "I moved away from the small town I grew up in, too. I moved back recently after more than two decades. My son is in college, my marriage fell apart, my parents are both gone, and I got tired of my life in the city. So I moved back. To the house I grew up in, actually."

Dante smiled. "We are both very lucky," he said.

"How so?"

"We had homes that we were drawn back to, happy places that would shelter us when life got stormy."

He did not know how true that was.

After an hour or so of chatting with this interesting, funny man, it was time to go.

I waved my goodbyes to Tony, and Dante and I walked out of the place together. It was nearing eight o'clock, and the streets were more bustling than they had been when I arrived. Many of the restaurants were readying for dinner, their doors open and inviting, windows blazing with light.

"I'm headed up this way," Dante said, pointing toward the piazza. "May I walk you home?"

I smiled and shook my head. "I'm fine," I said. "But I'll see you tomorrow at Luna's?"

"Looking forward to it," he said, tilting his head to the side and smiling.

"Me too," I said.

Dante laughed. "You might not be saying that if you knew about the carload of old folks I'm bringing. They can be . . . a lot."

I couldn't wait.

CHAPTER 15

Violetta

Violetta sat at the vanity dresser, staring into the mirror, brushing her hair. The same mirror where her mother Fiora and aunt Florencia had brushed their hair at night, getting ready for bed, for as long as Violetta could remember. One hundred strokes, they had always said.

But Violetta wasn't getting ready for bed on this particular evening. She was dressing for a visit from a man, something she had never seen her mother nor her aunt do.

A man. She chuckled to herself at the thought of it. Giovanni Moretti was coming by to take her for a walk, the same Gio who had come by to take her for walks and picnics and exploring the hills and helping her with the animals nearly every day of their lives. Much to his father's chagrin.

But this time was different.

One day the week prior, Gio had come to the barn carrying a basket and wearing a fine suit, not the work clothes he usually wore. His hair was combed, not wild and curly as it always had been. His shoes were shined. Violetta had been wearing an old dress as usual, the one with the floral print, and was in the midst of brushing the donkeys. Giuseppe was feeling the aches and pains of age, Violetta knew. She was always extra gentle with his brushing.

"What is this?" Violetta had asked Gio, gesturing to his clothes. "Did someone die? Are you going to a funeral?"

He gave her a smirk. "No, someone didn't die."

"Are you finally going to work for your father, then? Is that why you're dressed like a banker?"

"Yes, but not today. We can talk about that later. I've come to talk to your mother, Letty. Where is Signora Fiora?"

"Why do you want to talk with her?"

"Never you mind. Where is she?"

"Where do you think she is? She's where she always is. In the shop. With my *zia*."

He gave her a mock scowl. "I thought maybe she could be out tending the bees. It's about that time, isn't it?"

"That was yesterday."

Gio straightened his tie. "How do I look?" he asked her.

Violetta smoothed her dress and took him in. Gio was smiling, slightly. His hair, though slicked back, was so dark. His eyes, so deep. He smiled broadly then, and Violetta could feel it in her bones.

"You look wonderful, Gio," she said, leaning on Giuseppe's back. "The handsomest man in Santo Stefano."

Gio smiled even broader. "Exactly what I wanted to hear." He clapped his hands together. "Now. I'm off to have a talk with your mother. And then we're going for a walk."

"You and my mother?"

He stared at her. "Yes. Yes, Letty. That's right. I'm here to take your mother for a walk. Or perhaps I'm here to take *you* for a walk. Which do you think it is?"

Violetta laughed and threw a handful of hay at him.

"Why do you need to talk to my mother to take me for a walk? And we're going for a walk with you dressed like that?"

Gio put his hands on his hips. "Stop asking questions. I'll be back soon."

He set his basket near the door and strode out of the barn, Freddo at his heels.

As Gio took the stairs, two at a time, up to the house just off the piazza, he practiced his speech in his head. His stomach was in knots. Why he should be so nervous about talking to a woman he had seen nearly as much as he had seen his own mother, he did not know. But, as he stood at the front door and knocked, he took a deep breath. For courage.

Fiora opened the door and furrowed her brow at the sight of him. "Did somebody die?"

Gio let out his breath in an exasperated sigh. "No! Nobody died. May I come in? I'm here to talk to you for a moment."

Fiora opened the door wider and stood aside. "Please," she said, ushering him inside.

He saw that she had sprigs of rosemary and lavender and fresh lemons laid out on the table, along with a dozen or so glass jars. An earthenware pot of honey sat in the center, along with a large ladle.

"Making the new batch today, I see," Gio said, inhaling.

The Rossi home was always filled with sweet aromas, he thought. It wasn't always the aromas of cooking but the scent of the herbs and flowers and fruits and the honey itself that permeated its way into the stone and wood of the place. It smelled, to Gio, like magic. The everyday kind of magic, the healing kind, that the Rossi women practiced. To him, it was love.

Fiora smiled at him, this boy, now almost a man, who had come into their home, their lives, their world, when he was but a child. She knew what he was there for that day. She had seen it coming, heard the bees whispering about it as she tended to them, for months.

It had been inevitable, from the first day Violetta laid eyes on him, but inevitability didn't mean anything good would come of it. Not necessarily. After what had happened with her own true love . . . and with her mother and father, she wondered if it was true what her mother had said about a powerful curse being handed down upon them. Was it Violetta's turn to live out that curse?

"Florencia!" Fiora called out. "Gio has come to see us."

Florencia appeared then, through the kitchen door, wiping her hands on her apron. The aroma of stewing tomatoes swirled around her.

"Hello, dear boy," Florencia said, crossing the room and taking her sister's arm. "You've come here dressed for a funeral. Not ours, I hope."

Gio threw up his hands. "What's with everyone saying I'm dressed for a funeral? I just thought I'd put on some nice clothes today. Some respectful clothes."

The sisters so enjoyed teasing this boy. Florencia rested her head on Fiora's shoulder, and the two smiled at Gio.

Nothing was said. But the air in the room seemed to thicken. A delicate cord, a gossamer filament, materialized and floated around the three of them, then, there, in the Rossi house, swirling this way and that until it had bound them together.

"I think this calls for some wine, don't you?" Fiora said, breaking—for just a moment—the magic that was happening around them. She knew what the boy was here to say.

"I think so," Gio said.

Florencia crossed the room and retrieved three glasses out of the heavy wooden armoire where they kept their best dishes. She filled them with wine, which had been opened that morning by Fiora in anticipation of this moment, and passed them around.

When the two women, who were both saddened by the passage of time but cautiously anticipating the future, and the young man, whose heart was in his throat, each took a sip of wine, Giovanni Moretti spoke.

"I love Violetta," he said, his voice catching on the monumental importance of those three words. "I don't think that comes as much of a surprise to you."

Fiora squeezed her sister's arm.

"I am going to work for my father," Gio said. "He has been insistent for some time that I learn the ways of the bank. This, I will do. Because I want to provide well for Violetta. I want her to be my wife." He gulped and finished his speech with one long stream of words. "I'm here to ask for your blessing to ask her to marry me."

He was right in that it came as no surprise to the sisters. They had never seen any other man in Violetta's future. Fiora raised her glass. "One hundred years of happiness to you, Giovanni Moretti, and to my daughter, Violetta Rossi," she said, her voice cracking with the weight of it. "May the cold winds of life be shut out by the warmth of your two hearts."

"May your love grow better with age, like a fine wine," Florencia added.

The sisters enveloped Gio in a hug then, blessings floating around them like hummingbirds.

CHAPTER 16

Violetta

When Gio had left, the sisters sat together by the fire, sipping their wine.

"So," Florencia said. "Now it has happened. It was inevitable."

"It's going to take more than a few blessings from us, I'm afraid," Fiora said. "On the other hand, the two of them love each other, strongly. Fiercely. We've known that from the first day he appeared in the barn."

"Strong enough to break the curse? Love has not been good to our women."

"Or the men who have loved us," Fiora said, her voice breaking.

They had spoken of it. Out loud. Curses were the stuff of storybooks, of tales told around the fire on autumn nights. Even the talk of a curse could, and would, do real harm to women like them. And not magical harm. Truly human harm. Being branded a witch. Banished. And much, much worse. Burned. Tortured. Killed. Yes, they were living in modern times. But the old ways, the old beliefs, still lingered.

And how could she forget what had happened to her own beloved, when the curse was fresh and new?

Fiora put a finger to her lips and shook her head slightly. But the truth was, the sisters had been searching for something—an herb, a spell, a remedy—since the day Violetta had been born. She had written it all down in their leather-bound book, kept a careful log.

"If what we have done is not enough, we will have failed her," she said.

"That's the question," Florencia said. "Have we failed? We don't know. We need to bestow on them the most powerful blessings we can conjure up. All of the good luck we can give them."

"She already knows about warding off the *malocchio*," Fiora said. "You can bet his mother has been casting that evil eye on her for years."

"Oh, yes. Neither of Gio's parents have been happy he was 'mixing' with someone so low class."

Fiora smirked. "Which is idiotic, because he of all people knows how much money we have. He should be happy his son is marrying a girl of means."

Her twin shook her head. "People have long been suspicious of women with means. Very suspicious."

"People always have something to say." Fiora shrugged. "They can be so ugly. People weren't happy when our mother married our father, either."

"My point exactly."

The sisters were silent for a moment, remembering.

"Why can't love ever be easy?" Fiora said, her words catching in her throat, mingling with a heartbreak that would never leave her, no matter how many years had passed.

"It is the curse of our women," Florencia said, her voice gentle and, she hoped, soothing. "That is why I have never chosen it."

But Florencia didn't tell her sister about the quiet glances and conversation she had shared with Claudio, the shepherd whose flock oftentimes grazed near the bees' meadow.

She had noticed him for some time, but they had first spoken because of the dog, Freddo. He had accompanied Florencia to the hives that morning—that wasn't like him—and Claudio had remarked on the breed.

"Your Maremma dog should be herding my sheep," Claudio called out to her. He had seen the beautiful Florencia many times over the years but had never summoned up the courage to speak to her. He was ashamed to even think he could. What would a handsome woman like that have to do with a man like himself? But that day, and the dog, helped him find his voice.

"Maremma?" Florencia asked.

Claudio pointed to Freddo as he walked closer. "He's a Maremma. A sheepdog. Known for herding sheep in these hills. I have a few myself." He gestured over to the sheep and sure enough, Florencia saw three white dogs, similar to Freddo, keeping watch.

"The only thing this dog herds is my niece," Florencia said, tucking a curl behind her ear and hoping fervently she had brushed her hair that morning. "He's her protector. Ours too. My sister's and mine."

"I'm Claudio," he said, extending his hand.

"Florencia," she said. "My sister and I—"

Claudio nodded. "You have the shop off the piazza in town. I know."

"Your wife probably buys our honey," she said, wincing a bit.

"My wife passed away, these ten years ago now," Claudio said. "It's just me and the dogs."

"It's nice to meet you, Claudio," Florencia said.

"Maybe I'll see you again, here, sometime," he said. "The sheep like this grass."

Florencia felt a flush come to her face. She put one palm on her cheek, as if to ward it off.

"Say hello, if you do."

They had continued meeting like that, every so often, talking, walking with the sheep. Florencia hadn't mentioned it to her sister, and wouldn't. Considering what Fiora had been through. But Fiora knew all the same. And was secretly glad for her sister.

On that day, the day of Violetta's engagement to Giovanni, the sisters exchanged a glance, both sighing at the same time. Fiora pushed herself to her feet, groaning a bit at the effort.

"It's time to get to work," she said, beckoning her sister to follow her. And she wasn't talking about the honey.

∽❧∾

Back in the barn, Gio found Violetta reading from the leather-bound book that, he knew, belonged to her mother and aunt. She had washed her face and brushed her hair, he saw, and changed her dress. Although where she had found a clean dress in the barn, he wasn't sure.

"You look pretty," he said. And then, grinning: "Did someone die?"

She got to her feet and put her hands on her hips. "No, nobody died. That I know of."

"Then why have you dressed up?"

"Because you look like a banker today, and you threatened to take me for a walk. So I didn't want to look like a peasant by your side. People would talk."

"We should get going, then," he said, retrieving the basket he had left by the door.

The two walked together through the streets, followed by Giuseppe and Bianca, with Freddo bringing up the rear, watching everything from his post behind his charges.

They didn't speak on the way to where they were going. Violetta kept sneaking furtive glances at Gio, who seemed different somehow that day. More serious. Even a bit nervous. It made Violetta's stomach gnarl up as well.

They walked a familiar path, one they had taken often. Whether they ended up traversing the rocky hills, checking on the bees, or finding a shady spot under a tree in the meadow by the lake, that depended on the day. On this day, Gio led his little band of companions to Violetta's favorite spot by the lake.

He pulled a red-and-blue checked blanket out of his basket and unfurled it onto the ground, setting the basket on top of it and motioning for Violetta to sit. Then, out came bread, and meats and cheeses, and grapes, and a cold bottle of wine. They both sat down as Giuseppe and Bianca strolled off to a polite distance and began grazing to pass the time. They already had their love story, both of them thought. It was time Violetta got hers.

The air smelled particularly sweet that day, Violetta noticed, as a breeze wafted around them, blowing her hair slightly.

"You've made us a picnic," she said finally. She found herself to be strangely tongue-tied, casting about for something, anything to say to this boy, now a man, with whom she had spent nearly every day of their lives.

"Very observant," he said, grinning at her. "Nothing gets past you."

She threw a grape in his direction. "This feels like an occasion," she said. "Is this an occasion?"

"Yes, Letty," he said, moving closer to her. "I think it may be. I hope very much that it is."

The air between them seemed to buzz with electricity then, as though a thousand fireflies had descended around them.

He reached over and tucked a stray curl around her ear, then he gazed into the face of the most beautiful woman he had ever seen. The woman who had captured his heart long ago. The woman for whom he had been patiently waiting to grow old enough to marry.

She slid closer to him, and although her heart was pounding in her throat, she did not turn away. Not this time. She did not say anything lighthearted. Not this time. And when he put a hand behind her neck and gently drew her face to his, she did not pull back.

When he kissed her, for the first time, the way a man kisses his beloved, she kissed him back, deeply, with her whole soul, having waited patiently to grow old enough to do it.

She put both of her arms around him then and melted into his embrace, and the two of them lay back on the blanket, lovingly placed in the sweet grass of the meadow. He gazed down at her, stroking her hair.

"I love you, Violetta Rossi," he said, his voice not much louder than a whisper.

She reached up and placed her palm on his cheek. "I love you, Giovanni Moretti."

"Will you be my wife?"

She smiled at him. "Did you even have to ask?"

"I know," he said. "It was a silly question."

"Is that what you were talking to my mother and auntie about?"

He pushed himself up and poured wine for the two of them. He took a bite of bread and cheese. The nerves of the moment, the strange formality of it all, had dissipated, and he was just there, with Violetta, his only love.

"Yes, I asked for their blessing," he said.

She sat up, too, and took the glass of wine he was offering. "And what did they say?"

He laughed. "All sorts of strange and magical things," he said. "You know how they are. They gave us many blessings."

"They love you," she said. "They always have."

Gio thought about his own parents and winced. "I know my parents will be happy, too," he said, but both he and Violetta knew it wasn't true. She let him pretend.

The two of them lingered there, in their meadow, by their lake, for a long time that day, talking of everything and nothing. The bees. Gossip about various happenings in the village. Gio's plans to start work with his father, now that his tutoring was over.

"I made sure to tell your mother and Florencia that I would provide for you," he said. "I had to get that part of it in place before I asked."

Violetta had no doubt that he would provide for her. Working for his father in the bank was one of the best, if not the best, professions anyone in Santo Stefano—or the surrounding towns—could hold. Not all the hill towns in the region had banks, but Santo Stefano had been a center of commerce for so long, since the Middle Ages, that a banker was needed to handle the monies exchanged for goods in the piazza. It was a position traditionally passed down from father to son, and Gio's brother was already at his father's side, keeping the books. Now it was Gio's turn to take his rightful place and join them.

Any woman in town would be thrilled to be marrying such a man. But, having been raised by two independent women, Violetta didn't hold any traditional ideas about needing a husband to survive.

Her mother and aunt had taught her about the bees. They had taught her how to infuse honey and soaps and olive oil. They had taught her to count money and keep the books. But most importantly, they had taught her their ways, how they would go out into the meadows and forests in the early morning, when the plants and flowers were just waking up, to gather the herbs and flowers and grasses and mushrooms and wild grapes and other secret things to make their infusions, just at the right time. They had taught her to respect the whispers of women who came to them with requests.

My husband has lost his love for me.

My child is sick with fever.

Do you think my daughter's bad luck is from malocchio, the evil eye?

Those whispers and requests never left the confines of the Rossi kitchen, were never spoken of, even between the sisters. That is why the women of the town kept coming.

Fiora and Florencia had taught Violetta how to use the sight since she was a very small child, the line of sight that ran from Isabella to Rosa to Fiora and now to Violetta, gifted with the sight from Cecile as well. All of it was coursing through Violetta's veins, and she knew, somehow, that it—not a husband, not even her beloved Giovanni—would provide for her long into old age.

But she didn't say any of this to Giovanni that day. Instead, they planned their shared future. They talked of when they would marry— the next year—and how they would live.

While Violetta had always known she and Gio would marry, it had never occurred to her that she would live in any home other than the one she shared with her mother and aunt. That her room would be different from the cozy four walls she called her own, just down the hall from the kitchen. That she would curl up at night in a different bed. Wake up to sun streaming in from a different window. And what of Giuseppe and Bianca?

"You know my brother Geno and his wife live in rooms next to ours on the castle grounds," Gio said, wincing. "I have a feeling my parents will want us to move in there as well. What do you think about that?"

It was true that Giovanni's family was the wealthiest in town and lived in the grandest accommodations. Most women would have been happy with the prospect of setting up house there. Violetta wasn't so sure.

"Would it be possible for us to get our own house? Maybe near the piazza? I would like my own kitchen."

Gio stretched out on the blanket and crossed his legs at the ankles. "I had a feeling that's what you were going to say. There is a place a few doors down from my parents that might be available for us. So it's on the other side of town from your mother, but it is not connected to my parents' house."

Violetta knew the place. "Is that where your tutor lived?"

"That's the one. All of us have finished up our studies, so he went back to Verona a few weeks ago."

Violetta shrugged. "I guess that will be all right," she said.

Married women lived with their husbands, she told herself. These are changes, yes, but good changes. "But what of Bianca and Giuseppe? And Freddo?"

"They can stay in their barn," Gio said. "You'll still tend to them. And help your mother and aunt, if that's what you want to do."

"Freddo will come live with us," she said, with an air of finality. "He's getting old, you know. I want him near me."

The pang of that reality stung Gio's heart. He loved the dog as much as Violetta did. Freddo had always been there, one of them, lending his silent protection to them, and his wise counsel to the donkeys and the bees. But Gio had noticed how the dog now struggled to get up off the ground of late and complained as he lay down into a sleeping position. His joints were bothering him. Like an old man's. And he no longer ran in the fields, opting for a dignified walk instead.

"Of course he can live with us. I can't imagine he would have it any other way."

Violetta sighed. Partially out of contentment, but there was a sense of resignation, too. The next stage was upon them. And that meant letting go of the old, if just a bit. But not leaving it behind.

Later, when Gio had gone home, presumably to break the news to his parents, Violetta walked into their kitchen, where her mother was stirring a big pot of sauce.

Fiora turned away from the stove and gazed at her daughter. It was true, then. He had asked her to marry him. And she had said yes. What else would she say? Fiora could see the difference in Violetta's eyes. She opened her arms and her daughter flew into them, and the two cried together, not caring to be silent with their tears.

Florencia leaned against the doorframe in the kitchen, not wanting to interrupt mother and daughter at this moment, even though she had been as much of a mother to that girl as Fiora had.

It had always been that way, since Fiora's one true love, Violetta's father, Paolo Rossi, was murdered. And their parents, Constant and Rosa, fled to America. And they knew the curse was real.

CHAPTER 17

Cassandra

The next morning was dark and dreary, with gray clouds hanging low around the mountains. I lazed in bed for much too long. Slipping out of the covers and into my robe, I took a cup of coffee and sat outside on the bench next to my door, contemplating what to do with the rest of my day.

As fat drops of rain began to fall, chasing me inside, I knew it wasn't the day for wandering around the village or exploring the countryside. The last thing I wanted to do was drive down that mountain road when it was slick with rain.

I spied my computer on the counter and realized I had all but forgotten my promise of writing a travel piece, or even a series, for the newspaper. It was the official reason for me taking time off, after all.

So I built a fire in the fireplace and settled into the armchair beside it with a fresh cup of coffee, put my feet up and my computer in my lap, and got to work.

I wrote an email to my editor, telling him I was "making great progress" on the article, and sent him some photos I had taken during my travels. Then I started writing—journaling, more like it—about my trip and everything that had happened thus far.

Immersed in my travelogue, the day passed quickly. Before I knew it, it was time to make myself presentable for Luna's dinner party.

Bath taken, hair washed and dried—no more glitches with the electricity, thank goodness—outfit chosen (a black turtleneck, jeans, and a silver necklace), I grabbed my purse and slipped into my coat.

I cast an eye out the window. The rain had stopped earlier in the day, but at nearly seven o'clock, it was getting dark out there.

That's when I noticed the dog. He was pure white, with a few touches of orange that added depth—not so much color—to his long, fluffy coat. I put him at a hundred pounds, if not more. He was sitting by the wall directly across from my door, looking at me.

I remembered the dog I had seen on the mountain road the day before. Could it be the same one?

I wasn't sure what to do. Was he friendly?

I opened the door. "Shoo!" I said, waving my hand. "Go home!"

But he didn't move. He just sat there with an almost expectant look on his face. I noticed his tail was wagging. He seemed to be smiling, if dogs could smile.

"I'm going to walk down the street now," I said to him. A warning? Or just a notification? I took a few hesitant steps away from the door, and the dog got to his feet and followed.

Okay. He's following me. That's fine.

Old-fashioned-looking streetlamps gave the streetscape a yellowish glow, and the chilly wind swirled around me as I walked.

I hurried up, up, up the stairs, the dog at my heels, but I didn't see another soul (human soul, that is) anywhere. The windows of houses I passed glowed with light—people were snug in their homes, perhaps having dinner with their families or settling down to read or play a game by the fire. But nobody else was outside. I was glad now to have my furry companion.

As I made my way down the alley to La Oliva, it dawned on me that Luna's front door might be someplace else, on the other side of the building, say, or down some other alleyway. But as I peered in through the deli window, I saw her grabbing a bottle of wine out of the cooler.

I knocked. She looked up, a bit startled, but a warm smile crossed her face when she saw me.

"Hello! Hello!" she said, opening the door. "My entrance is on the other side of the building, which, now that I think about it, I never told you. Welcome!"

Once inside, the aromas wafting from the kitchen surrounded me and nearly knocked me to the ground with their deliciousness. It was almost as though the aroma was tangible enough to taste.

"It smells like heaven in here," I said.

She smiled. "Some people say heaven *is* an Italian kitchen. I quite agree."

I handed her my hostess gift and peeled off my coat, which she hung up near the door. I glanced out the window. The dog was still there.

I followed Luna through the deli and into her sitting room, where I found Renzo standing next to the fireplace, a glass of wine in his hand. He set it down and enveloped me in a hug.

"Hello!" he said to me. "How about some wine? Red or white?"

"White, please," I said, and he was off to the sideboard, where bottles of red sat next to ice buckets containing bottles of white. He poured a glass and handed it to me.

I took a sip. "Delicious!"

"Any more trouble with the electricity?"

"No," I said. "Not yet."

"I'll have my guys come by tomorrow, or sometime when you're not there to be inconvenienced by their boorish presence."

I laughed at this.

He shook his head. "Oh, they're terrible. But good electricians."

Then, a knock at the door. Luna opened it to find Dante with an older couple, presumably his parents, and a much older lady. She was dressed all in black and had the deeply lined face of someone who had lived a stressful life. His grandmother?

Luna ushered them all in, taking coats, exchanging greetings in Italian. Dante shepherded them out of the doorway and into the main room. He took the elderly lady's arm and guided her into an armchair by the fire as his parents made their way to the sideboard to greet Renzo.

The folks settled, Dante made his way over to me and gave me a quick kiss on the cheek.

"Cassie," he said. "So nice to see you."

"You too," I said, feeling the heat rising on the back of my neck.

He turned to his parents. *"Mamma e papà,"* he said, *"si chiama Cassie Graves."* Then, turning to me, in English, said, "Cassie, my parents, Alberto and Mia Caruso."

Alberto, a dapper gentleman, had his wisps of hair neatly combed to the side of his head and was dressed in a button-down shirt with a faint-blue stripe running through it, a navy-blue cardigan, and dark slacks. He bowed his head slightly and then extended his hand to me. "A pleasure to meet you," he said.

Mia, who wore a floral dress and sensible shoes, smiled and nodded, also shaking my hand after her husband did so. *"Piacere,"* she said.

"And this is my grandmother, Elena Caruso."

I had practiced "It's nice to meet you" in Italian all afternoon. *Here goes nothing,* I thought.

"Buonasera, signora," I said, my Italian faltering. *"È un piacere a conoscerti."*

The lady looked me up and down and then turned her rather stern gaze to Dante. She said something in Italian.

I gathered it meant "Get me a glass of wine"—I caught the *vino* at the end of the sentence—because he did just that, pouring an ample glass of red. He handed it to her and returned to my side. His parents had found their way to the sofa, where Renzo was chatting with them. Luna had disappeared back into the kitchen.

"I thought your grandma didn't travel much," I said to Dante. "Isn't that what you said?"

He nodded and took a big gulp of his wine. "Yes, I did and no, she doesn't. It took an act of God to get her ready. First of all, my mother, no spring chicken herself, wrestled with Nonna's stockings for an hour! And then just transporting her from the house to the car—I could have used a forklift."

I couldn't help but chuckle a little at this. I well understood the challenges of "elder wrangling," as Maria and I had called it when both sets of our parents suddenly, it seemed to us, got old. Just taking them grocery shopping, which they insisted on doing themselves for far too long, was an adventure of epic proportions.

"You are amused," Dante said, mock indignation on his face, trying to mask a smile of his own.

"I have had the same experience, taking care of my own parents as they aged," I said, putting a hand on his arm. "You have to laugh about it, or you'll cry."

"That is the truth," he said after taking another sip of wine. "Even with all of that trouble, she could not be dissuaded. When I told her you were the relation of the Rossis that ran the honey shop her grandparents bought, she said she needed to come to meet you."

"Wow," I said. "I would've been happy to drive into town and meet her there. She didn't have to come all this way."

"That's what I said to her," Dante said. "But she said she wanted to come. It had to be here, in Santo Stefano." He looked as confused as I felt. "I have no idea why," he said.

I caught her eye and smiled. A frown in return. *Strange,* I thought. *This woman made a real effort to meet me, and she has, so far, shown me nothing but disdain.* I shrugged at him and crossed the room to sit down next to her.

"*La mia famiglia era proprietaria del negozio di miele,*" I said, hoping I wasn't butchering the phrase too badly. I was trying to say that my family had once owned the honey shop.

She looked at me deeply then, reaching out a hand to touch my hair.

"Rossi," she said. "You are Violetta Rossi."

The hair on the back of my neck stood up. The room grew quiet, everyone looking at this old woman. She had just said my great-grandmother's name. But obviously she was confused.

"I'm not Violetta Rossi," I said gently. "My great-grandmother was Violetta Rossi."

"Strega," she said in a harsh whisper, pointing at me. *"Strega."*

CHAPTER 18

Cassandra

That was the second time in two days I had been called a witch. Or was it Violetta she was talking about? What was I supposed to say to that? Although . . . that death certificate. Did she know something? I wanted to ask her, prompt her to say more, but I didn't get a chance to do it.

Everyone in the sitting room fell silent as the old woman Elena cried in a strangulated whisper, "Witch," and pointed at me. And then, suddenly everyone was talking at once. Dante flew across the room to her side.

"Nonna!" he said, looking at her, then turning his gaze to me and then back to her.

"Mama, no!" Dante's mother said. "There are no witches." And then she said a lot more, in a string of rapid-fire Italian that I had no hope of understanding.

"Here we go again with the witches," Dante's father murmured, pouring himself a large glass of wine. "Always, the witches."

Renzo stood by the fireplace, a stricken look on his face, which was reddening. He caught my eye and winced. He put a hand to his chest and mouthed *Mi dispiace*. I'm sorry.

I smiled and shook my head. *È tutto a posto,* I mouthed back, telling him the equivalent of "Everything's fine."

As if on cue, a knock at the door broke the tension in the room. Renzo opened it to find another couple—a man, about a decade older than me, wearing a navy-blue suit that looked impeccably tailored, and a much younger woman in a white blouse, a floral-print scarf, and jeans, with high wedge heels. How she traversed the stone streets of this ancient town in those heels, I did not know. My snap judgment: rich man and trophy wife. I'd soon be proven wrong on that.

A second woman, who looked like an older version of Luna, stood behind them. Her mother, I assumed.

"Oh!" Renzo said, throwing up his hands. "Here you are at last! Good, good!" He ushered the group into the house and busied himself taking coats.

Warm embraces all around, laughter exchanged. Luna made her way out of the kitchen and greeted them as well.

"I'm so happy you could come!" she said to the couple. And then, turning to me: "Cassie, this is my mother, Aria." I nodded to the older lady, who smiled at me in return. "And these are the Morettis, Angela and Thomas."

I held my breath, hoping there would not be another "witch" outburst, but instead, Angela Moretti crossed the room and held out both hands to me. I took them in mine.

"Luna has told us you are from America, here researching your family history," she said. "I have brought some old photos of my husband's parents and grandparents, some papers and things, and some stories for you. We may be family!"

She enveloped me in a hug then. I could feel my own grandmother coming through that embrace. All at once, I missed her very much. And felt a pang in my stomach for judging this woman before she had even said one word to me.

"It is good you have come back to Italy," Angela said. "We need our roots, yes?"

I nodded, fighting back tears. Yes. Yes we did. "I am the first of our family to come," I managed to say. "My grandmother—a Moretti—never was able to make the trip. Her mother moved to America when she was a young woman."

Angela put a hand to my cheek. "We will talk about this," she said.

"But first, we eat!" Luna broke in, and herded everyone into the dining room. Why did that not surprise me? It was how we did things in my family, too.

"Can I help you with anything in the kitchen?" I asked her.

She shook her head. "Sit! Sit. Tonight, you are my guest. Next time, we'll cook together."

The dining room was a splash of color. The mahogany wood trim on the mullioned windows contrasted with the soft yellow of the walls, which enhanced the deep-red tablecloth and red cushions on the chairs. Candles flickered on every spare surface. The whole room seemed to glow from within.

The table was already set with boards of cheeses, meats, dried and fresh fruits, and nuts, along with bottles of wine and pitchers of water that were positioned down its length.

Renzo caught my eye and winked. "You're not going to go hungry," he said. "In case you were worried."

After a fair amount of fuss getting Dante's grandmother to the table, everyone else took their places. And then, it began.

Warm conversation, in Italian—parts of which I picked up, most of which I didn't—and in English, which I was grateful for, livened the table as Luna and her mother disappeared into the kitchen, and we delved into the salty sliced meats paired with hard cheeses, fruits, and nuts.

We talked and laughed—no more witch conversation, thankfully—until Luna and her mother emerged from the kitchen with steaming bowls of pasta carbonara.

At the first bite, I could not suppress my moan of sheer delight.

"You like the carbonara?" Aria asked.

"I love it," I said. "My grandmother used to make it."

She nodded and smiled, clearly pleased.

As we were all close to finishing the pasta, Luna and her mother pushed their chairs back again, disappeared into the kitchen, and brought out platters of lamb, along with grilled vegetables. I wasn't normally a fan of lamb—though I would never have told Luna—but the slightly spicy, tender meat melted in my mouth. Why had I not loved this all my life?

More laughter and conversation then, most of which I didn't understand. The combination of the wine and the food coma I was slowly slipping into hindered my ability to follow the Italian, and it seemed to hinder their ability to speak English.

But we weren't done yet. Next, it was salad, with a light and lemony dressing. Then came the plates of soft cheeses and fruits.

When Luna pushed her chair back once again, I thought we were finished, that it was time to clear the plates. No. It was time for tiramisu and espresso.

"I make tiramisu for the deli every day," Luna said, "but I put a little extra love into this batch."

The soft, creamy coffee-flavored concoction was only made better by a sip of espresso, which, I was told, was not typically drunk after dinner, only after a heavy meal.

And still we weren't finished. Luna and her mother cleared the dessert plates—I had offered many times to help, only to be rebuffed—and then brought out a tray of small glasses, along with a tall bottle of grappa.

"Digestivo," Luna said, handing the glasses around and pouring the herby, spicy drink.

"I have never eaten more in one sitting in my life," I said, sipping my grappa and hoping it lived up to its name as an aid in digestion.

Dante smiled. "Welcome to Italy."

In all the flurry and joy of the meal, I had been distracted a bit by Dante's grandmother staring at me from across the table. She didn't say much as we ate, and I was wondering what she was thinking. If she even remembered calling Violetta a witch. I was used to elderly folks and their . . . quirks. Mannerisms. I was all too familiar with the ravages of age, having seen it in my own family. So I wasn't going to make an issue out of this witch thing. But it nagged at me more than a little.

She had called Violetta Moretti a witch. And that was also what it said on her bogus death certificate, printed and signed here in Santo Stefano. There had to be something there. Something more than the ramblings of an elderly lady.

As we all took our glasses of grappa away from the table and I helped clear the plates, much to Luna's objections, I thought about how, and if, to broach the subject again.

In the kitchen with Luna and Aria, I turned to the older woman. "*Signora*, why don't you go sit by the fire with everyone," I said. "I can help Luna clean up."

Aria shook her head. "No, no—"

But Luna broke in. "Mama, she's right. You've been on your feet all evening. I know how they bother you. Why don't you go sit down, enjoy your grappa, and Cassie and I will get this done."

Aria shrugged but smiled all the same. "My feet are a little tired."

"There!" Luna said. "You see? Now, go. We will be right in to join you."

After Aria shuffled out of the kitchen, Luna and I began stacking the dishes in her dishwasher and wiping down the countertops. I wanted to talk with her about all this but didn't quite know how to begin.

She began for me. "Dante's grandmother . . ."

I shook my head. Tears came to my eyes, but I wasn't sure why.

Luna put a hand on my arm. "I know. I'm so sorry. I had no idea she'd react like that."

I took a deep breath and let it out. If I was going to tell anyone about the death certificate, now was the time.

"There may be something more to it," I said. "Luna, I came upon something very odd when I was looking through my grandmother's things. It all started with my cousin researching our family history."

"Yes, I know that," she said. "But what is this thing you came upon?"

"Well . . . okay," I said. "It involves a little backstory. We had always been told my grandmother, Gia Moretti, was born in Portofino and came to America with her parents, Violetta and Giovanni Moretti, in around 1912."

"Then . . . how did you make the connection to Santo Stefano?"

"That came up during this research my cousin and I were recently doing," I said. "I found photos of the two of them, taken here in town. One outside of the shop Dante now runs. Also, my grandma had a painting of a landscape that hung on her bedroom wall all of my life— we all knew it was a scene from Italy, but none of us knew where it was. Until now."

Luna leaned back against the counter. "And what was this odd thing you said you found?"

"We were researching online and couldn't come up with any immigration records for either Violetta or Giovanni. But I did find a birth certificate for my grandmother Gia, and . . ."

Luna leaned in. "And?"

"And it contradicted everything we had been told. It recorded her birth in New York, 1912, to Violetta Moretti."

"So she was born there and not here," she said, shrugging. "I guess that's not so unusual."

I shook my head. "It listed the father as 'illegitimate.'"

Luna furrowed her brow. "So Violetta was a single mother . . ."

"No," I said. "Her last name, her maiden name, was Rossi, as I've now found out. Moretti was Giovanni's last name. Luna, my family has talked about their great love story all of our lives. We were told Giovanni died in the United States during an epidemic in 1918. So Gia wasn't illegitimate, but that's what her birth certificate says."

Luna shook her head. "This is getting confusing."

"But that's not the only thing," I said, steeling myself to continue. "I was looking through my grandmother's things. I found a death certificate for Violetta. It was in Italian, filled out here in Santo Stefano, and it stated she died in 1911."

"Wait a minute," Luna said. "Your grandma was born in 1912, and Violetta was her mother, so—"

I broke in. "Exactly. Luna, my great-grandmother Violetta lived until she was almost one hundred years old in the town where I grew up. I remember her!"

Her eyes grew wide. "So this death certificate from Santo Stefano . . ."

"That's what I don't understand. It says she died here, which she obviously didn't. It's bogus. It has to be."

"I can't imagine how or why that death certificate was filed."

"Neither can I," I said. "Nor can I imagine why my grandmother kept it among her things. I think it's an important piece of this puzzle. But there's something else about it that I need to tell you."

She leaned in and whispered, "What?"

I took a deep breath. *Here I go.*

"Violetta's cause of death, on that certificate, was listed as witchcraft."

CHAPTER 19

Cassandra

Luna and I stood in the kitchen, just looking at each other, for a long moment. Neither of us said anything.

"Elena called her a witch in my sitting room just now," Luna said. "How could she . . ."

"I know," I said, my voice dropping to a whisper. "Dante's grandmother wasn't even born when Violetta was here in Santo Stefano. How could she possibly know something like that?"

"Okay," Luna said, rubbing her hands together. "Let's try to make the pieces fit. The Rossis owned the shop . . . until, when?"

"I have a photo of Violetta outside of the shop in around 1910."

"So we know they owned it until at least that time. Do we know who the Rossis are? Mother and father, I'm assuming?"

"I'm assuming that, too, but we don't know. There's no genealogical information going back further than Violetta."

Luna considered this. "The Caruso family has owned it for a few generations. I know Dante's great-grandparents bought it, so it's likely it changed hands around that 1912-ish time period. That just makes sense, timeline-wise. It could be you are related in some way to them—businesses were passed down in families back then. Or they could have bought it, as Dante said."

Luna stared out the window for a moment before continuing. "But that doesn't tell us why. It seems like there's a whole lot of energy swirling around that time period in your family. Birth certificates. Death certificates. Witchcraft."

"And no records at all about Giovanni."

She shook her head. "Now I see why you came here," she said, hugging herself. "I'm intrigued by this already, and it's not even my family. I'd do the same thing if it were."

I wasn't sure whether to say what I wanted to say next. *Should I tell her about the lady at the market?* Somehow, Luna picked up on that.

"What?" she said. "There's something else."

"I know this is probably nothing, but yesterday when I was at the market . . ." I took a deep breath. "An older lady there called *me* a witch."

Luna frowned. "No, no, no. Are you sure?"

"Pretty sure," I said. "She glared at me, followed me around, and then whispered '*strega*' when she passed by me."

Luna held my gaze for a long minute and then fingered the amulet around my neck. "I see I gave you this for a reason."

"And that's not all," I said, leaning in. "Last night at Il Caminetto, Tony started talking about witches, just for no reason! He told me about a neighboring town that has a witch festival every year. He had no idea about any of this!"

"You come here, and suddenly witches are everywhere," Luna said, shaking her head. "I don't know what to tell you about that . . ." She paused a moment before continuing. "But I know someone who might."

She crossed the room and pulled open a drawer, looking around briefly before fishing out a business card. She handed it to me.

It had the words "Sogni Italiani" written in an old-fashioned font and an image of a painting of an arched stone alleyway, much like the ones in Santo Stefano.

I turned it over and saw a name—Anna Ricci—and a phone number and address.

"She's a friend," Luna said. "An artist. But she is . . . gifted in other ways. She lives in Castel del Monte—the town Tony was talking about. That spider is spinning its web around you, Cassie. You're caught up in something. I just don't know what. Tell her about it."

I slipped the card into my pocket. "Do you think I should just go over there? To her studio?"

"I'll call her in the morning and let her know you'll be coming."

Voices and thuds brought us back into the present. A clatter in the living room.

As we joined the others, we found the Carusos and Morettis fumbling with their coats, dropping canes and purses, and creeping toward the door.

"Oh, you're not leaving already?" I asked, wishing they'd stay. We hadn't even had the chance to talk about our family connections.

Dante was helping Elena with her formidable, long black coat. She tucked a tissue into her sleeve. "They are getting tired," he said, nodding at Elena.

"Us too," Angela Moretti piped up, pulling on her coat. "But I do have these papers and photos to show you, about the Morettis."

"They are all staying at the hotel," Renzo said. "Nobody is driving down the hill tonight. So we were thinking we can meet for lunch, after everybody gets up and gets into the day, to continue this conversation about the past. Yes?"

That sounds like a very good idea, I thought with a yawn.

We all said our goodbyes, with handshakes and hugs and kisses all around, and Dante and Renzo went to shepherd the crew to their rooms in the *diffuso*. As he was pulling the door shut behind them, Dante turned to me.

"I'll just get them settled and come back to walk you down to your place," he said.

"Oh, you don't have to worry about me! I'll be fine."

He smiled. "I know. But indulge me. This won't take a minute, and I'll be back."

Luna put her arm around my shoulders. "She'll wait for you." And then, turning to me: "You shouldn't walk alone."

Luna's mother, too, bid us good night and padded down the hallway, presumably to a guest room. That left just Luna and me. We both settled onto the couch.

"It feels good to sit down," Luna said, sighing.

"What a wonderful dinner," I said.

"It was fun to have an excuse to cook for a crowd," she said. "My mother or I usually cook Sunday dinner. Sometimes it's just us, but sometimes Renzo comes with his family. He has a couple of kids who live in town. His son is in college. The daughter is getting married next year."

I took a sip of the spicy grappa. "What about you? Do you have kids?"

"I have not been so blessed," she said, smiling—a bit sadly, I thought—and swirling the liquid in her glass. "You?"

"My son, Henry, is in college," I said, thinking of his sweet face. I wished he were here with me.

"And you are divorced, yes?"

I winced. "The lawyers are handling it. It's just a matter of paperwork now."

"I'm sorry for your trouble. Are you dating anyone?"

"No," I said. "I'm pretty out of practice at that."

She raised her eyebrows. "Dante has been talking about you."

"He has?"

She nodded. "He finds you delightful. Hey, the man has eyes. Of course he finds you delightful."

I considered this. I was finding him delightful, too.

"And you and Renzo?" I asked, not sure if I should. "Are you a couple? It seems as though you are."

"Ah, that man," Luna said, shaking her head. "Yes, we are together. Have been for a long while. He's talking marriage, but we haven't done it yet."

"Why not?"

She shrugged. "Life gets in the way sometimes."

Just then, Dante knocked on the door and came right in, collapsing onto an armchair.

"Getting elderly people settled in for the night should be an Olympic sport," he said with an exhausted laugh.

I got that. Only too well. "I have been on the USA Elderwrangling Team for the past few years," I said. "I get how tiring it is. But it's the best work you'll ever do, taking care of your family like that."

"Elderwrangling," Dante repeated, chuckling. "How American, and how true."

The three of us chatted about other things for a moment, mostly offering accolades about the meal—The lamb! The pasta! Those lemony roasted vegetables!—until I pushed myself off the couch.

"I should get going," I said, feeling the weight of all that food. I was having trouble keeping my eyes open.

"I'll walk you down," Dante said, and I didn't bother protesting this time. The truth was, I wasn't looking forward to walking alone in the dark at that hour. It had to be nearly midnight.

After thanking Luna again and pulling on my coat, we headed out into the night air. The white dog was waiting there, sitting by the wall outside the door.

"Funny," I said. "He escorted me up here. He was outside my door."

"Your bodyguard," Dante said. "I noticed him when I arrived, and just now, when I was getting my parents and Nonna into the car. I think he was waiting here for you all night."

I leaned down and put out my hand. "Hey, boy," I said. The dog sniffed my hand and gave it a quick lick.

"You'd think he'd be more interested in all the cats in town," I said as we began walking down the street.

"He's more interested in you," Dante said. "Smart dog."

He held my gaze for a moment. Was this man flirting with me? It had been such a long time, I had almost forgotten what it felt like. Was I going to flirt back?

I stumbled a little as we walked down the ancient stone steps, and he took hold of my arm.

"These things can feel like they're crumbling beneath your feet," he said. "But they are solid. I ran up and down these steps every day as a boy."

I could imagine him doing just that.

We made our way down my street, under the archway, and finally to my door. The dog was still at our heels. Dante reached down and gave him a quick pat on the head. "He made sure I didn't try anything."

"I wasn't worried," I teased him. "Thank you for walking me home."

"My pleasure," he said, leaning against the doorframe. "Santo Stefano is among the safest places you can be. But you can never be too careful. Plus, I just wanted to spend a little more time with you."

A sizzle shot through me. "You did?"

"I did. I'm shamelessly trying to impress you. How am I doing?"

"Well, your eldercare skills earned you a perfect ten tonight," I said, grinning.

He looked into my eyes then. It was easy for me to get lost in his. Deep and brown and comforting.

"I should probably go inside," I said.

"That's probably a good idea. Although in Italy, it's customary to invite men into your home for a nightcap."

I wrinkled my nose at him. "Is it really? I've never heard that."

"Well, no," he admitted with a laugh. "We don't have that custom at all."

"Nice try," I said. "Plus, this isn't a date."

"That's true," he said. "And we won't have a date tomorrow, either, but we'll see each other. For a similar reason. I hear we're all meeting for lunch."

"That's the plan," I said. "We're getting to be quite the group."

His face took on a more serious tinge then. "I need to apologize again for my grandmother." He shook his head. "I don't know what got into her. It was terribly rude."

"First, you don't need to apologize," I said. "Older people—you never know what they'll say." I took a deep breath. "But the other thing is, there might be a little truth to what she said."

He furrowed his brow at me. "What do you mean?"

And so I told him about the death certificate. And the mystery surrounding it.

"That's crazy," he said. "How in the world . . . ?"

I could see his thoughts went exactly where mine had. How in the world could his grandmother have known that my great-grandmother had been branded a witch? Were there stories about her?

Of course, there was no answering that question right now. After seeing me safely inside, Dante went on his way. I peered out the window to watch him go. He reached down and gave the great white dog another pat on the head as he passed. A nice man, I thought. One I would like to invite in for a nightcap. Perhaps next time.

I started the fire I had laid before I left for dinner, and as it blazed to life, I went back to the window and looked outside.

The dog was still there. Sitting so nicely, staring at my door.

I slipped into my pajamas, brushed my teeth, and washed my face, intending to sink into the armchair and devour a few chapters of the mystery I was reading before bed. But instead, I padded over to the window again. My sentinel was still there. In the same position. Staring at the door.

I wondered: When was the last time he had water? Or any food? He seemed lonely out there. Against all my better judgment, I opened the door.

"Do you want to come in, is that it?" I asked him.

The dog trotted inside. I closed and locked the door behind him.

I hunted around and found what looked like a dog bowl in the pantry, filled it with water, and set it on the floor. He sniffed at it for a moment and lapped up some of the water, wagging his tail politely. I fed him some cheese, a bit of deli meat, and a piece of crusty bread—not the ideal fare for a dog, but it was all I had. He took it from my hand like a gentleman.

Then, he turned in a circle a few times and curled into a ball in front of the fire.

"I guess you're staying the night, then." A thump of his tail on the rug was his response.

I glanced at the clock—nearly one. With the time difference, it would've been a great time to call Maria. I started to key in her number but realized I didn't have the energy for the conversation. There was a lot to unpack about the evening—all the people, the outburst, the food, Dante—and I figured I'd do that myself, in my own mind, before talking with her.

Dinner went really well, I texted to her instead. The Moretti couple has some paperwork and photos that we're going to look at together tomorrow. He's a bit older than us, and at first I thought she was a trophy wife . . . but she turned out to be really nice and now I feel like an ass for thinking that. She's the one who seems interested. I'll tell you all about it after I talk with them tomorrow.

I didn't mention anything about Signora Caruso's witch comment. Nor did I mention anything more about Dante. She'd call me for sure if I hinted at any of that.

So I turned off the light, slid under my covers, and fell asleep by the warm glow of the fire, wondering what the morning would bring.

CHAPTER 20

Cassandra

The next morning, after fighting with the stove, igniting it (finally), and setting the kettle on to boil, I padded to the bathroom to shower for the day. It wasn't until I had dressed and dried my hair that I realized the dog was gone.

It took me a moment to even register that I had let an animal into the house the previous night. Hadn't I? I knelt down to check under the bed—not there. I opened the pantry. No. I even, inexplicably, looked in the tub. Of course he wouldn't be in there, and he wasn't.

I let him in the house last night, right? I started to doubt my memory. I had been exhausted, after all. But then I noticed the bowl of water was still on the floor where I had placed it the night before. Did I, somehow, let the dog out in the middle of the night without realizing it? The thought sent a shudder through me.

My phone rang, dissipating those wonderings.

"*Buongiorno*, Cassie!" Luna's voice sounded like music. "You slept well?"

"Very well, after that beautiful meal last night," I said. "Thank you again for that."

"Oh, it was no trouble at all," she said. "I love cooking for my friends."

I smiled. She was that, I thought. A friend. And a lovely one.

"So!" she continued. "I spoke to Anna a moment ago. She's at her gallery all morning, so if you want to go to see her, she'd be happy to talk with you."

My stomach did a quick flip. "What should I tell her?"

"Everything," Luna said. "The more I think about it, it all has to be connected. You come here looking for your great-grandmother, who was called a witch, and all of a sudden, witches everywhere. And strange visions."

Visions, indeed. First the spider, then the woman by the hives and that weird donkey apparition—if that's what it was—and then the dog. But the dog was different, wasn't it? I wasn't the only one who had seen the dog. Dante had seen him, too. I was sure he had. This was an actual dog, not something I had dreamed up.

But then I thought: *What about the old lady in the market? Was she real?* Was anything?

"You go see Anna," she said, soothing my minor inner panic attack. "It's not far. Twenty minutes at most. You have the address, yes? Then come to La Oliva for lunch with everyone. We can talk after, if you'd like."

I was doing it, then. We said our goodbyes and I took a deep breath, grabbed my purse, and shut the door behind me.

Soon, I was zipping down one twisty mountain road and up another like a native, absurdly proud of myself for mastering, at least, the skill of driving on these roads. As I pulled into the town of Castel del Monte, I realized Tony had been right. With its cobblestone streets and winding alleyways, this village was much like Santo Stefano. Was he also right about the witches?

The town was bustling with activity, people coming and going in and out of shops, couples sitting at tables in the piazza, people walking here and there. I took a few wrong turns before finding Anna's gallery, Sogni Italiani, Italian Dreams. A bell clanged as I pushed open the door and walked inside.

The walls were covered with colorful paintings of the town, the countryside, people. Sheep. A slice of life in Abruzzo.

A woman of about sixty, with streaks of gray in her dark hair, came out of a back room. She was wearing a white gauze top embroidered with flowers and a pair of skinny black leggings, bright-red high heels on her feet.

"Buongiorno!" she sang.

"Buongiorno," I said, getting more confident in my Italian by the day. "I'm Cassie Graves."

"Ah, yes, yes," Anna said. "Luna said you'd be stopping by. I've been expecting you."

"Your paintings are beautiful," I said.

"Grazie mille," she said, smiling. "But you didn't come to talk about paintings."

She motioned to two chairs positioned by the window, and we crossed the room to take a seat. A teapot and two cups sat on a small table between the chairs, and Anna poured tea for the two of us, the smell of cinnamon and clove and citrus swirling through the air.

As I took a sip of my tea, I found myself a bit tongue-tied, there in that beautiful shop on a bright, blue day, with all manner of normalcy going on outside the door. And I was there to talk about witches.

"Luna mentioned a bit about your . . . situation," Anna said. "Did she mention anything to you about me?"

"Only that I should talk to you about some of these weird happenings," I said. "It all might be nothing, but—"

She raised her cup. "It's never nothing," she said. "It's always something. I have known that since I was a girl. I have certain . . . sensitivities, you might say. And the moment you walked in, I knew you did, too. So, why don't you tell me about your something."

Me? Sensitivities? I wasn't sure about that, but I told her why I was in Santo Stefano and what had been happening to me. Finding Violetta's "death certificate." All of the witchy coincidences, or whatever they had been. The vision of the spider. The donkey. The dog.

"It just seems like there's a thread connecting all of it," I said finally. "But I don't quite know what it is."

Anna took another sip of her tea and gazed at me over the rim, her eyes fixed and intent.

"We have a couple of things happening here, as I see it," she began. "And I think they're connected. First, you come to Santo Stefano to find out the truth about your ancestors, specifically a woman who had been called a witch. I think the very act of you coming here, being in the same town where she lived, walking on the same streets, awakened something in you."

I set my cup down on the table. "In me?"

"Have you always had it?"

"Had what?"

"Chiaroveggenza," she said. "Second sight."

Electricity crackled through me as she said the word.

"My grandmother always told me I had it," I said. "I guess I have been sensitive to things. But not always. I missed a pretty big 'something' in my own life recently." I was thinking of my marriage. "I shrugged it off as women's intuition."

Anna smiled.

"Women's intuition," she said, reaching over and putting a hand on my arm. "In this woman, it's more than that. And, from what you have told me, I think you're going to be feeling it more and more."

Great, I thought. *Just great.*

"I don't know whether your ancestor was a witch or just branded as one," Anna continued. "But I can tell you we have a long history of witches in this part of Italy. Persecution in the early days, yes. Hundreds of years ago. But not when your great-grandmother lived here. However . . ."

"However what?"

"Those old superstitions about witches ran deep," she said. "Even into modern times. Do you know about the Festival of the Witch that is held here every year?"

"I've heard a little about it, yes."

"The whole town becomes a stage. At the heart of it is a reenactment of an old ritual," she said, and my skin began to crawl. All at once, I didn't want to hear any more about any reenactment. But Anna continued. "The ritual was used to break the curse of a witch."

"So, not to hurt the witch herself . . . or the woman accused of being one?"

"No, not that we know of," she said. "This is the story behind it. When a child fell ill in town without any real explanation, naturally that was the work of a witch, right? That's what they believed then. So the child's mother would watch over the child for a number of nights, and if he or she didn't get well, it was time to take action.

"The mother would gather some of the child's clothes that were obviously infected with evil spirits, sent by the witch, and walk through town. Other women of the town would join in. They would reach the piazza and put the clothes in a pile and beat them with sticks to wake those evil spirits, and then they'd set the clothes on fire."

That chill was wrapping around me, tighter and tighter, just like that spiderweb.

"When the clothes had burned into ash, the spell was broken, and the child would recover."

"What if they didn't?"

"That part of the tale is a little more vague," Anna admitted. "I imagine it was not good for the woman. And I imagine women who were accused of being witches, or looked upon as such, would have created protection around them. Which brings me to my next point."

I wasn't sure I wanted to hear her next point, but she continued.

"The spider is definitely a warning," Anna said. "Luna was right about that. Now, the white donkey . . . that's a well-known symbol of protection. Same with the white dog. You know those dogs have been protecting our sheep here in Abruzzo for hundreds of years. It's what they're bred to do."

I mulled this over. "It makes a kind of sense," I said. "But what do I have to be protected from?"

She wagged a finger at me. "Here's where it gets interesting, if you weren't interested before. Your great-grandmother had a fake death certificate that indicated she died of witchcraft. She ran the honey shop—those bees are well known!—and passed down some of those skills to your grandmother, and she to you, right?"

"Yes, that's right."

"And your grandmother said you had the sight."

"That's right, too."

"Maybe she really was a witch, Cassie. And maybe she ran into some trouble because of that. You said you don't know why she left Santo Stefano. Maybe that's why. And she is doing what she can now to protect you because you are here in this place that she fled."

As I drove back to Santo Stefano that morning, I was lost in thought. Could Violetta have been a witch? And what did that mean, exactly? My belief was that many, if not most, of the women branded as witches throughout the ages were more like healers. Women who knew about herbs and remedies and teas and things like that. Not old hags who stirred cauldrons of dubious ingredients, casting spells on people.

I knew Violetta. She was a lovely, elegant woman . . . who was unnaturally gifted when it came to the bees. And her inn was never without customers. And, come to think of it, my brother and I never had any sort of illness, ever, growing up. It was like we were living a charmed life.

Maybe we had been.

~❀~

I pulled back into the parking lot in Santo Stefano just in time to hurry up to the piazza for lunch.

When I arrived, I saw Dante's parents and grandmother already seated at a table in the sun, with the Morettis and Luna's mother at the next table. Luna came around the corner carrying a tray of bread and meats and cheeses. Dante followed with a tray of what looked like Bellinis.

"Cassie!" he called out. *"Buongiorno!"*

"Buongiorno!" I said, and everyone started responding at once. Signori Moretti and Caruso both got to their feet and gave me a quick bow; the women waved and called their greetings. Their happy faces warmed me from the inside out. It felt like coming into a gathering of family, my family, even though I had just met most of these people the night before.

"Come, Cassie, sit, sit," Angela Moretti said, waving her hand at an empty chair at her table. She looked so effortlessly chic with her long green coat and green-and-blue scarf wound around her neck.

"Beautiful day," I said, taking a seat. And it was. The sky was a deep shade of blue. The rolling hills seemed to glow, and the white peaks of mountains beyond glistened in the sun.

As I pulled out a chair at her table, Renzo appeared and set a glass of wine in front of me, patting my shoulder.

"Are you ready?" he asked, his voice in a low whisper.

I squinted at him. Ready for what? He answered my question without me asking it. Nodding to the Morettis, he said, "They have paperwork for you to look at. About your ancestors, maybe?"

My stomach did a quick flip as I noticed the leather satchel beside Angela. Renzo was right. What I had come to Italy to find might well be right there, within reach. *Was* I ready?

Small talk fluttered between the tables then—how everybody had slept, the beautiful weather—until Dante collapsed into a chair next to me. He downed his Bellini in a gulp.

"It took my grandmother upwards of a full hour to get out of the hotel room today," he said, a grin on his face.

I squeezed his arm. "You're doing the Lord's work," I said.

I was about to ask him about the dog when Thomas Moretti set his glass on the table with an air of finality and turned to me.

"Now," he said, placing his hands on the table. "You have come to Italy to research your roots, no?" His English was heavily accented but very good. It occurred to me it was the first time I had heard his voice. He hadn't spoken much at dinner the night before.

"That's right," I said.

"Then, let us speak of the Morettis of Santo Stefano," he said, nodding. "My people. And possibly your people, too."

CHAPTER 21

Fiora

Fiora had defied her parents, yet again, and made her way to the other side of town. Her twin, Florencia, had become used to covering for her, saying Fiora was in the woods or down at the hives or shopping in town. But Fiora wasn't doing any of those things. She was meeting Paolo Rossi down on the riverbank.

The twins first met Paolo years earlier, when he came with his mother into their kitchen to see their mother, Rosa, for reasons unknown to the girls. When they were young, they didn't understand, exactly, what Rosa did with her time, what she conjured up in their kitchen. But as they grew, they came to realize their mother ministered to the women of the village, mostly for female ailments. Aches and pains and infertility and infidelity and baby troubles and even love. Reversals of the evil eye, those were commonplace also. So, what Paolo's mother was doing in their kitchen they didn't quite know, but they knew she would likely leave with a small satchel of herbs.

Paolo was a very young man then, helping his mother walk down the bumpy streets at night toward the Broussard house. He would give her his arm as they walked and wait outside the kitchen door as she spoke with Rosa, not wanting to intrude on her privacy. That's where Fiora first spoke with him.

"You're Paolo," she said one dusky evening as the sun was setting. It was too forward for a young girl to begin a conversation with a young man, and Fiora knew this, but she had grown tired of waiting.

"And you're Fiora," Paolo said. "I know. I've seen you here."

"Why haven't you spoken to me before?" she asked.

Paolo shrugged and looked down at the street. He moved his feet back and forth. "You are so beautiful," he said finally. "I couldn't think of anything to say."

Fiora smiled. "How about hello?"

"Hello, Fiora."

"Hello, Paolo."

And that was the beginning of it. Rosa saw the whole thing, standing at the window, preparing her concoction for Paolo's mother.

Rosa watched through the window at her girl chatting with this darling, dark-haired, shy young man, whose eyes shone with intelligence and love. Constant's eyes shone with something else when he saw Paolo.

Despite how her father felt, it was evident to Florencia very early on that this handsome boy fancied her sister. And that Fiora fancied him, too.

She wasn't happy about this but saw the inevitability of it. It wasn't up to her to object, even though she felt a gnarling in her stomach when she thought about it. Something was not right. She couldn't put her finger on it. Paolo was a fine boy, she had no doubt. But it seemed to Florencia that he was carrying something . . . a dark shadow of some sort.

Rosa had the same feeling. The shadow settled over their household every time Paolo and his mother would come.

But Fiora saw nothing of that. She saw only this handsome young man, of whom she grew more fond with every passing day.

The next time his mother visited Rosa, Paolo accompanied her, carrying a book. A slim volume. "Do you like to read?" he asked Fiora, his eyes bright and expectant.

"Yes," she said. "Our mother has given us many books. We discuss them."

"I thought so." He held the volume out to Fiora. "I found this interesting. Since I have so much trouble finding my voice whenever I see you, I thought maybe you could take this and read it. And then we could talk about it the next time."

Fiora took the book from Paolo's hands and held it to her chest. "Thank you," she said, trying to contain her smile. "I will read it and give it back to you. And we can talk about it."

Paolo nodded. And the two stood there, by the kitchen door, in silence for a few moments until his mother was ready to go home.

"Signora Rossi," Fiora said to her as she came out of the door. "Good afternoon."

"Good afternoon, Fiora," she said. "I hope my son hasn't been bothering you."

"Not in the least, *signora*."

As they walked away, Signora Rossi looked back over her shoulder at Fiora. She did not smile.

Fiora and Paolo were not encouraged to see each other, nor did either set of parents give their consent. They had not been formally introduced. And Paolo got the same feeling from his mother that Fiora got from hers—there was something not right. They shouldn't be meeting. Their families would not approve.

But young people in love don't much care about approvals or consents or families. The two young lovers met in secret during those early days, down at the river as the sun was just beginning to set. Fiora loved that time of day. Everything was bathed in a warm glow. So was she.

One particular day, she found him under their favorite sycamore tree, the one that had stood on the river for decades. Maybe longer than that. She slid down next to him and sighed as he took her in his arms. It was not the first time.

"Your father has asked me to come to the barn and help him today," Paolo said.

Fiora's father, Constant, made his living in Italy as a blacksmith, despite being a highly educated man. It was difficult, in those days, for a man of color to attain or even remain in professional status, and when his benefactor went back to America, Constant had continued as a professor for a time at the university, but after an ugly incident with another professor, he realized he would need more reliable income to support his family.

So he turned to the trade he had learned from his father and found no shortage of customers. Honest work, Constant was fond of saying, and he was gifted at it.

"Help him?" Fiora said. "How will you help him?"

Paolo shrugged, with a laugh. "I don't know. But this is the first time he has asked anything of me. Or even spoken to me kindly. So I'm going."

❦

About that same time, Paolo's mother was knocking on Rosa's kitchen door. As she sat down at the table, she sighed. Rosa could see the darkness swirling around her, like an unholy mist. It did not dissipate as she poured her visitor some tea.

"Let us speak as women, as mothers," Signora Rossi said, taking a sip of her tea. "I have something important to talk with you about. A situation we must put right."

Rosa pulled out a chair and sank down into it. She had a feeling about what the other woman was there to discuss.

"I think we both see the growing love between my son and your daughter," Signora Rossi said. "Fiora is a fine girl. And you are a fine family."

Rosa nodded—but this was not what she had expected. Maria and Edoardo Rossi were well above their station. The husband was in city government. The family lived in a grand house in the best part of town and traveled abroad frequently, as Maria had told Rosa during their visits. Rosa was expecting a conversation of that sort. What could a family such as theirs offer the Rossi family? And that Constant was a Creole man . . . perhaps they didn't want grandchildren with that bloodline. So Rosa braced herself for what she was about to hear.

"I know about the power of love," Maria said. "My love for Paolo's father took me away from my home. My family came from Santo Stefano—you may not know this."

Rosa did not. "Oh?" she said, wondering how this conversation would find its way to her daughter.

"But sometimes, love isn't the most important thing in a marriage," Maria continued. "And it doesn't always last." This, Rosa understood. Maria came to her often with requests for teas for her husband, to revive the love that she thought had been lost.

"And how does this relate to Fiora and Paolo?" Rosa asked.

Maria took a deep breath before continuing. Whatever she was about to say hung in the air, even before she spoke it aloud.

"Paolo is betrothed," she said finally.

"Oh no," Rosa said, the image of her daughter's face swimming into her mind.

"It's true. The arrangement was made years ago, when Paolo was just a boy. My husband sought to unite our family with a powerful merchant family in Venice. It means money and land and business opportunities for both families."

Rosa rubbed her forehead—she felt a twinge of pain coming on. "A financial arrangement, then?"

"This has to stop between them," Maria said, not answering Rosa's question. "My husband has no knowledge of it, but word travels, even in a town as large as Rome. He will not have it."

Rosa took a sip of her tea to have a moment to digest this news. Although she knew there was no alternative, no path for happiness for Fiora. This meant heartbreak, there was no doubt. A vision appeared on the edges of her mind then. Arguing and wailing and grief, her daughter running in the night.

"When will the wedding take place? To this girl from Venice?"

"Not until she becomes of age. Two years."

"Does Paolo know about this?"

"No," Maria said. "We planned to make the introduction during a visit to Venice this summer."

Rosa nodded slowly. "So, my daughter and your son have to give up their love for your monetary gain."

Maria's face flushed. "I am very sorry to say it."

"My daughter's heart. And your son's. That's what we speak of here."

Maria gazed down into her teacup. "It's not their hearts I'm worried about," she said. "My husband will fly into a rage if this arrangement is broken. The family could sue us for breach of promise. Fiora also would be tainted by it. But that's not the worst of it. Edoardo would retaliate against your family. Your husband. There is no doubt in my mind."

As Rosa thought about it, she realized the mother, the wife sitting across the table from her, was right. This was the dark cloud she had seen every time Paolo came to the house. It had only darkened with every visit. Now she knew why.

But she did not know that Paolo, at that very moment, was speaking to Constant, who knew nothing of this.

CHAPTER 22

Rosa

When Constant summoned the young man to the barn, it wasn't help he wanted. Paolo saw that immediately. The older man set down his tools and turned to him.

"What are your intentions with my daughter?" he asked, resting a hand on his belt.

Paolo took a breath. If he was tongue-tied around the daughter, he was absolutely mute around the father. Especially because he knew the older man did not approve of him seeing Fiora.

"I—" he began. No more words would come.

Constant put up his hand. "Don't bother. I know your intentions. But do you know what you're getting into?"

Paolo shook his head.

Constant opened his arms, wide. "Look at me," he said. "I am a Creole man from New Orleans. Fiora has this blood flowing through her veins."

"I know," Paolo said, finally finding his voice. "And from where I sit, you are a very fine man. And Fiora is a fine girl. I'd be lucky to have her as my wife. And you as a father."

Constant folded his arms across his great chest. "You have more courage than you seem to."

"It doesn't take courage to love."

"Hell yes, it does. Very much. And you'll need it, boy. What do your parents have to say about this? They can't be happy about it."

Paolo winced. He knew this man was right. "I haven't spoken to my father about it," he said finally.

"I see trouble ahead," Constant said. "This doesn't feel right. In my bones."

Paolo just looked at him, not knowing quite what to say. They stood like that for a moment, one man who had seen life's adversities, cruelties, and harms and was afraid his consent would unleash all those beasts upon his beloved daughter. The other man, who was looking to the future with cautious optimism, the possibility of a life with Fiora still hanging in the air, waiting for him to grasp it.

"If Fiora loves you," Constant said finally, "there's not much more to say."

"Do I have your blessing to ask for her hand? To ask Fiora to be my wife?"

Visions of Fiora floated through Constant's mind then, almost as though they were playing themselves out in front of him. He watched her grow up again, in that instant, in the barn, with the man who wanted to take her away.

The dangerous birth of his twin daughters, expertly attended to by Rosa's mother. The girls playing outside as Rosa hung out the wash. Constant carrying both daughters in his great arms down to the riverbank. A lifetime of love and laughter, his girls' faces, his intense pride as he looked at them. Constant never knew he could love anything so much.

"You have my blessing," he said, his voice shredded by the sheer weight of those words. He wiped a tear from his eye before patting the young man on the back. "Now her mother? She's the one you have to worry about. Like I said, you'll need that courage."

Paolo held out his hand, shaking Constant's for the first time. He did not know it would be the last. "Thank you, *signore*. Your daughter will want for nothing. On this, I give you my word."

Paolo hurried out of the barn then and back down to the river, knowing Fiora was waiting for him. He could not wait to tell her their life together had begun.

But Rosa, glancing out her kitchen window, saw Paolo running out of the barn, smiling from ear to ear.

What just happened? But she didn't need to be told. The look on the boy's face spoke volumes. She would talk with her husband later. First, she had important work to do.

"What is it?" her mother Isabella said, sweeping into the room in her long floral dress. "I sensed something. What's happening?"

And so Rosa told her mother the news about Paolo's betrothal.

"I just saw him coming from the barn," Rosa said, pacing from the hearth to the table and back again. She sat down with a huff.

"They were talking about Fiora."

"Yes! And by the look of the boy, Constant has given him his blessing to court her. Or even marry her."

Isabella pulled out a chair and joined her daughter at the table. She held out her hands, which Rosa clasped.

"It's time to burn those letters," Isabella said.

Rosa had not told Constant about the barrage of letters from his mother Cecile, the Creole woman—a witch, many people said, with "the shine" darker and deeper than their own family leanings. Their use of herbs and plants and spices to concoct recipes was one thing. Cecile's was something else. Something they had never seen.

Constant had told the girls stories about the great Cecile, the woman who helped feed the hungry, cure the sick, heal the heartbroken. And that was all true, as far as Rosa knew. But Constant did not know about the latest letters from his mother. The ugliness. The threats. There was a devil side of Cecile, Rosa saw clearly in the letters. Isabella saw it, too.

Come back to New Orleans, Cecile wrote to her son. *You have been gone too long. In a country that is not your own. With people who are not your own.*

Constant knew his mother wanted him to come home. He had always known. But his life was in Italy now. With Rosa. The girls. He had no wish to return to a country where many of his people were enslaved, building cities and towns at the crack of a whip. Toiling in the fields for someone else to get rich. The brutality that he had heard about and seen. Treating people like animals.

No, Constant had no plans to return to New Orleans and had written to Cecile to let her know, gently, that he loved her but needed to remain in Rome because he had found true love with Rosa. He had invited her to join them. But she would never leave the bayous of New Orleans. He knew that before he asked.

Cecile sent letters in return. After reading the first one, Isabella had intercepted them all and given them to Rosa.

The first was just a simple plea to return. *Bring the lovely Rosa! Build a life on the bayous! Make this your home!*

When Cecile's pleas for Constant to return fell on deaf ears, the messages grew stronger. Stranger. Deadlier. Until one contained what was clearly a curse. It was directed at Rosa.

You have left me alone, childless, no comfort from my boy in my old age. All because he loves you. This is not love. You have cast a spell on him. So I will cast one on you.

As the wind whispers through the bayous, tangling in the vines

I curse the woman's love to be lost time
As long as love blooms across the sea
Many years their beloveds will not see
For generations on, from love's first kiss
Your line will languish alone in the eternal abyss
As I have done for so many years
They will suffer from the weight of my tears.

Isabella and Rosa looked at each other, both women wrinkling their noses in confusion.

"Has she cursed our family? Is that what this is?" Rosa asked.

Isabella shook her head. "I'm not sure. I've never seen anything like this before."

"It sounds like she's threatening the men we fall in love with," Rosa said, squinting at the words, as if to get a clearer picture of their meaning.

"Not yours, surely. He's her own son."

But then, mother and daughter looked at each other, both realizing the meaning at the same time as a chill descended around them.

"She means Fiora and Florencia."

"And any women who come after."

That very night, they performed the ritual to dissipate the evil eye, better safe than sorry, but both felt the situation needed more than that. It went deeper.

Rosa spoke to her husband, brandishing the letter.

"I know you all believe in these curses and powers and things," Constant said after hearing her out, his eyes on his mother's words. "But this is the modern age, Rosa. A curse? She would never really hurt my daughters. It's unthinkable."

But as he handed the letter back to his wife, Constant felt a gnarling in his stomach. "Is there anything I can do?"

"Write to her and ask her to reverse it," Rosa said. "It has to come from you."

Beyond that, Rosa and her mother weren't completely sure what to do. If anything. This wasn't their magic. It was not of their world. These things were delicate, Isabella had said to her daughter. You chanced making things worse if you did the wrong thing. Said the wrong words at the wrong time.

Time passed, and soon the letters stopped coming. So, the two women felt, perhaps letting it be was the best course of action after all. They hadn't given the curse any power. Hadn't said the wrong words trying to defuse it. And maybe Cecile had done as her son had asked. As the years passed, Isabella and Rosa had hope that all was well.

Until Paolo came along. Until his mother told Rosa about his betrothal. Was this the stuff of the curse, sent across the ocean by a Creole woman?

"We cannot let this stand," Rosa said. "We need to do something. The best of what we know. Now."

So, when the girls had gone to bed for the night and Constant was asleep in his chair by the hearth, Rosa and Isabella stole outside. They made their way down to the river, where Isabella had laid a fire earlier in the day. As they were preparing to light it, they noticed other women walking down to the river. What was this? Would they have to stop what they were planning to do?

No. The women, their neighbors, those whom they had helped and healed and listened to over the years, came to join them. How they knew to do it, Rosa and Isabella never knew. But they came to stand with the women as they lit their fire, and Isabella placed a packet of letters on top of it. They made a circle, clasping hands, as they watched the paper burn, the smoke rising into the night sky.

Isabella began to speak.

"I command this fire shall set us free
From her wicked words of destiny
Our love denied, our passions cold
No longer bound by doom foretold
I hereby sever this web of lies
I break her spell as embers rise
The wind doth take this jealous screed
I claim ours spirits now are freed
As night becomes day, the curse undone
May love surround us, everyone."

What Isabella and Rosa, and all the women there that night, did not know was that the burning of the words unlocked their power. Now they were alive.

Rosa did not hear it, but Cecile was laughing as she sat by her own hearth, in her own home, alone, in the darkness of a Louisiana bayou.

CHAPTER 23

Rosa

What did Rosa expect to happen when she burned Cecile's letters? She did not know. She only knew she had to do something to avoid the darkness coming toward her daughter. She did the best she could.

During the following few days, the Broussard household was still and quiet. Everyone was seemingly holding their breath, but for different reasons.

Rosa did not mention anything to Constant about burning the letters. Rosa and Isabella did not speak of the letters or the curse between them. It felt like silence was what was needed. A respectful, reverential silence. Rosa hoped they would be done with it.

Constant was silent, too. He did not tell Rosa about Paolo's intentions, giving the conversation he had had with the young man some time to settle in his mind before talking about it with his wife.

Florencia knew something was not right. She felt it, in her bones, the way her father felt things in his. She walked carefully through those days, not wanting to upset the stillness that had descended on their household.

But Fiora and Paolo were anything but silent, not with each other. The young lovers were eagerly planning their life, their future, as they lay together under the sycamore tree by the banks of the Tiber. True happiness surrounded them then and held them close, knowing how fleeting its presence in their lives would be.

Paolo tucked a stray curl behind Fiora's ear. "I will tell my father tonight," he said, his voice stronger and more confident than Fiora had ever heard it.

Fiora laughed. "Shall we marry tomorrow?"

"Maybe not tomorrow," Paolo said. "I'm sure your father and mine will need to speak of this, and our mothers will want to plan a wedding. But soon. In the summer?"

She pulled him closer to her then, and kissed him, holding her whole self against him. She could feel his heartbeat on her chest. No. Not on it. In it. As their hearts beat together, she thought, *This is the man of my life.*

When Fiora was busily writing in the journal about her day—becoming engaged to Paolo Rossi!—she did not know all the hope and happiness of the two young lovers and the stillness of the Broussard household would be shattered later that evening, when Edoardo Rossi knocked on their front door.

Isabella and Rosa were together in the sitting room, Rosa reading by the firelight and Isabella knitting, when the knock came. And then, the shouting.

"Broussard! Constant Broussard! Open up!" Rossi's voice sounded, to Rosa, like that of a monster. A man enraged could be just that, she thought.

The two women exchanged a glance.

"Where is he?" Isabella asked.

"I think he's still in the barn," Rosa said, rising from her chair. She turned and whispered to her mother, "Take Fiora out of the house through the kitchen door."

Isabella pushed herself up and held her hands above her head as Rossi bellowed on. She closed her eyes and whispered an incantation. *"Peace to all who enter here."*

The candlelight flickered, just a bit, and the fire burned brighter with a whoosh. A mist seemed to fall over the room.

Isabella nodded to her daughter. "Now," she said.

When her mother was out of sight, Rosa walked to the front door, step by slow step, as the man shouted.

She pulled it open, causing Edoardo Rossi's clenched fist to stop in midair.

"Good evening, Signore Rossi," Rosa said, smoothing her skirt. Her voice was a calming balm. "I hope you are well. What can I do for you?"

"Where is your husband?" he demanded, pushing his way past her and through the doorway.

"Broussard!" he shouted, attempting to stomp farther into the house. But Rosa stood in front of him and put up her hands, as if to stop the flow of anger—as well as the man—from entering.

She smiled, exuding peacefulness. "Please come in," she said, eyeing him up and down, silently pointing out that he had entered without being invited. "I will let my husband know you are here."

Edoardo took another step into the room. That's when Rosa noticed the pistol in his hand.

"Would you like some tea?" she asked. "Or something stronger?"

Edoardo's eyes flashed. "No," he said, his voice measured and low. "This is not a social visit. Just summon your husband. I must speak with him. Now."

"Please, sit down," Rosa said, gesturing to one of the chairs by the fire. "Are you sure I can't get you a drink? I have an excellent grappa on hand."

Signore Rossi squinted at her. "No," he said, and Rosa could sense his anger dripping away. The spell for peace was working.

"I won't be a moment," Rosa said. "Please excuse me as I fetch my husband for you."

Rosa walked slowly from the room, but then hurried to the kitchen, where she found Isabella and Florencia standing together by the back door.

Rosa looked from one to the other. "Why are you here?" she said to her daughter, her voice a harsh whisper. "Fiora—"

"She is not in the house," Isabella said.

"Where is she?"

Both women turned toward Florencia, but the girl didn't get a chance to answer. Edoardo Rossi burst through the kitchen door.

The peace that had settled over the man in the sitting room had all but evaporated. "You," he said, pointing at Florencia, his voice measured but filled with anger. "You have bewitched my son. All of you women in this house. Witches!"

Florencia shook her head. "No," she said.

Rosa put her arm around her daughter. "Your son Paolo has been here at this house nearly every week," she said, pausing for emphasis. "With your wife."

"And this girl," he said, his face reddening.

"Your son's friendship has been with my daughter Fiora," Rosa said. "This is her sister."

"My son will not have a friendshi—" Edoardo began, his hands twitching. But he didn't get a chance to finish his thought because Constant opened the kitchen door. A whoosh of chilly air followed him in, swirling around Signore Rossi and attempting to cool him down.

That's when Rosa noticed Isabella was gone.

While Rosa had been keeping Signore Rossi occupied in the kitchen, Isabella had stolen out the back door and hurried down to the river, where she knew the young lovers would be together. She found them entwined in each other's arms, under the ancient sycamore tree.

Upon catching sight of her, both sat up immediately, Fiora smoothing her skirts, Paolo running a hand through his hair. "Signora Isabella," he said, scrambling to his feet.

She shook her head and put a hand out to stop his words. "Don't you worry about that now," she said, casting a sad smile at her granddaughter. "I am the least of your worries. Paolo, you need to know your father is now in our home, talking to Signore Broussard."

Paolo furrowed his brow. "Why? If this were happy news, you would not have the countenance on your face that you have. Is there a problem . . . ?"

Isabella grasped his forearm. "You are betrothed to another. A girl from Venice. This is a monetary arrangement made by your parents and hers, long ago."

Fiora let out a strangled cry. But Paolo took her hand and pulled her to her feet. "No," he said, "this will not stand. I will refuse. I have asked for Signore Broussard's blessing and received it."

"I have accepted Paolo's proposal," Fiora said.

Paolo turned to Fiora then. "You must be prepared," he said. "This may get ugly. If there truly is a betrothal, there might be some repercussions. And we certainly won't be able to rely on my family for money."

Fiora squeezed his hands. "We will rely on ourselves."

Paolo pulled his future wife close and kissed her cheek. And then turned to her grandmother. "My father is up at the house now, as you said?"

Isabella nodded. "Do not go up there and confront him. You must flee. Both of you. Right now. From here. Send word to me, and Fiora's mother, of where you are. And we will help you, if we can. We will bring clothes and supplies and money."

Paolo grasped Fiora's hand. "No," he said, with a strong voice Fiora had never heard. "I will not flee into the night like a criminal. I will talk with my father. I will tell him I will choose my own wife. And I have."

And with that, the two young lovers walked off into the night, toward the house, toward their fate. Isabella shook her head, but just for a moment. She gathered herself and whispered every incantation she knew for peace, silence, love, and even paralysis on her way back up to the house.

CHAPTER 24

Rosa

"Signore Rossi," Constant said, wiping his hands on a towel he was carrying. "Welcome to our home. I'm sorry I wasn't here to greet you." He put out his hand to the man, who did not take it.

"We have no time for pleasantries," Rossi said. "I must speak with you. It's urgent."

Constant and his wife exchanged a quick glance.

"Of course," Constant said, gesturing toward the door. "Let's go into the sitting room. My wife will bring us something to drink."

He put his hand on Rossi's back and ushered him out of the kitchen, catching his wife's eye over his shoulder. She understood. He was taking the angry man away from her and Florencia.

Rosa nodded toward the hallway. "Go to your room," she said to Florencia. "Do not come out for any reason. If anyone knocks at your door, or if you hear anything, you go out of the window and run down to the barn. Do you understand me?"

"What about Fiora?"

"You have to know she is with Paolo," Rosa said. "Where else would she be?"

Rosa and Florencia held each other's gaze for a moment then, a lifetime of words unspoken, but known.

"I love you," Rosa whispered as she watched her daughter hurry down the hallway.

After Florencia entered the room, Rosa stole down the hallway to the closed door. She kissed the tips of her own fingers and ran them across the door's lintel and down the wood framing on both sides. One last protection.

In the sitting room, Constant gestured for Signore Rossi to sit down in a chair by the fire. He could feel the calming spell his wife and her mother had cast in the air and did his best not to be caught up in it. He needed his wits about him.

As Rossi glared at Constant, he noticed how much bigger the Creole man was than he. The gigantic chest. Shoulders. Arms. Rossi fingered his pistol, glad to have brought it.

Constant noticed the pistol in the other man's hand. And knew all the diplomacy he could muster was needed at that time. It might have been just fine, then. If that was all that had transpired. If the two men had talked things through, like the reasonable people they were. And if the love between Fiora and Paolo hadn't been so fierce. So strong. If they could've seen the inevitability of the agreement Rossi had made. But it did not happen that way.

"I understand from my wife that my son is enchanted with your daughter," Rossi said, gripping the chair's arm with one hand and the pistol in the other.

"And she with him. Is something wrong with that?"

Rossi told Constant about Paolo's betrothal.

"So you see, he cannot court your daughter," Rossi said. "His marriage has already been arranged. I have given my word. My promise. My consent." He spat the words out, each with more force than the last. "I came here, like a gentleman, to let you know this. Man to man. Father to father. We need to stop this before it starts."

Constant rubbed his chin. "There's a problem with that, I'm afraid."

Rossi's eyes flashed. "What is the problem?"

"I have already given your son *my* consent. My word. My promise. And he does not wish to simply court my daughter. They have known each other for half of their lives. He asked for my blessing to marry her. I gave it to him."

Rossi pushed himself up from his chair. "That will not stand."

"It is not up to me," Constant said, shaking his head. "Or you. I gave my consent to your son this afternoon. There is no doubt in my mind he has already told Fiora of this. I have not seen her since I talked to the boy—I can only assume the two of them are together. The question of marriage between them has undoubtedly been asked and answered."

Rossi ran a shaking hand through his hair as he paced. "This will be dissolved," he said, his voice wavering. "It must be. My son has been betrothed since he was a child."

"Does he know that?"

"No," Rossi said. "I planned to tell him in the summer, during a trip to Venice to meet the girl. And her family. Their union is not negotiable."

"Why can't that promise be dissolved? Paolo did not know anything of this. His promise to my daughter Fiora is pure. It is you that has contaminated it—and your son's life—with your secrets."

Rossi looked at Constant, up and down, with the eyes of an animal and the sneer of a superior. "You may know nothing of our Italian ways," he said, enunciating each word, the implied insult clear to the Creole American. "But my son is bound to another. I made a promise. And that promise will be kept."

Now it was time for Constant to get to his feet. He was about to give Rossi an answer to the question he had not asked—what would happen if he tried to enforce his edict—when the door to the kitchen swung open and Paolo and Fiora walked through it, hand in hand.

Signore Rossi shot his son a look. "What have you done?"

"What have I done? Asked the woman I love, and have loved for all of my life, to marry me. With the blessing of her father. And she has said yes. So we are celebrating. The question is, what have *you* done?"

Fiora had never heard Paolo so forceful, so confident. He was now a man, she had no doubt.

"We are leaving this house now, Paolo," Rossi said, his hand twitching. "And we will never return. Not you. Not me. You will never see this girl again."

"I'm sorry, Father," Paolo said. The two young lovers stood side by side, resolute. Nothing more needed to be said.

Signore Rossi shook his head. "You don't understand. You are betrothed. You have been since you were a boy."

The anger between father and son swirled around the room then, like a red mist, growing more and more intense between them until it caught them, fast.

"I knew nothing of this," Paolo said. "It is your mistake for not telling me sooner. Not that it would have made any difference."

His father stood firm, just as firm as Paolo and Fiora. "It is the merger of two great families. There is no possibility—"

The anger in the room grew into a deep red.

Paolo snickered. "The merger of two great families? So you are gaining in wealth because of this? We are living in the modern age, Father. I have received consent from Signore Broussard, and from Fiora."

"You do not understand, my son," Rossi said, his tone almost pleading now. "This is a signed contract."

Constant could see the desperation in Rossi's face. He had seen that desperation before. Nothing good came of it. He stood between Rossi and his son, his great chest a barrier between them.

"This will ruin our family, don't you see that?" Signore Rossi bellowed at his son.

"I think it's time you leave my house, Signore Rossi," Constant said. "Leave this be, now. We can sort it out in the morning. When everyone has a clearer head."

But clearer heads would not prevail. Not in the sitting room. Not that night. Anger was growing stronger. Fiora could feel it.

In the kitchen, Rosa, whispering with Isabella, heard the shot ring out.

And then, the wailing.

It was a sound the likes of which none of the women had ever heard. Grief, given awful, terrible voice. Rosa burst through the sitting room door.

She found Edoardo Rossi standing, frozen, with a gun in his hand. His only child, Paolo, lay on the floor, on his back. Fiora was kneeling over him, wailing. Her grief, astonishment, abject fear, and disbelief seemed to be a living thing, crouching around her. Closing in. Engulfing her.

Constant took the gun from Rossi's hand. He looked at his wife and shook his head.

Rossi slumped down onto a chair; his bones had seemingly lost their strength. "I was aiming at him," he said, gesturing toward Constant, his voice so weak Rosa could barely hear it. "What have I done?"

Rosa knelt down and wrapped her arms around her daughter. "Summon the police," she said, looking over her shoulder at her husband.

"No," Constant said, setting the pistol down on the table. "No police."

Rosa frowned at him. "Why?"

"I'm a Black man, and a foreigner, and the son of a prominent Roman has been shot in my house."

About that time, Isabella swept into the room, carrying her satchel. Her presence, so large, so looming, brought silence with it. Even the wails had no voice.

Gently, she drew Fiora away from the body of her love—for it was but a body now. A shell. Isabella could see that. But she would do what she could, for Fiora's sake. For Paolo's mother's sake. She checked for signs of life. Whispered strange and foreign words nobody there had ever heard before or would ever hear again.

But it was no use. Paolo Rossi was dead.

CHAPTER 25

Rosa

While Florencia led Fiora—stunned into a state of shock—away, Rosa and Isabella took charge.

Rosa ran to the kitchen for a bottle of olive oil and, back in the drawing room, sprinkled it on the doorframe and threshold, along with a generous dose of salt. And then Isabella began to whisper ancient words of protection. They did the same for the kitchen door.

The women were warding off any further evil from coming through their doors into the house. Both were angry they hadn't done so before inviting Edoardo inside.

That done, Isabella returned to the drawing room, where Edoardo was still crying in a heap on the chair.

Isabella clapped her hands, seemingly to jolt the man out of his stupor. She well understood what would rain down upon their household if Paolo was discovered there. That was her only focus now.

"Look at me," she said, snapping her fingers. "Look here. *Signore!* Look to me."

Edoardo looked up, blinking several times, as though he just awakened.

"Unless you want to hang for your son's murder, a few things are going to happen right now. Do you understand me?"

Edoardo nodded, happy to have someone handle the worst day of his life.

Within very short order, a man came to take Paolo's body down to the riverbank, whereupon police were summoned by Edoardo, who said he had been out walking by his home and found his son had been shot.

Paolo Rossi was buried in his family's crypt, the victim of a robbery on the streets of Rome. Nobody who was not in the room that night, with the exception of his mother, ever knew what really happened to the young man, who died for love.

⁓❦⁓

The next days and weeks passed in a blur for the Broussard family. Fiora, consumed by her grief, took to her bed and scarcely emerged, even for mealtimes.

But Isabella soon began to take meals to her granddaughter, small portions of soup or bread or pastas. "You must grow strong," she whispered to Fiora, who didn't much care if she did anything again.

But Isabella knew why her granddaughter needed to grow strong. And she knew she and Rosa had failed her that night when they burned the letters. This was the work of the curse, there was no doubt in her mind. Rosa knew it, too, and was inconsolable.

Meanwhile, life grew more and more difficult for Constant and Rosa Broussard, there in their quiet Roman neighborhood. Customers stopped coming to Constant for his blacksmithing skills, which, he suspected, was the work of Edoardo Rossi. Women stopped knocking on their kitchen door, as whispers of witchcraft and scandal swirled through the air. People stopped greeting them at the market or on the streets.

A sense of dread began to waft through the house. Constant knew well that sort of dread, and it didn't lead to anything good. Untended, it did not go away.

"I think it's time we left here," Rosa said to her husband one evening. "We should pack up and build a life elsewhere."

Constant leaned back in his chair. "How does New Orleans sound?"

Rosa considered this. They had received word, shortly after Paolo's death, that Cecile was in ill health—perhaps tending to her would be the right thing to do, the only thing to do to break this curse. If not for Fiora's sake, then for Florencia's. And for whoever came after. They had lost to the powerful magic of Cecile and now must do what she had asked.

They had enough money for passage for themselves, Isabella, and their daughters, and if they sold the house, the barn, and all Constant's blacksmithing tools, they'd have a tidy sum with which to start a new life in America.

But the question was, Would Fiora leave Italy? Could she make the trip?

As the weeks turned into a month and her daughter did not bleed, Rosa knew she could not. Isabella knew long before that. Even before Fiora knew.

Rosa sat on the edge of her daughter's bed. She stroked Fiora's hair, her heart breaking a bit more with each stroke. The thought of her daughter, with the child of a man who had been murdered in front of her. A child who Fiora would have to raise on her own.

"Fiora," Rosa said, as gently as she could. "You must sit up and look at me."

Fiora sighed and did as she was asked.

"My beloved girl," Rosa said. "Soon to be a mother."

A flood of tears then, as Fiora cried in her mother's arms.

"Paolo lives on in you," Rosa whispered to her daughter.

And that is how, and why, Fiora rose from her bed, began eating again, and came back to the living.

That evening, Rosa walked out to the barn to speak to her husband. She looked him in the eyes, and they shared a smile.

"We're going to be grandparents," he said, his low voice reverberating in Rosa's heart.

"How did you know?"

"I must've got a little of my mother's shine somewhere along the way," he said. "Not that I'm happy about this situation. A child without a father."

She noticed that he had not packed up his tools, as he said he would, for the man who was coming to buy them.

"We can't leave yet," he said, answering her question before she asked it. "I told him to come back in a few months' time."

Rosa wrapped her arms around her husband's waist. "That's just what I was coming here to ask you. The trip will be long."

"Let's let the child come into the world," he said. "And then we will decide what to do. This baby may be a reason to stay here after all."

But that was not to be. Some months later, Constant appeared in the kitchen and sat down at the table next to his wife. He was holding a letter.

"What's this?" Rosa asked, furrowing her brow. "It looks important."

Constant exhaled. "I think it is, honey," he said, nodding.

"So?"

The big man cleared his throat. "When we started talking about leaving Rome and going back to New Orleans, I wrote to my former mentor, the professor who brought me to Italy all those years ago," he said.

"To meet me." Rosa smiled at her husband, remembering those early days. They seemed like a lifetime go. And yesterday.

Constant squeezed her hand. "Yes," he said. "I wrote to him, asking for a job."

Rosa held her breath. This was good news. She could feel it. He pushed the letter across the table toward his wife. She took it out of the envelope and smoothed the paper flat on the table.

"My English isn't . . . ," she started, squinting at the letter, written in more complicated, professional language than she was used to. "Can you read it to me? Or just tell me what it says?"

But Rosa had a feeling, deep down, she knew what it was.

Constant looked at her with hope and anxiety in his eyes, almost like that of a little boy's. Rosa's heart melted. How she loved this man.

"Tulane University is offering me an assistant professorship," he said, smiling broadly at his wife. "In the History Department. They also asked me to teach a course in Italian language and history. It's not too much money to start, but the idea is for me to work toward—"

Rosa's hands flew to her mouth. "Oh, Constant!" she squeaked out, pushing back her chair and running to him. He stood up and took his wife in his arms.

"I am so proud of you," Rosa said softly in his ear. "And happy for us."

Constant pulled back. "You know this means we're really going to America," he said.

"You gave up your career to stay here in Rome with me," she said. "You had achieved so much but made your living as a blacksmith here because of me. I will go to America with you."

"For a Black man, at this time, to be offered this sort of position," Constant said. "It means so much."

"They are lucky to get you," Rosa said. "But now you realize you need to teach me better English."

Rosa did not tell her husband she was harboring ill will in her heart for his mother, who had all but ruined Fiora's life. Mending fences might be the only way forward, but deep inside Rosa wanted to declare war.

CHAPTER 26

Fiora

As the family made plans to immigrate to America, Fiora's future was about to unfold.

Violetta was born on a rainy spring day, as Paolo lay next to his beloved, watching his daughter come into the world. The daughter who would never know him. Who he would never hold and guide and make giggle with his silliness.

Fiora had made no sound during the birth, her grief strangulating any joy she may have felt. As Rosa scooped up the baby to wash and swaddle her, Fiora, still a bit delirious from the whole experience, rolled over and put her head on Paolo's chest.

"We have a daughter," she said to the only man she would ever love, her words slurred with approaching sleep.

"We shall name her Violetta," he whispered, filled with grief at his life unlived. "For the color of her startling eyes."

"You will be the most wonderful father to our Violetta," Fiora said, curling into his embrace. And he cried tears of bitter regret and crushing sadness, yearning for the one thing the Fates would not allow him.

Shortly after the child's birth, there was a knock at Rosa's kitchen door. It was Maria Rossi.

Rosa shook her head. "I have nothing for you, *signora*," she said. "Please go away."

"Please, let me in," Maria said, smiling slightly. "Or come out. I must talk with you."

So Rosa opened the door to Signora Rossi, who took a few steps into the kitchen, her face wet with tears. She was holding a large, fat envelope sealed with red wax. She held it out to Rosa.

"This is for your daughter," she said, grasping tight to Rosa's sleeve with her other hand. "I know how Paolo loved her. I watched their love grow, day after day."

Rosa took the envelope. "What is it?" Rosa asked.

"It is enough money to live on for a lifetime, and the deed to my father's house in Santo Stefano. Far away from here."

Rosa held her gaze for a long moment. "You are funding my daughter's life?"

"Yes," she said, "People are talking. They have heard about the baby. They are saying it is Paolo's. Rumors are running wild. I'm telling you, Fiora needs to leave this place. Now."

Rosa squinted at Maria. "Why? Why does she need to leave? For your reputation because they were not married? Or because Fiora isn't from a fine family? Or worse, if this family from Venice gets wind of the scandal and could still sue for breach of promise to save their own face?"

"All of that, yes, but none of it matters in the least." Maria leaned in, closer to Rosa. "My husband intends to begin legal action to take the baby. To raise it as our own."

Rosa's hand flew to her mouth. "No!"

"You have been such a friend and confidante to me over the years. You have helped me. I wish no ill on your family, Rosa. That is why I am here, unbeknownst to my husband, to tell you to leave. Not just Fiora and the baby. All of you must go. He is blinded by his grief and determined to ruin you all."

"Oh no," Rosa said again.

Maria nodded. "Yes. He blames your family for the loss of ours. He is powerful, Rosa. He can and will destroy you."

Rosa looked into the desperate face of this woman and knew she was telling the truth. She took the envelope from Maria, set it down on the table, and squeezed her hands.

"I must tell you that we have already made plans to leave Rome," Rosa said. "My husband has secured a teaching position at an American university, and we are leaving any day now. So Fiora doesn't need this money. Or the deed. And you can tell your husband to drop this vendetta because the Broussard family will be gone very shortly."

Maria shook her head. "No," she said. "I will not tell him, until you are gone and there is no chance he can retaliate against you. And keep the deed. And the money. I know Fiora. She is a fine girl. She may want to raise the baby in a place connected to Paolo."

As she mentioned her son's name, Maria's voice cracked and her eyes filled with tears.

Rosa's heart broke for this mother, who had lost her only child, and now, too, her grandchild.

"Would you like to see the baby?"

Maria shook her head, a tear escaping one eye. "More than anything. But I cannot. If I see her, I will never let Paolo's daughter go. It took everything I had to come here, to not let my husband take this child from its mother."

The sacrifice this woman was making for Fiora took Rosa's breath away. She called upon her ancestors to speak important words through her, an incantation.

"May you find peace, Maria Rossi," Rosa said. "May the intense grief for your beloved son soften and grow less harsh with every passing day. May his memory reside in your heart forever. And may your husband drink in your peace to cool his anger and his rage. May your life become calm and settled once again. And may you know, the women of my family, Fiora, Violetta, and all who come after, will know your name."

The two women embraced each other, and stood like that for a long time. Two mothers' hearts breaking as one.

Signora Rossi left the Broussard house that day, never to return. That evening, the family sat together, Violetta in Constant's arms, to discuss the future.

Constant told his daughters of his new position, which would begin the following autumn at Tulane University. They would be traveling to America together, effective immediately.

After hearing her parents' plan, Fiora spoke. "I don't want to go," she said. "Paolo's spirit is here. I have felt it. His daughter should be raised here, as an Italian. Not as an American."

Constant and Rosa exchanged a glance. Fiora knew nothing of Signore Rossi's plan to take the baby. Rosa had whispered it to her husband, who then said, "Let me see him try." But they both knew the best course of action was to simply leave. No more trauma, no more altercations, just an exit from a life that had run its course.

The big man tried to convince his daughter to reconsider, but his wife put a hand on his arm to stop it.

"Fiora, there's something you don't know," Rosa said. And she told her about Maria Rossi's offer, the money and the deed.

"A home in Santo Stefano is waiting for you," she said, tears in her eyes. "If you are determined to stay in Italy, that is where you should go."

Fiora took this all in. "Why can't I stay here?"

Rosa and Isabella exchanged a glance. "Violetta is in danger if you do" was all Rosa said. "Do not ask any more about this. Just know it is the truth."

Florencia crossed the room and took a seat next to her sister. "I will go to Santo Stefano with you and the baby," she said, surprising no one.

"Take this deed," Rosa said. "There is money for you to live on for the rest of your lives. This is your opportunity to create a new life for yourselves and the baby. I see good things for you three there."

Isabella nodded. "Yes," she said. "I see it, too."

Constant rubbed his forehead and was silent for a time. "We will all leave together," he said finally. "I'll hire a coach in the morning. From Santo Stefano, we can go south, where we can get a boat to travel to America. If that's what we choose to do. Maybe we'll stay on in Santo Stefano with you."

But Rosa shook her head. "No," she said. "A new life is awaiting you in America. A better life than we could have here. That's where we will go."

Isabella cleared her throat. "I have something to say," she said, looking around the table. "I'm staying here."

Rosa frowned at her mother. "What do you mean, staying?"

"This is the house of my mother and her mother before her," Isabella said. "We have been tending the bees in Rome for many generations. Serving the women of this neighborhood for longer than either of us has been alive. You were born here. The girls were born here. Violetta was born here. This is my place."

"But you'll be alone!" Rosa said, tears stinging at her eyes. "I will not leave you alone!" It had been more than a decade since Rosa's father had passed.

"Alone." Isabella waved her hand. "How? You know that my sister and her children and grandchildren are across town, a short carriage ride away. I have our neighbors and the church and the *Signore* from the market down the street. And the bees."

She turned to Florencia and Fiora. "And I will be here, in this house, as I always have been, just in case you do not find happiness in Santo Stefano and wish to return to Rome. You always have a home here."

Rosa tried to argue on, but ultimately she knew she could not change her mother's mind.

Rosa and Isabella held hands under the table then, as their family's future unfolded. Isabella would stay in Rome. Rosa would go with her husband to America. Fiora and Florencia would create a life together in Santo Stefano for baby Violetta. And one day, the family would be all together again.

It would take much longer than she imagined it would. A lifetime longer.

CHAPTER 27

Isabella

After a long goodbye, Rosa, Fiora, Florencia, and Violetta climbed into the coach that had pulled up outside their home as Constant loaded their things. Rosa had agonized over what to bring with them to America but ultimately decided on clothes and a few special items of significance—a silver mirror passed down from her grandmother, the brightly colored bowl they kept on their kitchen table, lace tatted by Isabella. She would have to buy whatever they needed to set up housekeeping once they arrived in America rather than drag all those things across the sea.

The girls did the same, knowing they'd have the money they needed to make a home for themselves and Violetta.

As the coach pulled away, Fiora put her head out of the window and waved to her grandmother, watching the faded yellow house with the terra-cotta tile roof disappear as they turned onto the main boulevard, the house where her bedroom window overlooked the garden with its olive trees, the house where she and Florencia had learned to walk and talk and read. She knew she would never see that house again, the house where she had met her great love Paolo outside their kitchen door, where their love had blossomed and grown. The garden where he had taken her in his arms for the first time, taking her breath away as his lips pressed against hers, the place where Violetta had been conceived and born. The house where the love of her life had his taken from him, and from her, and from their daughter.

As the horses clopped along, Fiora knew she was leaving all of that behind. Not just the house and everything she knew, but love as well. Her love died when Paolo took his last breath in her arms. She would never give her heart to another, never lie down with another man at night and wake up with him in the morning. She knew this in her bones. Her life was Violetta.

As Isabella watched the carriage disappear, carrying her family away, she knew exactly what Fiora was thinking, and knew the truth of it. Edoardo Rossi had taken much from her granddaughter. He had taken much from Isabella herself, driving her family away. He had never paid any price for it. Cecile Broussard had been the cause of it all. And now she was getting exactly what she wanted—Rosa and Constant, in America with her. Tending to her. Helping her as she grew old. While Isabella died alone.

This would not stand.

A chill wind swirled around Isabella then, whispering in her ear. She pulled her shawl over her head and went back inside the house. She had important things to attend to.

In the kitchen, she closed all the shutters and lit a dozen candles, placing them around the room. She poured water into the black cauldron hanging in the fireplace and lit the logs that had been laid there earlier in the day. The water would soon boil. She stepped into the pantry and searched the shelves for a powerful recipe her grandmother had handed down to her when she was a young woman. It was not to be used lightly, her grandmother had warned, only in the most extraordinary of circumstances. That time, Isabella thought, was now.

Dried holly, nightshade, buttercup, gypsyflower, adder's tongue, slowworm, and others. Some of the ingredients were native to this land. Others had been acquired in secret from traders who specialized in the dark ways. They had been combined and stored for a generation, as their power grew.

When the water in the cauldron was boiling, she closed her eyes, took a deep breath, and sprinkled the mixture into the water. It sizzled and crackled, and aromatic steam rose from the pot and swirled around the room, as if alive.

She reached into her pocket and pulled out a piece of fabric. Edoardo Rossi's handkerchief that he had left behind that fateful night. Isabella had taken it on the hunch she might need it one day. Today was that day. She dropped the fabric into the pot. Next, she drew one of Cecile's letters from that same pocket. One she had held on to, for just this reason.

As she gazed into the cauldron's boiling water, she recited the incantation her grandmother had taught her, in secret, nearly a lifetime ago.

> "By the new moon's light
> I curse you, Edoardo
> With every step, your path shall twist into darkness
> Shadows will rise from dark corners and sur-
> round you
> Despair shall dwell in your heart
> A river of sorrow shall engulf your every moment
> I bind this curse upon your head
> Until the end of your woeful days
> And by this new moon's light
> I curse you, Cecile
> May your own evil words dictate your fate
> By the heat of grief's fire, it is now too late
> May they arrive, safe and sound, at your door
> Only to find you had gone long before
> I bind this curse upon your head in the name of
> your boy

Condemned to watch from the ether, a life you
cannot enjoy."

With the last word, an ice-cold wind snaked through the room,
extinguishing the candles in a whoosh.

It was done. The man might not hang for his son's murder, but he
would pay the price all the same. And Cecile would not grow old with
her beloved son tending to her. Fiora's heartbreak was avenged.

With that, Isabella opened the shutters and let the sunshine stream
in, chasing out the darkness.

⁕

The trip from Rome to L'Aquila in the coach was long, but it was not
arduous. The roads were as good as could be expected, Violetta was
sweet and happy most of the time, and there were many inns along the
way for the family to stop, spend the night, and rest the horses. The
coach company had sent word to their regular inns along the route that
the family would be coming, and the approximate times of arrival, so
they always had cozy rooms with fireplaces waiting for them. Wonderful
dinners of pastas and soups and breads. Savory sauces and sumptuous
desserts.

For most of the trip, the women rode inside the coach and Constant
took a seat on top, with the driver. He was immersed in thinking about
the future, his new position in the land of his birth, and how he was
going to manage it all without his girls. And how Rosa would manage,
as well. He was also thinking about his mother, Cecile, and how—and
if—she would welcome Rosa.

The girls savored the countryside, the mountains and rivers and
gorges and hilly trees—all of it breathtakingly beautiful. So unlike the
city Fiora had known all her life. She had never before ventured outside
the city walls.

They were also cherishing this time together. This adventure into a new part of the country none of them had ever seen. They were building memories along this road that would have to last them a lifetime. All of them knew their time living together as a family would be short.

As the coach rocked along, Rosa became more and more aware of the fact that her time with her daughters and granddaughter was fleeting. And her time with her mother was gone, perhaps for good. When the coach arrived in L'Aquila, they would prepare to go their separate ways. And every hour, that day grew closer.

When that day came, the sun was shining, illuminating the mountains that surrounded them so they shimmered like glass. The coach pulled to a stop in L'Aquila, the town below the hill that the medieval town of Santo Stefano was perched upon.

The family would spend several days together there until two coaches would arrive at their inn to transport them in separate destinations. One would take Rosa and Constant on to a port in the south, where they would board the ocean liner that would take them to America. Constant had already sent word and booked passage.

The other coach would take Fiora, Florencia, and Violetta up the winding mountain road to Santo Stefano, where they would make their new home.

Nobody in the family was happy about this parting. But it felt like destiny had a hand in what was transpiring. That the river of time was flowing fast and furious, and they were caught in it, come what may.

While the rest of the family was at the inn enjoying baths and a delicious supper, Rosa stole out into the night, her cloak drawn close over her head. Isabella had told her of a dark part of town, the mysterious neighborhood where she could get some help. Isabella and Rosa were not women who would leave their girls' lives to chance.

After enjoying several days in town, it was time for the family to go their separate ways.

As their coaches waited, each packed and loaded but headed in different directions, the family stood on the road between them.

"Is it time?" Constant said to his wife, his eyes filling with tears.

"Not quite yet," Rosa said, noticing a figure walking down the road, toward them. "Good," she said. "Here they come."

Constant squinted at her. "What's this?"

Rosa smiled. "You'll see."

A young boy neared, holding the reins of a donkey. A large white dog followed behind.

Rosa took the reins from the boy and thanked him, handing him an envelope. "Give this to your mother, along with my thanks."

The donkey was handsome, with a bright red-and-blue bridle and a black saddle. Rosa stroked the fur on his nose and turned to the twins.

"This is Giuseppe," she said, handing the reins to Florencia. "His job is to shoulder your burdens, take your worries, carry you through your life, and stand beside you. He will never complain, never be obstinate, and never turn against you. He will only give you peace and see that others do the same."

She bent down and patted the head of the white dog with shaggy fur that, Rosa noticed, had been washed and combed for the occasion. He had a bright smile and was upward of 130 pounds.

"This is Freddo," Rosa said. "His breed is unique to this region. They are known for guarding the sheep that produce the exceptional wool that comes from here. But he will not be a sheepdog. His job is to protect the three of you. He will be your best companion, your loving pet, and a sweet presence in your home. But make no mistake about it—he will stand between you and the world."

Fiora didn't know quite what to say. She didn't know anything of animals like this. But when she looked at the two great beasts, holding Violetta in her arms, she felt a sense of calm that she had never felt before.

"These two souls are your protection and your companionship, because we cannot be there with you on the next part of your journey," Rosa said.

Constant wrapped an arm around his wife's waist and nodded. "Good thinking."

"Pet them, say hello," Florencia said to her sister.

"Giuseppe," Fiora said, stroking his fur. He nodded, seemingly in response. Violetta reached out with her tiny hand and touched his back. She giggled.

And then, the time came. The time they had all been dreading.

Rosa hugged her daughters and granddaughter tightly, tears flowing down her cheeks, whispering incantations, prayers, and spells of protection.

She reached into her satchel and pulled out the journal they had all used, logging entries, recipes, infusions, and spells.

"Don't forget this," she said, handing the book to Fiora. "My girls, this is your lifeline. Your connection to me, your grandmother, and all the women of our past."

Fiora took it from her mother and held it to her chest. "Florencia and I will keep it safe, Mama." She tucked it into her satchel.

"I will use it every day," Florencia said. "She's not good at keeping the log. That will be my job."

Constant took his turn next, holding Fiora, Florencia, and Violetta all close to him at once. "You and your mother are the blessings of my life," he said, his voice ripped to shreds. "I will hold you in my heart until we meet again."

The girls' driver tied Giuseppe's reins to the back of the coach as Constant helped his daughters and granddaughter climb inside. Freddo hopped in with them. Rosa and Constant held their daughters' hands through the window, imprinting their faces into their minds, not knowing if they would ever see them again.

"I will write to you as soon as we arrive in America," Rosa said. "And you must write back right away. We will want to know you are safe."

Constant nodded at the driver and the coach began to move, carrying their loves away. Rosa and Constant stood there, arm in arm, watching them go until it turned and disappeared from view.

The coach made its way up the winding mountain road as Fiora and Florencia watched, breathless, out the window. The hills were rocky and green, and they were ascending to quite a height. They noticed a flock of sheep grazing on the hillside, guarded by three dogs that looked just like Freddo.

Soon, a castle tower, surrounded by stone buildings, came into view.

"Our new home," Florencia said, her stomach fluttering. She looked at her sister. "Are you scared?"

"Yes," Fiora said. "But we can't show it."

"What do we do when we get there?"

"I think we need to find the mayor or whoever is in charge, show them the deed, and tell them what Mama said we should tell them."

"That we are the grandchildren of Leonardo Leone and have come to claim the house."

"That's right. Remember that, now. Leonardo Leone. And we are Rossis now. To honor Paolo."

Fiora fished the envelope her mother had given them out of her satchel. There was the deed, and the money, and another paper—a will, showing they were the owners of the house.

Finally, the winding road straightened out and the coach came to a stop. The driver hopped down and opened the door. "Is there an inn where I should be taking you? I don't have any direction other than simply getting you to the town."

Fiora and her sister exchanged a glance.

"No, thank you," Fiora said. "We will walk in from here."

The driver helped them out of the coach and secured their bags on Giuseppe's back.

"Good luck to you," he said. "The piazza is straight ahead, around the castle tower."

And so, Fiora, Florencia, Violetta, Giuseppe, and Freddo took their first steps into Santo Stefano, turning a new page in the journal of their lives.

They had no idea that, more than one hundred years hence, another woman in their family would walk those same steps, having braved the journey alone, to find them.

CHAPTER 28

Cassandra

Thomas Moretti made his pronouncement and then gestured to his wife—apparently she would be doing the talking.

"You may know that the Morettis were the bankers in Santo Stefano for many generations," she began. But then he broke in.

"Since the Medicis!" he said, referring to the infamous, powerful Italian family that had put Santo Stefano on the map, among their other endeavors. "We believe the Medicis started the banks that the Morettis ended up running."

Angela gave her husband the side-eye. "We're not sure about that. But we do know that Thomas's relatives were the bankers here in this town and elsewhere in the 1800s."

"We still are," Thomas added.

Angela reached into her satchel and drew out a huge book, leather bound.

"The Moretti family Bible," Thomas said, again breaking in. He turned a few pages. "Here is the time period we're talking about. Look, look!"

I fished my glasses out of my purse and put them on, peering at the yellowed pages. It was a family tree.

"See, here," Thomas said, pointing to a limb and a prominent leaf. "Silvio and Sofia, my great-grandparents. Silvio was the banker in Santo Stefano. They lived right here." He waved his hand toward the castle tower.

I saw the names of his sons, Geno and Giovanni—my heart skipped a beat at seeing his name. And next to his, Violetta's.

"There they are!" I said, tears forming in my eyes. "Giovanni and Violetta! They were my great-grandparents!"

"But look," Angela said, her voice gentle. "There is nobody after them. No children. And look at the death dates."

Giovanni Moretti, died 1911, Santo Stefano
Violetta Moretti, died 1911, Santo Stefano

That lined up with the death certificate I had found in my grandmother's room. But it wasn't right. It couldn't be. All at once, anger surged, seemingly bubbling up from the ground. I pushed my chair back from the table and walked away, trying to contain my tears. I turned back around, seeing that everyone was watching me. I took a deep breath.

"That's not right," I said, my voice louder than it should've been. "They are my great-grandparents. Giovanni and Violetta. If they had died here in 1911, I would not exist. My grandmother would not exist. My mother would not exist. Something is wrong."

"Or maybe your facts are wrong," Angela said. "Maybe you have the wrong Morettis."

"I don't think so," I said, trying to measure my voice. "It might have been, before I had seen your family Bible. But their names are right there." I pointed to the page. "How many married couples named Giovanni and Violetta Moretti could there be? This is the right family."

Thomas and Angela exchanged a glance. His brow was furrowed. "So you were told they were your great-grandparents. Giovanni and Violetta Moretti. From Santo Stefano?"

"Yes, that's what I was told, but I wasn't just *told* about them," I said. "I knew Violetta. She lived until she was almost one hundred years old. Into the 1980s! I remember her. Half of Wharton, the town where I grew up, remembers her. She was well known there. She ran a hotel and a shop much like the one she had here. Honey, soaps, oils."

"Lady stuff," Renzo added helpfully.

I picked up my purse and pulled out a photograph, handing it to them. "This is Violetta and Giovanni. Here. In Santo Stefano."

Thomas squinted at the photograph and turned to his wife. "Do you have the Silvio Moretti family photographs?"

Angela nodded and dove back into her satchel. She set an old black photo album on the table. As she turned the pages, I saw they were of heavy black paper, with black-and-white photographs sitting in white photo corners, four or five to a page.

"Here," she said, turning the album around to face me. It was a large sepia-tinted photo of a family. A man with dark eyes, slicked-back dark hair, and a small mustache, dressed in a suit. His wife, wearing a heavy dress, her hair piled atop her head. And two young men, both dark, with curly hair and devilish smiles. One was significantly older than the other.

Under the photo, written in a careful, practiced hand: *Silvio and Sofia Moretti, Geno and Giovanni, Santo Stefano, 1908.*

The younger of the boys was Giovanni. My Giovanni. I had no doubt. He was younger than he had been in the photograph with Violetta. But it was the same person.

Thomas held my photo next to the one in this age-worn album. He placed it on the table with an air of finality.

"It is the same person," he said to me. "You are correct about that."

Both tables in the piazza were abuzz, all talking at once.

"But this doesn't answer the big question," I said. "They had a daughter. My grandmother Gia. She told me all about them. They came to America. They did not die here."

Angela and Thomas exchanged a glance. "That's what I was always told," he said. "Geno Moretti was my grandfather, and he told me his brother died here in 1911. I can take you to his grave."

"If that were true," I said, "how and why would I have this photograph of Giovanni and Violetta? How could this photo possibly have gotten to America if they died here in Italy in 1911?"

Thomas held my gaze. I could see he was working the mystery out in his mind.

But then, something occurred to me.

"You asked me, just a moment ago, if I had always heard about Giovanni and Violetta from Santo Stefano," I said, trying to untangle this web in my mind. "I just thought of something you don't know. My grandma Gia always told us she was born in Portofino. But her birth certificate says different. I only learned about Santo Stefano from the photograph, and from the death certificate we have from Violetta, saying she died here."

Thomas held up a finger. "This plot is thickening."

I shook my head. "Yes, that's what I'm saying. This is the mystery I came here to solve. She could not possibly have died here in Santo Stefano because—as I said—I knew her."

He nodded, thinking.

"And you have proof, in your family Bible, that your Giovanni was married to my Violetta."

"The only thing in doubt is the date and the place of their deaths," Dante broke in. I hadn't realized he was standing right behind me.

"And why Portofino was involved at all," he continued. "You were not told about Santo Stefano, yes?"

"Yes," I said. "I hadn't ever heard about it until recently."

"As you said, Thomas, this plot is thickening," Dante said. "Because now my family gets involved. We know, without question, the Rossis were here. My great-grandparents bought the shop from them. The shop in this photo."

Tangled webs, indeed. I started to understand why I had dreamed I was encased in them.

Dante placed a hand on my back and looked around at the people sitting at the tables, in the piazza, in Santo Stefano on a beautiful, crisp morning. All of them had something to do with my family. And some of them may have information that would help us untangle this mystery once and for all.

"Mama," Dante said to his mother. "Did you bring the papers your grandparents signed, purchasing the shop and the bees?"

She nodded and opened a slim leather folio she had in front of her on the table. "I looked for these before our dinner last night," she said, sliding the folio toward her son. Dante examined them.

"It says here that my people, the Carusos, 'took ownership' of the shop in 1911," he said, looking up at me, furrowing his brow. "It doesn't say anything about buying it."

He was silent for a moment, reading further into the document.

"It says the 'former owner' was Fiora Rossi." He held my gaze for a long moment. "There is no bill of sale."

We all took a collective breath as everyone leaned in.

"I was always told we bought the shop," Dante said, breaking the silence, looking from his parents to his grandmother. "Did we buy the shop? Or did we 'take ownership' of it? There's a difference."

His parents both shook their heads. "The shop was passed down to me," Dante's father Alberto said, frowning and shrugging his shoulders. "From my parents. It has been in our family for generations—the bees."

Renzo was looking over Dante's shoulder at the paperwork.

"Is everybody seeing what I'm seeing?" he asked.

I took a closer look and then turned my gaze to him. "What?"

Luna, who was now standing behind Renzo, was nodding, smiling. "I know!" she said. "I was thinking the same thing."

Dante and I exchanged a confused glance. What were they seeing that I wasn't?

"It all happened in 1911," Luna said. "The supposed deaths of Violetta and Giovanni. The Carusos 'taking ownership' of the shop."

Thomas was paging through the family Bible and stopped when he got to what he was looking for. He nodded, frowning.

He turned his gaze to me. "That is also the year Silvio and his family left Santo Stefano."

"That's a lot to happen in a small village in one year." Luna crossed her arms and narrowed her eyes. "All of it, 1911. There has to be more to this. Much more. What happened here in that year?"

Everyone fell silent as Dante's grandmother pushed herself to her feet.

She brandished her black wooden cane in my direction.

"*Terremoto,*" she said. "Those Rossi witches. They were the cause of it."

Terremoto. My Italian had improved since I got here, but I didn't know that word.

Dante hit his forehead with the palm of his hand and took a couple of paces back and forth. Renzo and Luna were both looking at me, their mouths agape. The Morettis and the Carusos were all nodding. "Of course," Thomas said.

"What?" I asked them. "You all look like you know something I don't."

"I can't believe I didn't think of it as soon as we saw it was 1911," Luna said, running a hand through her curls. "Now it's starting to make sense."

"What?" I asked again.

"Earthquake," Dante said. "Luna's right. Part of this is making sense now."

I frowned at him. "A literal earthquake? Here?" I looked around at the group—everyone was nodding. Recognition on their faces. This was not news to them.

And then, the old woman began to speak.

CHAPTER 29

Cassandra

Her words were Italian, but somehow, some way, I understood what she was saying. It was as though those words swirled in the air and translated themselves before they reached my listening ears.

"My mother and grandmother spoke of it often," Elena Caruso said. "The great earthquake of 1911. My family was living down the hill in a town that isn't a town anymore. Destroyed, all of it, the entire town, by the shaking.

"Hundreds of people died, including my grandfather and several other relatives. He was on his way to work at the train station when the quake hit. That's how it was for people: they were on their way to work or to the market or school for the children and then—poof—gone. My mother told me the house was turned to rubble in an instant. She and her mother were saved because they had been outside hanging clothes on the line. If they had not been"—she snapped her fingers—"we would not be sitting here. I would not have been born."

Luna's mother Aria was nodding along. "Our family speaks of it, too," she said. "The region was devastated. Here in Santo Stefano, in the town center, there was not much damage. That's why most of these buildings are intact. But just outside of town, yes, buildings fell.

People were crushed. And down the hill, much worse. Whole towns were destroyed."

"Children lost their parents, and many were taken in by other families," Elena said. "My own family—my aunt and uncle—took in two boys whose parents were killed. It seemed that everyone helped out like that, in some way or another."

I shook my head, imagining the devastation. "I had no idea," I said.

"That is how and why my family came to Santo Stefano," she continued. "Our town had been turned to rubble. There was nothing for us to do. Some people began to rebuild their homes but—why? There was no market and no piazza and no churches, no nothing. My father was a young man and came here several months after the quake, seeking a new life, a new opportunity. A way to support his new wife, my mother. They married after the earthquake, you see. When they came to Santo Stefano, they brought my grandmother with them. And it was a good thing, because she was the key to it all."

"And that's how we got the shop?" Dante asked.

Elena nodded. "The story goes, they found the shop abandoned. Bottles broken, shelves on the floor, tables overturned, honey oozing everywhere, so he has told me. But the building, like most in Santo Stefano, was strong. My father went to the mayor to inquire about the shop."

"To buy it?" Dante said. "That's what we've always thought, right?"

"Yes," she said. "To buy it."

"But from whom? If it had been abandoned?"

Elena shrugged. "This, I don't know. I only know it became ours. My grandmother knew the ways of bees—that is why she was the key— and soon they had a business that has been in our family ever since. When I was born, she taught me of the bees, how to talk with them, calm them down, ask for honey, and give thanks to them for it."

I was entranced by Elena's story about her family's endurance after such devastation, but my mind was stuck on one part of that story. *Abandoned.*

Where did they go? And something else nagged at me.

"Signora," I said to her, my voice as gentle as I could make it, "last night, you said Violetta was a witch. If her family ran this shop, and the shop was abandoned by the time your family got to it, how could you possibly know anything of her?"

"Violetta Rossi," Elena said, pounding her cane on the stone street. "She was the witch of Santo Stefano. She and her mother."

"Signora," I said, with the last pretense of politeness I could muster, "you are talking about my family. My great-grandmother, who I knew. And loved."

Dante broke in. "Nonna," he said. "Why do you say such things?"

"Because it's true," she said, shrugging and frowning. "She and her mother. People said they were the cause of the earthquake."

"Caused an earthquake? That's . . ." I struggled to put my thoughts into words. The last thing I wanted to do was offend this lady, but what she was saying was ridiculous and, if I was honest about it, offensive to me.

But she was nodding as though it were gospel truth. "My mother spoke of it only once," she said. "I overheard her talking to my grandmother, in the shop. She said people had whispered about the Rossis and the earthquake, as though they had caused it somehow. The witches."

"No, no, no," Dante broke in. "After devastation like that, people try to make sense of it by coming up with these kinds of crazy theories."

"That may be," Elena said. "But one thing I know is true. They were witches. Of that, there is no doubt."

"You weren't even born when Violetta lived in Santo Stefano," I said. "And since she was gone by the time your family came here, how could you know?"

The old woman held up one hand and then bent down and picked up a satchel with the other. Out of it, she drew a leather journal. She set it on the table with a thud. "This is how I know."

All the nerves in my body seemed to begin vibrating, tingling.

I saw the cover was etched with curlicues and swirls and patterns, and the faces of women young and old. They looked familiar to me. I took the book into my hands. And then, for reasons I can't explain, held it to my heart.

"This belongs to my family," I said, not having any idea I was going to say it. "At least, I think it does."

"Then you are a witch, too," the old woman said, sitting back in her chair with a groan. "All of your women were."

CHAPTER 30

Violetta

As Giovanni suspected, his parents Silvio and Sofia were none too thrilled about his engagement to Violetta. The girl had been raised by her mother and aunt—no father in the picture. Always in the barn with those animals. Or in the meadow, tending to the bees. Her hair wild. Not exactly the picture of sophistication their older son Geno had chosen, a respectable girl from a good family. She had already produced two sons.

Still, Sofia had visited the Rossi sisters on regular occasions, and they had somehow always helped with whatever she needed. Honey for her family's meals, candles for their table, soaps for their bath. And much more. Silvio's wandering eye mysteriously turned back to her, and only her, after he drank tea sweetened with the sisters' honey. Her hair became more lustrous and thick—those hints of gray that had been alarming her had somehow vanished. She, like many of the women in the village, didn't know how the Rossi sisters did what they did. They couldn't explain it. The local priest certainly wouldn't approve of any of it. But they all knocked on the Rossis' door more often than any of them cared to admit.

And Violetta was a lovely girl. The most beautiful in the village, for certain. The children she and Gio would produce—stunning! Sofia could fashion a lady out of this girl, with a little work, and help her create little Morettis out of the children when they came along.

That's why she invited Violetta to the Moretti home one afternoon.

Sofia led the girl through the house to a sunny courtyard outside the kitchen. Flowering plants sat in pots on the stone tile floor, and a fountain bubbled in one corner.

The glass-topped table was set with a plate of sliced meats and cheeses, bite-size sweets, and a dainty bowl of olives, all on the most magnificent china Violetta had ever seen. It was a deep shade of white with yellow, blue, and red designs and curlicues. A bottle of white wine sat in a silver ice bucket, and as they settled into their chairs, a woman Violetta assumed was the housekeeper poured the wine into two red glass goblets before evaporating back into the kitchen.

"This is all so lovely," Violetta said, happy to have worn her best dress.

Sofia waved her hand as if to shoo the compliment away. "Just some light refreshments," she said. "It's pleasant to sit here in the afternoon, with the sun streaming in. I'm sure you'll come to enjoy it yourself, after the wedding. It's a wonderful spot to sew, or read, or simply contemplate."

Violetta imagined herself relaxing there but knew, she would never be the lady of that grand home.

"Have you thought about the wedding?" Sofia asked.

Violetta smiled at her, and all at once, Sofia felt a bit . . . unnerved. Those eyes. Were they violet? This girl had a magnetic quality to her, Sofia saw this right away. No wonder Gio had been so entranced.

"Yes," Violetta said. "But isn't that for you and my mother to plan?"

A good sign, Sofia thought. "It is," she said, taking a sip of her wine. "But I wanted to know if you had any preferences or wishes we should take into account."

Violetta gazed over the rim of her goblet at Giovanni's mother. She had known her for most of her life, of course, but this was the first time they were talking like two women, just the two of them.

"I had been hoping we would have something small," Violetta said.

Sofia set her goblet on the table. "Of course you were," she said. "But we do need to include some of my husband's clients from around the region, our families from Rome and Siena, and, of course, your people."

Violetta winced. The only "people" she had were in the honey shop, just steps away in the piazza.

"My grandparents live in America," she said. "In New Orleans. They immigrated when I was a baby. You likely know I am an only child, and my aunt has never been married. So it is just us. The three Rossi women. That's all the family I have."

Sofia reached across the table and put a hand on Violetta's. She gave the girl a knowing look. "We will be your family," she said.

Gio already was, and always had been, Violetta thought, but didn't say it out loud.

"And the wedding dress?" Sofia asked. "Have you chosen one?"

"I thought I'd wear my best dress," Violetta said. "My mother intends to make it for me."

Sophia pushed herself up from the table and extended her hand to her future daughter-in-law. "I have another idea."

Sophia led Violetta back through the house to a bedroom—an elegant affair with thick curtains, a fireplace, ornate furniture, and a stunning brocade spread on a four-poster bed. Laid out on the bed was a dress that took Violetta's breath away. She had never seen anything like it.

The dress was a deep, dark blue, the V of the neck adorned with delicate lace. The wide skirt was embroidered with the same color blue thread, in patterns of flowers and curlicues.

"Oh my," Violetta murmured, lost in the depth of the blue.

Sophia smiled at her. "This was my wedding dress, and my mother's before me," she said.

"It's beautiful," Violetta whispered, crossing the room to touch the fabric. It was thick and sturdy, but seemed to be flowing and wispy at the same time.

"Do you like it, my dear?"

"I have never seen anything like it," Violetta said.

Sofia stroked Violetta's hair. "It is for you, to wear when you marry my son."

This grand dress? Violetta took a breath. She touched the older woman's hand. "I would be honored."

"It is yours now, to pass down when your child marries."

As Violetta ran a hand over the dress's embroidery, Sofia smiled. She hadn't given the dress to Geno's wife, and was now glad of it. She had always wanted it to go to the girl who would marry Giovanni. And Violetta would look stunning in it. A breathtaking debut into polite society.

⁓✲⁓

At the honey shop, Fiora and Florencia were also busy with wedding preparations, but they were not so concerned with the usual trappings associated with the wedding of a daughter. They only wished for Violetta's happiness—which they were certain Giovanni would bring—and also for creating a day filled with the magic and love and mystery befitting a woman of their line.

Neither Fiora nor Florencia had had a wedding, and they were drawing on stories of the day Rosa had married Constant to create a suitable tableau for Violetta.

The night before the wedding, Violetta awoke to the sound of singing. It was coming from outside her window. She slipped out of bed and into her robe and opened the window to find Giovanni's brother, Geno, and a dozen or more young men Violetta knew from around town, standing there, each holding a bouquet of flowers. They were singing to her.

Fiora and Florencia were by her side in an instant. "It is your wedding serenade," Fiora whispered to her daughter. "For good luck and a happy marriage."

Violetta leaned out her window and gazed at these handsome young men, all dressed in fine suits, smiling and laughing and singing songs of love under the night sky, filled with stars. In a lifetime of magical moments, this was the most blessed, she thought.

"Beautiful, beautiful!" she called out.

When it was over, they all tossed the bouquets toward the house. Geno caught Violetta's eye and tossed his bouquet directly to her in the window.

"From the lucky groom!" he called out. He put his hand over his heart and bowed slightly. "Welcome to our family, Violetta."

Fiora had to step away from the window to wipe her tears. It was all too wonderful for words. The serenade. A dark cloud had crept its way into her vision in the days and weeks leading up to the wedding. She was not sure why it was there, but she and her sister did everything they could to keep it at bay.

The next day dawned, blue and bright and crisp.

As Fiora and Florencia helped Violetta into her dress and styled her hair, the people of Santo Stefano stepped out of their houses, lining the streets, waiting for the procession to pass by. As the procession passed, families would follow it to the church, which was just off the piazza.

Women whom the Rossi sisters had helped, and their grateful husbands. Town dignitaries, like the mayor, who was happy for the fine commerce the Rossi sisters brought to the village. Many bankers—colleagues of Silvio's—from nearby towns.

A flurry of talk and activity rippled through the crowd in the piazza as Giovanni's parents, Silvio and Sofia, arrived, he in a smart black suit, she in a shimmering green dress. They waved to the crowd as they entered the church.

But those whispers were not all happy ones, especially not from the families with young daughters. Giovanni Moretti was the most eligible bachelor in Santo Stefano, and the entire region for that matter. The handsome, funny, whip-smart son of a banker who had been educated by the finest tutors from Rome, Venice, and Florence.

People had always known Gio was spending time with Violetta—the two of them grew up together, always with the donkeys and the dog and the bees—but nobody thought he would actually marry the girl. Raised by her mother and aunt in a shop that sold honey . . . and much more than that. It wasn't respectable. Not respectable enough for the Morettis.

How could such a young man choose an unsuitable girl? Enchantment? People thought, in their own secret imaginations, that the Rossi women were witches. Nobody wanted to say the word aloud—witch persecutions were a dark part of Italy's past, and it had certainly never happened in Santo Stefano, and in modern times, those old beliefs just seemed silly. Or did they? The whispers around town said Violetta had put a spell on the Moretti boy. Their daughters never had a chance.

Giovanni arrived at the church, dressed in his best black suit, flanked by Geno. If the people of the town had thought Giovanni Moretti was handsome before that day, they were awestruck by his appearance on his wedding day. His dark hair, usually a riot of unruly curls, was combed back. His black suit had been tailored perfectly—in Rome, people whispered—to accommodate his broad shoulders and tall frame. His shoes gleamed. But it was his countenance that caught people's words and held them hostage. His dark eyes sparkled. His smile was stunning. His face radiated happiness.

Giovanni waved and exchanged greetings with the crowd, all calling their blessings and good luck, and then disappeared into the church, careful to be inside before Violetta arrived. It was extreme bad luck, he had been told, to see the bride before the wedding, and there would be no bad luck on that day.

And then she came. The cheers of the crowd preceded her, and they parted as she entered the piazza.

Violetta was sitting on the back of the donkey Bianca, whose bright-white coat had been washed and brushed and adorned with wreaths of pink and yellow and red flowers. She gleamed in the sun like an angel. Giuseppe walked solemnly behind Bianca. His own coat had been brushed until it shone, and he proudly wore the flowers from the meadow that had been woven into his mane. Freddo, similarly washed, walked at Violetta's side, his face a mask of protection, pride, and joy. He scanned the crowd, looking for danger, and found none.

Fiora and Florencia, in dark-red dresses they had sewn for the occasion, walked on either side of Bianca, each carrying a lit candle.

Violetta's long, wavy hair hung freely around her face, and her dress, the one gifted to her by Gio's mother, had been adorned by the two sisters with pearls, hundreds of them. The dark navy-blue of the fabric contrasted with the soft white of the pearls made it seem as though Violetta was the night sky incarnate.

The crowd went silent at the sight of her. Nobody had ever seen the likes of Violetta Rossi on her wedding day. Stories of it would be handed down in families, who would tell of the most bewitching beauty they had ever seen, wearing all the stars in the night sky as a dress, riding into the piazza on a snow-white donkey with flowers in its mane, to marry the most handsome man in town.

When they reached the heavy wooden doors of the medieval church, Violetta slid off Bianca's back and, petting her nose, thanked her for the ride, for her love, and for appearing in the meadow all those years ago. Bianca nodded, as though she understood. She did. Her work was nearly done, she knew. It would not be long now.

Violetta moved on to Giuseppe and rested her forehead on his, whispering words of love and thanks. He returned the emotion, for he loved the girl deeply, the one who he had walked beside all her life, and his.

Violetta then turned to Fiora and Florencia and took their hands as they, along with Freddo, walked into the church.

The people in the crowd found their voices and broke out into a cheer. They did not notice the shadowy, almost transparent image of a grandmother and great-grandmother, there to witness this important event, this culmination of true love.

Inside the church, she was greeted with the sight of hundreds of candles, flickering in stained-glass holders. It was like something out of a Renaissance dream.

Violetta knew the candles were made from the wax of their beloved bees, painstakingly crafted by her mother and aunt. The fragrance told her all she needed to know. Her mother and aunt had infused them with happiness and love and peace and contentment, everything they had given to her throughout her life.

Violetta saw her childhood rolling out before her eyes then, as if on a spool. Her aunt, reading to her from the leather-bound journal when she was a baby. Her mother, in the kitchen whispering incantations and blessings and recipes. Playing in the meadow with Giuseppe and Freddo as silent guards. Bianca appearing out of nowhere. The whispers, as she'd fall asleep at night, from older women, wisps in her room, who Violetta somehow knew were family but had never met. The lessons they'd impart. The tales they'd tell.

And through all of it, there was one boy. Giovanni. In the barn with the animals. In the meadow with the bees. Laughing as the two of them ran through the town.

Giovanni, who made her heart flutter every time he came near. Giovanni, who dressed in a fine suit to ask her to be his wife. Giovanni, whose low voice made her shiver. Giovanni, who she knew would stand between her and the world forever, the man who would father her children, the man who loved her so much his heart nearly burst each time he looked at her.

Now, he was a man who stood at the altar. He gasped aloud and placed his hand on his tender heart as he saw the love of his life in her wedding dress.

Violetta linked arms with her mother and aunt, who walked their girl down the aisle and into her future, with the only man she could ever, or would ever, love.

As she clasped hands with Giovanni, she saw tears in his eyes. She reached up with one hand and wiped a tear away, and the people in the pews took a collective sigh. She left her palm on his cheek for a moment, and the two lovers gazed at each other as vines of devotion worked their way out of the floor of the church, up through the very earth itself, and wove around them, binding them for the rest of their lives.

As they said their vows, Violetta wasn't even focusing on the words. She was only looking into the eyes of the man of her soul and knowing all this ceremony and fuss wasn't necessary. Their union had been destined long before.

CHAPTER 31

Cassandra

Silence filled the air when Elena gave me the book. Everyone was staring at it, and at me.

"What is that book, Nonna?" Dante asked. "I've never seen it before." His parents were frowning, too.

She nodded, her lips a thin line. "No, you haven't," she said. "I thought it best. My mother passed it down to me, and once I realized what it was, I probably should have burned it. But I couldn't do that."

She turned her eyes to me. "It was as if the book itself told me to keep it. As if it knew, somehow, you'd be coming for it one day."

"What is it?" Dante repeated.

"It is a spell book," she said. "My mother told me it was left behind when the shop was abandoned. Her mother found it and first thought it was simply a recipe book for making infusions of honey. She used it! But then, she realized it was more than that."

I gazed down at its leather cover, soft and well-worn with age. And the strange markings on it, which seemed to move, vibrate, and change as soon as I looked away. It had belonged to Violetta and her mother. I wondered why she had left it here when she made the trip to America.

Was this the reason I was compelled to come to Santo Stefano? To get it back? Anna's words from that morning were whispering in my ear. Were the Rossis really witches? Did that make me one?

The Morettis and I exchanged a glance. Angela shrugged and shook her head, as if to signify she didn't know anything about it, but Thomas looked away and fiddled with his collar.

"Signore?" I asked him. "It seems like you might have something to say?"

He let out a sigh. "I have heard stories."

Elena Caruso frowned, and then nodded at me. "See?"

I turned back to him. "What stories?"

"Passed down through my family," he said. "I didn't pay them any attention and didn't put the two together until Signora Caruso brought up a witch . . . who may have been your Violetta, the wife of my grandfather's brother. And now this book."

I waited for him to continue.

"There have been stories about my grandfather's brother being enchanted by a . . . well, a witch," he said. "Who caused his death. Nobody quite believes this story. You know how old family stories are. They can get embellished over time, no? But now . . . ?"

His words caused a chill wind to waft around me. The book itself felt cold in my hands.

"Caused his death?" I repeated, my head swimming, trying to make sense of what I thought I knew.

I had always been told—by Violetta herself—that Giovanni had died during the flu epidemic in 1918. In the United States. But his death, and hers, were recorded in the Moretti family Bible as having happened in Santo Stefano in 1911.

Now, Elena Caruso was calling Violetta a witch and had produced a book she believed was a spell book. She also claimed Violetta had somehow caused the 1911 earthquake. Ridiculous, yes—as Thomas Moretti said, those stories can be embellished as they are passed down, one generation to another. But they get passed down for a reason.

Thomas was now claiming that *his* family had a story about a witch causing Giovanni's death in 1911, the same year as the earthquake.

The Carusos "took ownership" of the honey shop, which had been abandoned in disrepair, that same year.

The elder Morettis left Santo Stefano that year as well, moving to a neighboring town, where Thomas and Angela—and presumably the rest of their family—still lived.

I let it all sink in. It was a lot. That spider, with its tangled webs, was making more and more sense.

I looked around, at these people who were strangers to me just days ago. All were here to help me unravel my family mystery, this web of confusion that had wrapped itself tightly around me. But it occurred to me, it was their mystery, too.

Elena's parents and grandparents had "taken ownership" of the shop and the bees, creating a life for themselves that stretched for generations, on the backs of the business my ancestors had built. The Morettis had married into my family, and my ancestors into theirs. And the earthquake had happened to all of our people.

Everyone in the piazza now were tied together by one thread. And that thread was wrapped around Violetta and Giovanni and woven through all of us.

"Does your family believe Giovanni died in the earthquake?" I asked Thomas, finally finding my words.

"We are not sure, but it makes sense," he said, paging through the photo book. "There are no photos of him after 1911. Many people fell victim to it, were crushed in their homes. Not so much here in Santo Stefano but down the hill in town. All we know is, he wasn't seen again after 1911. As I said, his grave is here."

He paused for a moment, looking off into the distance as if trying to catch sight of a memory.

"Something is worth noting," he said. "As I'm thinking about his grave, which is in our family's plot—Violetta was not buried next to him, even though in this Bible we have them listed as passing away in the same year."

I felt a gnarling in the pit of my stomach, deep inside my core. In his family story, the "witch" that had caused Giovanni's death was not buried beside her husband. Of course she wasn't. She lived a long life after that.

Family stories that are handed down over generations are powerful ties to the past. But Thomas Moretti's and mine were different strands of the same tale. And they did not converge. So whose was correct? What really happened in Santo Stefano in 1911?

The leather book seemed to be vibrating in my hands. Calling to me. All at once, I knew what to do. I wanted to hurry back to my room and read that book.

"Thank you, everyone, for taking the time to talk about my family," I said, looking around. "I truly appreciate it. This is the reason I came to Italy, and I can't thank you enough for helping put some pieces of the puzzle together."

Turning to the Morettis, I said, "I hope we can talk further. I'd love to show you photos of my grandmother—the daughter of Violetta and Giovanni—and of her children, my mother and my aunt. And my brother, who passed away years ago, and my son. You have a family in America you have never known."

Signore Moretti got to his feet. "We invite you to our home." He glanced at his wife. "You make the arrangements, *cara mia*. We will sit, and we will talk of our family. Maybe we can make all these stories of the past make sense. And if not, we will talk of the present. I want to hear all about my American family, and tell you all about ours."

The party broke up then. After a long Italian goodbye, which consisted of kissing everyone and talking for what seemed like forever, I tucked the leather journal under my arm and headed toward the stairs off the piazza that would lead down to my lair. I was anxious to open the book and see what it contained.

Dante caught up with me and put a hand on my shoulder. "I'm going to wrestle my parents and grandmother into the car—pray for me, for the love of God—and drive them home, but then I'd love to come and look over that journal with you."

"You're interested?"

"My grandma kept this book hidden for all of this time. These old ladies and their secrets! I tell you, no good comes from it. I've never seen the book, and I don't think my parents have, either. But it convinced my grandmother that your women were witches." He shrugged, with a mock frown. "Maybe you are, too." He raised his eyebrows and grinned. "So of course I'm interested."

I smiled at him. "Meet me down at my place when you get your elders squared away," I said.

"It's a date," he said, turning back to his parents. But then he turned around again to me. "Is it? We've had three non-dates. Maybe this is a non-date, too."

"I'm not sure," I said. "But I'll open some wine, just in case."

As Dante herded his family out of the piazza, Luna caught my eye and hurried over to me.

"Are you okay?" she asked. "This was a lot."

I grasped her hands and gave them a quick squeeze. "It was a lot."

"And what about Anna today? Did she shed any light on things?"

"What she said is helping this all fall into place," I said. "I need to process it all. But I am so grateful to you for organizing this, for bringing everyone here."

"In Italy, we're all family," Luna said. "We love nothing more than talking about family, about our elders and ancestors, especially if there is a mystery or scandal involved." She laughed, and it sounded like music. "These family stories, they are like lifeblood to us. And I'll say this to you. If your women were really branded witches, they are in good company."

I hugged her tight and kissed her on the cheek.

"I'll be at La Oliva until we close around six o'clock," she said. "Come on up if you feel like talking."

"I will," I said. "I'm planning to read what's in this book this afternoon."

She raised her eyebrows. "If you don't feel like company after that, come up for coffee in the morning," she said. "I'm interested to hear all about it. Maybe some spells I can use, no?"

She laughed again and made her way across the piazza, back to the deli, and I turned to trot down the steps toward home.

That thought, *home*, stopped me short. I had been in Santo Stefano only a few days, but it already felt like I was home.

As I trotted down the wide stone steps, I wondered what this book would tell me about my ancestors' life here.

As I jiggled the key into the lock, I half expected to see the white dog waiting there for me when I opened the door. He wasn't.

I placed the book on the table and hurried to the bathroom to wash my face, brush my teeth and hair, and make myself presentable for when Dante arrived. Was it a date? I wasn't sure. Did I want it to be a date?

I hadn't had a date for decades. Not since John and I were first getting to know each other. A pang of guilt sizzled through me—was this appropriate? Another man? But then I shook my head. Even if the divorce papers were not yet signed, John had long since left our marriage. The text exchange with a woman who was obviously sleeping with him had made that clear, if the original affair with Cynthia hadn't.

Couples get through affairs, with work on both sides. But multiple affairs? With women who were close enough to sleep in his bed—in *our* bed—and check his cell phone? John and I had been living apart for months, but it felt as though I had been pushed over a cliff by that call.

It's hard to accept the reality of a beloved spouse cheating. At first, you make excuses. It can't be true, you think to yourself. Not my husband. Not my soulmate. There's no way. You try to pretend it didn't happen. Then, when you realize it did, you wish so much to walk back in time and prevent it from happening in the first place, if you could somehow be there during the moment they meet. To remind him of your love for each other. The happiness you've shared.

But, when you know what you know, there is a filament of stark reality that keeps pulling you forward through all that lying to yourself, toward what you finally have to admit. And when you get there, you realize you have had enough.

It occurred to me that I had realized that long ago. I just had trouble untangling myself from the web of memories that surrounded me.

So whether this was or wasn't a date, I wanted to dress for the part. I figured I had about an hour until he came by, so I hopped in the shower for a quick refresh. Then I pulled on a deep-purple knit top with a V-neck and put a little effort into my face—concealer, a light gel bronzer, and a dash of lipstick—and gazed at myself in the mirror. I was good to go.

It felt like I had jumped out of an airplane with a parachute that I hoped with all my heart would open.

Despite the fact that we had just eaten, I assembled a plate of snacks, the usual cheeses and meats and bread, with a little fruit thrown in for color—I was in Italy, there had to be food. I opened a bottle of wine. And, as if on cue, I heard a knock on the door.

I opened it to find Dante standing there, with the white dog at his feet.

"There you are!" I said, bending down and giving the dog's great head a scratch. And then, looking up at Dante, "And hello to you, too. Please come in."

"Thank you," he said, giving me a kiss on the cheek and handing me a bottle of wine. "He was sitting outside your door when I got here. A sentry. I wasn't sure he was going to let me knock."

"Dogs have keen instincts about strange men," I said, raising my eyebrows.

"Apparently they also love witches," he said.

I ushered them both into my flat. The dog trotted into the room and hopped up on my bed, turned in a circle, and lay down, head on my pillow.

"As long as he's comfortable, I guess that's the main thing," Dante said with a grin.

"I do what I can to make strays feel at home," I said.

Dante turned in a circle himself and gazed around the place.

"I've been wondering what it looked like in here," he said. "Renzo couldn't stop talking about it during the renovation. Jacuzzi this and recessed lighting that. You'd think he was creating the Sistine Chapel."

"It is beautiful," I said. "But not quite as beautiful as that."

I poured some wine for both of us, and we settled down at the table.

"So, how are you doing after today?" Dante asked. "My grandmother can be quite the formidable figure. She's a force of nature, that woman. I hope she didn't offend you."

"No," I said. "Not at all. Mine was a force of nature, too. It's just a lot to try and make sense of."

"Witches, earthquakes, death records but not actual deaths . . ." he said.

I glanced down at the book on the table in front of us. "Maybe this will shine some light on it."

All at once, I wasn't so sure I wanted to share the book with Dante. Whatever it contained, it had been written by my ancestors, the women in my family.

But then, I thought, the book had been in his family, too. Passed down from mother to daughter as it had been in mine. But for a different reason. The women in my family had written it. His wanted to hide it.

And there we were, descendants of both sides, coming together to read it.

CHAPTER 32

Cassandra

It occurred to me then, with a laugh, that whether or not I wanted to share the book with Dante, I had to. I needed his help for a practical reason. It was written in Italian.

I took a deep breath and opened the soft leather cover. I saw that the first pages, yellowed with age, were written in beautiful script. It looked to me like a log of some kind. The first word on the top of the page was a name, written larger than anything else.

Isabella

I didn't recognize that name—her name—in my family history. It was becoming abundantly clear to me I really didn't know too much about the women who had come before me. Even my own great-grandmother Violetta, whom I had actually known, was proving to be a mystery.

But just gazing at the name, a hazy image swam into my mind, the face of a woman with long, dark hair. Or was I just imagining it?

Dante squinted at the pages, looking closely at the script. Clearly, he didn't see what I was seeing. That vision was only for me.

"So Isabella is the writer of this journal, then?" I said.

"Yes, I think so. That seems right."

The air vibrated and sizzled with electricity. *Something is happening,* I thought. But I didn't know quite what. It felt intimate, seeing these words written by my family so long ago.

"These first entries are from the late 1700s," Dante said. "So it goes back a ways. These are like, how do you call it? Log entries? People's names—mostly women's—the herbs and spices and concoctions they were given, and why."

He was silent for a moment, running his finger down the page. Dante read on . . .

The first dandelions that poke their way out of the snow in the spring, chopped finely and added to honey to give strength. Lavender to calm fussy babies. Rosemary for headaches.

The pages were adorned with drawings and doodles in the margins and around the corners, vines threading in and out of the words, animals keeping watch, a woman's face peering through the lines. Was that Isabella?

This didn't look like a spell book so much as the records of a natural healer, someone who had a deep knowledge of how to use plants and flowers and other things for common ailments. Someone who helped her friends and neighbors, not a witch who cast spells on them.

As it turned out, Dante was thinking the same thing. "Scary witches," he said, rolling his eyes. "It looks like they were more like doctors. I don't know what my grandmother was thinking."

"Agreed," I said. Until we turned a few more pages.

Incantesimo d'amore

Even with my limited Italian, I knew what that said. "A love spell?"

He raised his eyebrows and nodded. "Should I read it out loud?"

"What can it hurt?"

"If we wake up tomorrow and find we got married, we'll know where it came from," he said with a laugh. Then he began to read.

10 leaves lemon balm

10 red rose petals

1 small sprig lavender

Infuse in a large glass of red wine

Set glass on the hearth of your home for 3 hours

Transfer the infusion into a clean glass, straining out the leaves

Carry the glass into the night of a full moon, only if there is starlight. And, with your beloved's countenance held firm in your mind, drink the elixir and say:

In the darkness of the forest

When the night creatures roam

As I drink from this chalice, tasting my longing made real

I conjure my true love's spirit

And ask the night and the wind and the earth
and the stars to whisper to him, my heart's
desire

To love me, with all of his

Dante and I looked at each other. "Feel anything?" he said.

"I don't think so. But then again, we don't have the infused wine, so . . ."

He gazed down at the page. "Seriously. That's magic, isn't it? An incantation. Or a spell."

"It seems to be," I said, nodding.

"Okay, so they were witches after all," he said, laughing.

I shrugged and couldn't contain a chuckle. "I guess they were. Good witches, though. I hope."

I turned a few more pages. More spells and incantations. More log entries of people who were given infused honey and other concoctions. More doodles and drawings. Recipes.

After many pages, almost a quarter of the book, a new name was written at the top of a page.

Rosa

Different handwriting, but similar. Different doodles and drawings. But similar. A different woman's face drawn in the margins. Rosa. Was she Isabella's daughter?

The first entry wasn't a log or an incantation but a few paragraphs that answered that question.

My mother says this book is mine, now. I am
old enough to learn the ways. I will be the one
logging in the remedies, who comes for them,

what they come for. I am also permitted to write my thoughts and ideas. I like that!

My father is not happy about this—he does not understand our ways. But he says girls must learn from their mothers in the kitchen to cook and clean and do all of the things women do. Isn't that what this is? I think so. She has already taught me to read and write. He doesn't have to know anything else.

"She sounds a little *tutto pepe*," Dante said, grinning down at the page. "Full of pepper. Spunky, I think you'd say."

As we paged through the next few entries, he stopped on one. "Oh, look here," he said. "*Api*. She's talking about the bees."

Mama is teaching me the ways of the bees. We tend many hives. At first, I was afraid I'd be stung, but Mama is so calm. So peaceful. The bees seem to enjoy it when she comes. I am learning to thank them for their gifts to us. Mama says I have a special way with them. I hope that's true.

"It goes back that far, tending to the bees," I mused. "Honey was a big part of their . . . magic, I guess you'd say. Honey infused with herbs and spices and other things."

Dante turned his eyes to me, and I took a quick breath. It would be so easy to get lost in them. I shook those thoughts out of my head. We read on.

Today, Mama, Papa and I visited St. Peter's Square at the Vatican. The Pope gave a special *mass, and hundreds of people were there. Maybe thousands. Too many. I couldn't see anything! I prefer it when there isn't an event, when I alone can walk in the square and contemplate all of the history there.*

I had been to the Vatican, too, just days ago, walking the same streets Isabella and Rosa walked, many lifetimes ago.

Then, something occurred to me.

"Oh . . ." I said to Dante, squinting down at the page. "They must have lived in Rome if they were going to the Vatican for an afternoon. Right?"

"It looks like they did," he said. "They'd have to have lived in the area—the way this was written, they popped over there for an event. They didn't have to travel from outside the city to get there."

I took that in. "Unbelievable. I had no idea my family ever lived in Rome."

"You are learning much about your people from this book," he said. "I'm so glad my grandmother saved it all these years."

He was right. I had begun to think that the reason I had traveled to Santo Stefano had been to find this book.

As we turned more and more pages with more journal and log entries, drawings, recipes, and spells, it felt like years were passing. Rosa's handwriting got more sophisticated, more womanly. There were passages about getting her first period, seeing boys at the market. She was growing up as I turned the pages.

I noticed a drawing of a black man, stretched out on a riverbank. Rosa's words were written around him.

I was walking by the Tiber and met a man! The most handsome man I have ever seen. His name is Constant Broussard. He is an American, a Creole from Louisiana. He is here in

Rome with an American professor. Mama says she knew I'd meet him—of course she did—and that he will be my husband one day. I felt it, too, when I spoke to him and looked in his eyes. We are meeting by the river again tomorrow. I am going to take a bath and wash my hair. What will I wear? I am nervous but I can't wait for tomorrow to come. Is this what it feels like to be in love?

I could almost see it, Rosa as a young woman, fluttering around the house getting ready to meet an exciting new man. A few pages later, sure enough, a drawing of Rosa and Constant, intertwined.

Today, I will be a bride. I will marry the man of my heart, my true love, my destiny. The man who had to travel across the ocean to find me. He said he'd go around the world if he had to.

I looked up at Dante. "She married a Creole man from America? I can't wait to tell my cousin Maria. This is unreal. We had absolutely no idea we had any American ancestry on our mothers' side, let alone Creole. That's really interesting."

"Creole," Dante said, furrowing his brow. "Is that the same as Cajun? Like, in New Orleans?"

"I'm not sure," I said. I fished my phone out of my purse and looked it up.

"Okay," I said. "It says here Creole people have a mixed heritage that includes French, Spanish, African, Haitian, and others. Cajuns descend mainly from French Canadians. But both live in and around New Orleans."

I stared at my phone for a long moment, reading about Creole and Cajun cultures. I knew about the famous cuisine, of course. I had never even been to New Orleans, and now I was finding that a branch of my family tree grew right there.

"Here's something else interesting," Dante said, rubbing his chin. "I don't know much about New Orleans, but I do know that thousands of Italians made their way into the United States through there."

I frowned at him. "Really? I've never heard that."

"Yes," he said. "There was a great migration of Italians to the United States—you know this of course; you're the product of it. Many immigrants were from Southern Italy but some from this region as well. Most went through Ellis Island, but many went through New Orleans."

And then it dawned on me, as though a light went on above my head. I just stared at Dante, open-mouthed.

"What?" he asked. "You look like you're going to say something."

I shook my head. "My cousin and I have not been able to find any information about Giovanni Moretti. No birth or death records, and no immigration records for him or Violetta."

"Okay," Dante said, "and . . . ?"

"We were looking at records from Ellis Island. What if they came through New Orleans instead?"

Dante raised his eyebrows and wagged a finger at me. "You may be onto something. If they had people there—Constant's people—it makes perfect sense for them to have gone through there. Of course they would."

I sat back, hard, in my chair. "Nobody in my family has any idea about this New Orleans connection. I thought we were at a dead end, researching online, but I was looking in the wrong place."

"People think they can find anything online, but that's not always true."

"Exactly what I said to my cousin before I came here," I said. "Sometimes you have to get away from the computer and into places in the real world you never thought to look."

"Like in an elderly and rather difficult Italian lady's dresser drawer, or wherever she kept this book all of these years," he said, sniffing. "Without telling anyone it existed until now."

We shared a laugh then. I found myself always laughing around this man.

Then we returned our attention to the book. After being married, Rosa didn't write so many journal-type entries. I guessed she had other things to occupy her time. A new husband. Setting up a home. She still kept the log of infusions and elixirs she and her mother made for women of the neighborhood, adding a few notes here and there, along with the drawings and doodles. Bees buzzed through those entries, leaving trails behind them.

A few pages later, Rosa gave me more information that I couldn't find online.

> The twins were born weeks ago—thank goodness for Mama. She attended me and made sure the birth went fine. I am back on my feet, but feeling tired, which Mama says is normal for a new mother of one baby, let alone two. Constant says Fiora and Florencia inherited "the shine" from his mother Cecile and the second sight from me, so we need to watch out for them. I'm just happy they're healthy and thriving.

"Twins!" I cried out. "Rosa had twins! My mom is a twin. And my cousin Maria had twins!"

"They run in your family," Dante said.

The name "Fiora" jumped out at me then.

"That was my grandmother's middle name," I said. "Fiora. I'll bet she was Violetta's mother."

"Your . . ."—Dante squinted into the distance—"great-great-grandmother Fiora. Daughter of a witch and a Creole. A powerful combination."

A sizzle ran through me. *Yes, it was,* I thought. *Yes, it was.*

We spent the rest of the afternoon going through the book, reading stories of Fiora and Florencia as babies—given lavender when they were fussy—then toddlers running on the banks of the Tiber. As always, more recipes, spells, and incantations.

Then, we turned a page to see two new names written on top of it.

Fiora and Florencia

And the journal, and all the knowledge in it, was passed down once again.

CHAPTER 33

Violetta

The women of the village had walked through the streets at sunset, a mother carrying a set of her child's clothes. It was a ritual, handed down by generations of women before them. It was the only way, their grandmothers had said, to break a witch's curse. People had long since abandoned these old ways, these outdated beliefs. They had no place in this modern age. Or did they?

Little Alessandro was delirious with fever, mumbling strange and otherworldly words . . . if they were words at all. Obviously the work of a witch.

As the mother walked, the women of the village joined her, emerging from their houses one by one, and together they made their way through the tunneled streets until they reached the piazza. In front of the fountain, all the women said a silent prayer, an incantation, to themselves—*please let my own child escape this curse*—as the mother set a torch to the clothes and lit them on fire. The women stood in a circle around the burning bundle, watching the flames engulf it.

Fiora had been with them. She had to go, she said, for appearances. And she had hurried home to the shop to warn her daughter that the women might turn on them.

As she entered the shop, she saw Violetta had lit the candles, and they were set on the shelves, and on the tables, and along the window-sills, shimmering with a soft glow.

"I think it's time you left this place," Fiora said to her daughter. "Long since time."

Violetta thought the whole business was nonsense. Leaving Santo Stefano was out of the question.

These women and their superstitions, Violetta sniffed to herself, even her own mother and aunt. It was silly to think a "witch" had caused the boy to fall ill. As if she or her mother would ever do such a thing. The women who marched through the streets that night were their neighbors and their customers!

But her mother had been insistent. If the boy died . . .

"These people aren't as modern as you think," Fiora had said. "I want you safe, away from here. We've overstayed our welcome."

She had told Violetta that some of the women in town were already talking. She was the prettiest girl in Santo Stefano—though Violetta didn't think that for a moment—and had married the handsomest, most eligible man. Now *that* was true.

Her mother was clearly overreacting, telling her to flee. Although . . . from the little Fiora had told her about the circumstances surrounding her family fleeing Rome, Violetta felt Fiora, of anyone, had the right to overreact.

But then came the knock on the door.

Violetta and Fiora grew silent. The air seemed to change and coalesce around them, vibrating with a buzz Violetta could scarcely hear but knew was there.

The moment seemed to stop in time, stretching backward through the generations of their family. That knock at a witch's door was etched into their bones. Their very cells. Neither woman breathed. Fiora reached for her daughter's hand.

"Go to the barn," she whispered. "And then, use everything in your power to get away. Hurry."

The knock came again. Louder this time.

But Violetta didn't do as her mother asked. She pushed herself to her feet at the same time as Freddo crept in from the back rooms. He growled low, in his throat, at the door. Violetta had never seen him do that before. He'd never had to. The dog's reaction, more than anything else, caused a chill to rise up her spine and settle between her shoulder blades, wrapping its cold fingers around her body.

"Go!" Fiora screamed in a whisper. "I told you to go out the back way and rush down to the barn. Giuseppe and Bianca and Freddo will protect you there."

Violetta shook her head. "Freddo is here."

She crossed the room and, with shaking hands, opened the door. Several women stood on the street—all women they knew. The mayor's wife, Angelina, whose son Alessandro was ill, was among them. She was carrying the remains of a broom that had been burned on the fire along with some of the boy's clothes.

She threw it into the house. The charred stick hit the stone floor with a thud.

Freddo sniffed the stick and positioned himself between the women at the door and the women in the house. He was on alert, growling.

Fiora's face went white, remembering what had happened the last time someone angry had come to her door. She had lost the love of her life on that night. She opened her mouth to speak but didn't get a chance. It was the younger Rossi woman, now a Moretti, who took the mantle, just as she had taken possession of the journal.

"What is this?" Violetta growled, glaring at the women, looking from one to the other with enraged eyes.

"The curse is broken," Angelina said, jutting out her chin. "Now my son will recover."

Fiora crossed the room to stand with her daughter, and Florencia materialized from the back room as well, carrying the scent of the night air on her. The three women stood together.

Violetta kicked the broom back toward the group on their door-step. It clattered over the threshold and stopped at the feet of the may-or's wife.

"How dare you come here with this nonsense," Violetta said, her voice harsh and low.

"Witch!"

Freddo began to bark, a low, threatening sound. The group of women outside the door took a collective step back.

But Violetta threw back her head and laughed. "Don't give me that. Just because we live in a town that was built in the Middle Ages doesn't mean we believe the ridiculous superstitions of the past," she spat. "You are our neighbors. And our customers. You have told us all of your ailments and secrets and problems and heartbreaks."

She looked, again, from one to another of the women and held each of their gazes for a moment.

"When your husbands snored or had wandering eyes or fell out of love, haven't we always been ready to help? When you had female trouble or were unable to conceive, where did you go?"

The women stood, eyes downcast. Some of them began to shuffle their feet back and forth.

"When your children had rashes on their legs or coughs or were fussy at night, who did you come to?"

"But Alessandro . . ." the mayor's wife said.

"Yes," Violetta said. "Let's talk about Alessandro. My mother just told me he has a fever."

"He was here in your shop the day before," someone in the crowd said. "You spoke to him. Did you give him the evil eye? Did you cast a spell?"

Violetta waved her hand, as if to dismiss those words as nonsense. "A fever burns," Violetta said. "It's burning out a sickness your son is carrying. We have all had fevers, every one of us. Don't even try to tell me you don't know what they are."

"But this is not like one I've seen before," Angelina said, tears welling up in her eyes.

Violetta crossed the room to their herbs, seeds, and mortar and pestle.

"You should have come to us instead of parading through the streets like clowns," she said, mixing dried ginger, coriander seeds, and black pepper and crushing it with the pestle. She poured the mixture into a small jar of honey and thrust it out toward Angelina.

"Pour a spoonful of this into a mug, squeeze a bit of lemon on it, and then add boiling water. Stir. Let it steep for a bit while the water cools slightly. Tell Alessandro to drink it down—not too fast. He should savor it. This will help."

Angelina took the jar as a tear fell down her cheek.

"Put a cool cloth on his forehead, and if he's feeling up to it, give him a lukewarm bath. Not a cold bath. But lukewarm."

Violetta stared at the women and shrugged. "Every single one of you knows what to do for a fever," she said, putting her hands on her hips. "Yet you come here like a medieval mob looking for a witch. You should all be ashamed of yourselves."

Then she stomped across the room and slammed the door in their faces. The sound reverberated through the shop like an echo.

Fiora and Florencia were holding on to each other, staring at this girl, now a woman, who had just stood up to exactly the kind of mob that had threatened women like them for hundreds of years.

Violetta took a deep breath and sank onto a chair, her hands shaking. Fiora dropped to her knees in front of her daughter.

"I have never seen anything like that in my life," she said. "What courage you have!"

Florencia petted Freddo's great back. "What nerve they had," she said, sniffing. "Violetta was right. How dare they come here with that nonsense. Not after we have spent half a lifetime helping them. You are so strong, Violetta."

"I was raised by two strong women," she said, smiling at her mother and aunt. But that smile wavered, just a bit. In truth, Violetta's stomach was in knots.

Just then, Giovanni burst through the door, his hair wild, as it always had been when he was a boy.

"What has happened?" he said. "I was finishing up at the bank and I saw the women walking through the streets. I had no idea what they were doing, so I didn't pay it any mind."

Violetta stood up and crossed the room and melted into his arms.

"You're shaking," he said, stroking her hair.

"They were breaking the curse we obviously put on Alessandro," Florencia said, her voice level and cold.

"My mother told me they were calling you a witch," Gio said. "I rushed over here as soon as I heard and passed by some of them. They all gave me the evil eye at once, I think."

Violetta smiled at this. "We can undo it," she said. "Don't you worry."

"Gio, you need to know that those women came here, to our door," Fiora said, putting her hands on her hips.

He looked from one woman to another, his mouth open. "What? They came here?"

"They did," Fiora said. "Your wife ran them off."

Stunned silence, for a moment. Then the twinkle returned to Gio's eyes and he couldn't help but grin. "What did you do?"

Violetta grinned back at him. "I scolded them. I told them how ridiculous they were and called them a pack of clowns."

Gio let out a laugh, and then Violetta, Fiora, and Florencia were laughing, too, at the thought of Violetta standing up to an angry mob.

"Remind me to never get on your bad side," Gio said.

The young couple left the shop then and, with Freddo at their heels, walked through town to their flat. Much to her surprise, Violetta had fallen in love with their new home, with its ample kitchen, huge fireplace, and spacious pantry. It wasn't a shop with rooms in the back but a proper home with a sitting room and two bedrooms—one for a baby. Giovanni's mother had given them her mother's dishes and glassware, fancier things than Violetta had ever had. Silver candleholders. Fine linens and thick duvets. All of it befitting a banker. But that's not what Violetta loved about the home. It was the fact that it was the place where she and her beloved were beginning the rest of their lives. It could have been a barn, for all Violetta cared.

When they reached it that night, she and Gio closed the door behind them. He took her in his arms, and all thoughts of the ugly incident flew from her mind. She was with the man of her life.

But back at the shop, Fiora and Florencia sat together in front of the fire.

"Violetta was so brave," Fiora said.

"For our ancestors, that sort of encounter didn't go as well as it did here tonight," Florencia said.

"Especially if town elders had been involved," Fiora added. "Women have been branded witches just for speaking their minds as Violetta did."

"I hope that's the end of it," Florencia said.

But both women knew this wouldn't be the end of it. They felt it, deep in their bones.

CHAPTER 34

Cassandra

Dante and I continued to page through the book, reading all about Fiora and Florencia and their lives in the yellow house with the red terra-cotta roof by the Tiber River in Rome.

It seemed as though Florencia did most of the writing of journal entries and the logging of remedies and women's names, who came to the house for what purpose. I noticed spells and incantations were written in a different hand—Rosa's? Isabella's? I wasn't sure.

Florencia wrote about picking flowers and plants in the garden and gathering them for their mother, and of learning the ways of drying them to keep for infusions.

One journal entry, illustrated with a boy's face peeking out of the text, caught my eye.

"What does that one say?" I asked Dante.

He gave a quick chuckle. "A boy comes on the scene."

I raised my eyebrows. "Love comes to the yellow house?" He read aloud.

I notice Fiora always makes it her business to be idling around the back door when Signora Rossi comes to call. This is why: Paolo usually accompanies his mother. Fiora is flirting and smiling and making him laugh.

I noticed the name. Rossi.

"Hey," I said. "Violetta was a Rossi. Their shop—your shop now—here in Santo Stefano was called something like Rossi's Honey."

Dante frowned. "I wonder if Fiora married this boy and became a Rossi."

"There's one way to find out," I said, turning the page.

"Here we go," Dante said.

Mama and Papa are not happy about this Paolo Rossi situation. It has become obvious to all of us—they are spending all of their time together. Stealing off to the riverbank. Walking in the olive groves. Fiora is in love with him. She told me, just last night.

"I wonder why they weren't happy about it," I said, staring at Florencia's neat script as though it could tell me more.

Dante scanned a few more pages, until he stopped abruptly and gasped aloud.

"*Mamma mia,*" he said under his breath. "Oh no." He looked up at me. "This is not good."

"What?"

Dante shook his head and began to read.

Out of all the entries in this book, this is the saddest. Fiora has taken to her bed and has lost all her will to live. Paolo asked Papa for his blessing to marry Fiora. He said yes. But then, Signore Rossi came to the house, angry, saying that Paolo was already betrothed—who

> knew?—and he and Papa argued and . . . oh,
> I hate to even write the words. God bless him,
> Paolo is dead. Signore Rossi shot him, in our
> house. But the worst thing is, Fiora is expect-
> ing his baby. Nobody knows this but me.

I stared at Dante and took a deep breath. "Whoa," I said, tears stinging at my eyes. This was a story on a page, yes, but it was about my people. My ancestors. And being here in Italy where it happened . . . I wasn't sure why, but it hit me, hard.

Dante reached over and took my hand. "I know. This is a sad, sad situation."

I ran through what I knew in my head. "That baby," I said. "She must be Violetta."

We turned a few pages and sure enough, there was the entry about Violetta's birth. My great-grandmother. And then, another surprise.

> We are leaving Rome, leaving our house, and
> leaving everything we know. Papa has secured
> a position at Tulane University in America,
> and he and Mama are going there. I would
> have liked to have joined them. But Fiora is
> insistent that Violetta be raised in Italy, as
> Paolo would have wanted. She does not want
> to leave this place, where he took his last breath,
> but we must. We are going to a town called
> Santo Stefano, where we have a home wait-
> ing for us. It belonged to Paolo's mother. She
> came here with the deed and money for us to
> live on, urging us to flee Rome. Our family
> is breaking up.

Dante slapped his palm on the table. "So that is how they came to Santo Stefano!"

I nodded. "Now all the pieces are starting to fit. We still don't know a lot of things, but—"

"But we're not done reading yet," Dante said, raising his eyebrows. He turned back to the journal, silent for a moment, and then read aloud:

> This is what Mama warned us about. The curse. It dooms the women in our family to lose our beloveds. She said it is the reason Paolo died. Something about Papa's mother cursing the love we find here in Italy.

I felt a gnarling in my stomach. A love curse on the women of our family? Dooming the men we loved here in Italy?

I snuck a look at Dante. Did that mean him, if I fell for him? But then I shook it off. It was a long-ago superstition, wasn't it? But then again, with everything that had happened to me since I had arrived, what Luna and Anna had said . . . I wasn't so sure.

"Wow, here's something wild," Dante said, shaking me out of my wonderings. He pointed at a word in the journal, directing my eyes there.

Maledizione

I squinted at the word. I didn't know what it meant, but I knew that "mal" never connoted anything good. "What does it say?"

"Cassie, this is a curse. Isabella wrote it, I think. Or Rosa. It's not Florencia's hand."

A curse, again? I took a breath in and held it as he read aloud.

To the women of my family: This is a powerful, dark curse to be used in only the most dire of circumstances, against only the most evil of people. This is the only time I will use it and I hope it is the last time. Do not use this lightly.

Sprinkle dried holly, nightshade, buttercup, gypsyflower, adder's tongue, slowworm into a cauldron of boiling water. Add an article belonging to the unfortunate recipient, in this case Edoardo Rossi.

By the new moon's light

I curse you, Edoardo

With every step, your path shall twist into darkness

Shadows will rise from dark corners and surround you

Despair shall dwell in your heart

A river of sorrow shall engulf your every moment

I bind this curse upon your head

Until the end of your woeful days

Dante stopped reading and turned to me, confusion and shock written on his face. My heart was beating hard in my chest. "That's harsh," I whispered.

Dante nodded, his eyes wide. "I wonder what happened to Edoardo Rossi after that."

"A ton of bad luck, it looks like."

I could feel it, somehow, cold air slithering off the page. A pungent aroma seemed to be traveling on it, wrapping around me. I tried to shake it off.

"That's nothing to mess around with," I said, pushing my chair back from the table and getting to my feet. "Do you feel like taking a break?"

"Absolutely," Dante said. "What do you think about a walk?"

It was late in the afternoon and the sun was beginning to set, bathing everything in a gorgeous yellow glow. The golden hour. We walked out of the village, down toward the lake and the meadow, the dog running ahead, wagging his tail. I could see the rocky green hills beyond, and a flock of sheep grazing in the distance. It really was beautiful here.

"I thought we could visit the bees," Dante said.

As we neared the hives, he reached out and took my hand. Was this an Italian thing? Or a romantic thing? I didn't know. But I didn't pull away.

"The most important thing to know about approaching a beehive is to be calm," he said. "The bees, they don't like agitation. Anger. Or even excitement, really. They enjoy the calmness."

I smiled. "My grandmother taught me about bees, remember?"

Dante was a calming presence. He exuded it. Confidence, calmness. Serenity.

"I do a good business because of these bees," he said. "Thanks to your ancestors."

"And yours," I said. "They took over the shop after mine left."

He turned to me then. "Let's go find out why they left. Maybe the book will clear everything up."

As we were walking through the meadow, Dante stopped, took my hand, and pulled me close. My entire body felt like it was shimmering with electricity inside when he put his lips on mine. I wrapped my arms around his shoulders and melted into him.

He pulled slightly away and smiled at me. "That has been coming for a long time."

A lifetime, I thought. "Yes," I said. "It has."

CHAPTER 35

Violetta

Angelina, the mayor's wife, did as Violetta instructed. Alessandro drank the honey concoction. She put him in a lukewarm bath, with a cold cloth on his forehead. And, sure enough, his fever broke that very night. *Just like magic,* Angelina thought.

Even so, she didn't much like being talked to like that by Violetta. A fatherless girl. Yes, she was married to a Moretti. But who in the village didn't believe she had bewitched the boy?

"Our son is better?" her husband asked.

"Thank goodness," she said. "I don't know if it was the ritual or the cure the Rossis gave me. But he's better."

He frowned at her. "What ritual?"

"You know. Walking through town. Burning clothes in the piazza. To break a curse."

Her husband laughed. "Don't tell me you and your friends marched around—"

Angelina held up a finger to her husband to stop his words. He wasn't going to mock her, too. But he went on.

"It's 1911, Angelina," he said. "Please, don't do that again. It doesn't look good."

"You don't know, Aldo," she shot back. "They have been doling out cures for everything for years. Who's to say they're not witches? What do witches do but that?"

Her husband just shook his head. "I'm going to check in on the boy and then go to bed," he said, walking out of the room. "Maybe you can bewitch yourself into a better mood before joining me."

Angelina pulled out a chair from the table and sat down, hard. Her blood was boiling. First Violetta had humiliated her. And now this. She rolled it over in her mind. Those Rossi sisters. Both without a husband, all these years. Women living on their own. The town gossip had it they were as rich as the Morettis—but how? By selling honey? That could not be.

She would talk to her friends in the morning. The ones who had walked with her that night. She wanted to know what they thought. In her heart, she already knew. But the question was, What would they do about it?

~❧~

The next morning, after making breakfast for Giovanni and seeing him off to work, it was time for Violetta to go down to the barn and tend to Giuseppe and Bianca.

It looked to be a beautiful day, and she thought they would enjoy some time in the meadow. Giuseppe was slowing down lately, but he always loved basking in the sun near the hives. She'd stop into the shop for a coffee before spending the rest of the day reading in the meadow with the two great beasts.

Violetta was glad for the nice weather. Gio would be traveling to L'Aquila to do some banking business, and she always fretted when he would head down that hill on a stormy day.

So she was smiling as she walked down the alleyway to the shop, where she poked her head in to say hello to her mother and auntie.

"How are you after all of that nasty business last night?" she asked, accepting a cup of coffee from Fiora.

Fiora wrinkled her nose. "I hope it blows over," she said. "I don't like it, Violetta. I have a bad feeling."

"In your bones," Violetta joked with her. "I know, I know. Where's Auntie?"

"She has gone down to the barn to get—"

But Fiora's sentence was cut off in midair when Florencia came through the door, her face ashen.

Fiora shot up to her feet. "What is it?"

Florencia was silent for a moment, her eyes filling with tears. She put her hands over her face and let out a great sob.

Fiora rushed to her sister's side. "What's happened?" she said, her voice gentler than Violetta had heard it in years. "Florie. Tell us."

"Giuseppe." His name was torn to shreds as she struggled to say it.

Violetta went cold. "No," she whispered.

Florencia looked up at her niece, and her eyes said it all. Violetta flew out the door and pounded down the steps toward the barn. She burst through the door and the morning sun shone down, illuminating a thousand tiny specs floating in the air. It felt like she had entered an ancient church. She was on holy ground. Violetta smelled the strong aroma of roses.

And there he was. The patient, loving soul. Her first and best friend. The one who had stood by her side all the days of her life. Who had protected her and calmed her with his peaceful ways. Who had walked in a procession with her to wed the love of her life.

Giuseppe was lying on a pile of fresh hay, his legs curled under him, as though he were sleeping. Bianca was lying next to him, her head resting on his back. Violetta could swear the white donkey had tears in her eyes.

It seemed to take forever for her to make her way to him, but when she did, she collapsed in a heap, wailing with the grief of the stricken. She burrowed her face in his soft neck and wept.

When she looked up, Fiora and Florencia were there, holding hands, their faces stained with tears.

Violetta stroked his mane and scratched his nose, just the way he liked it. "Thank you, my beloved Giuseppe," she whispered to him, remembering the delight she had felt the day she first laid eyes on him, as a baby. "Thank you for the love you have bestowed on me. Thank you for the peace you have brought to our household, and to everyone you encountered. I was lucky to have known you. You brought nothing but joy into my life, every day."

"May your passage into the next world be swift, my good friend," Florencia choked out.

"You rest now, sweet Giuseppe," Fiora said, bending down to kiss his face. "Your work is done."

❧

The three women helped each other back up to the shop, and as Violetta slumped into a chair, Fiora opened a bottle of wine.

"I know it's morning," she said, pulling the cork out of the bottle with a pop. "But I think we could all use this."

She passed the glasses around and then held hers aloft. "Giuseppe," she said.

"Giuseppe," Florencia said.

Violetta couldn't speak, but she raised her glass before drinking it down.

Fiora crossed the room and dunked a cloth into the water basin, squeezed it out, and handed it to Violetta, who held it to her face. The coolness calmed her, as it always did.

"I want him buried in the meadow," she managed to say.

Nobody said how unusual it would be to bury a donkey. If any beast deserved it, Giuseppe did.

Florencia nodded. "I will make arrangements for some of the workmen to come today and do it," she said. She took a deep breath, as if to steady herself, and smoothed her skirt. "In fact, I'll go and talk to them right now."

Fiora knew her sister was going to the shepherd Claudio, and she was glad of that. He would handle the burial, and give comfort to Florencia, too.

"Can I sleep in my old bed tonight?" Violetta asked.

Fiora's heart broke just a little to hear this. The girl wanted to grieve there, in their home. "You don't want to go home to your husband?"

"He won't be home," she said. "He has gone down into town with his father to do some business, and they are visiting two or three banks. So they are staying the night and coming back in the morning."

Fiora smoothed her daughter's hair, glad she'd be staying in the house again. "Of course you can," she said. "Would you like to rest now, for a little while?"

Violetta rose from her chair, wrapped her arms around her mother, and wept as Fiora rubbed her back.

"There, there, child," she whispered. "There, there."

After Violetta retreated to her childhood bed, Fiora made her way over to her flat to retrieve Freddo. She found him curled into a ball, lying in the sun, and for a moment, until he lifted his head, Fiora thought they would be mourning two deaths in the family that day. Freddo was terribly old for a dog, she knew. He had lost a bit of pep in his step. Gray fur dotted his muzzle.

Because she was napping, Violetta did not see Claudio and some of his men walking with the wagon to the meadow, Bianca following behind. She did not see the men burying her friend. She did not see Bianca kneel down next to Giuseppe's grave and bow her beautiful white head. And she did not see Claudio wiping away a tear at the sight of it.

But that night, Violetta awakened with the moon streaming in through the window. She slipped out of bed and padded over to close the shutters, looked outside, and saw two donkeys, Giuseppe and Bianca, grazing peacefully in the meadow next to the hives. She watched them, holding her breath, tears streaming from her eyes, for a very long time, until a cloud floated over the moon and blocked the light.

CHAPTER 36

Violetta

The next morning, Violetta awoke in her childhood bed and, for a moment, wasn't sure where she was. Then she remembered, and an icy hot pang of grief shot through her. She sighed but pushed herself out of bed. It was time to walk through the day. Giovanni was returning from his overnight trip, and she would have to tell him about Giuseppe. He loved him as much as she did.

In the kitchen, her mother and aunt were sitting at the table, drinking coffee.

"Did you sleep well?" Fiora asked.

Violetta smiled a sad smile. "I dreamed of Giuseppe," she said.

"I knew you would," Fiora said, glad of it. The donkey was comforting the girl, even now.

After breakfast, Violetta and Fiora washed the dishes together, just like they always had, and chatted about the coming day. And then it was time for Violetta to go back home.

"I want to take a bath before Gio gets here," she said, managing a smile.

"You run along," Fiora said. "I'm going to the meadow this morning to tend to the bees." They had probably been agitated with the events of yesterday, she thought, and could use some calming. She did not know that Giuseppe himself had been calming them, all night long.

"What'll you do today, Auntie?" Violetta asked Florencia.

"Keep Bianca and Freddo company for a while," she said, her words catching in her throat.

And so, Fiora was in the meadow with the bees, Florencia was in the barn, and Violetta was walking through town toward her flat when the shaking started.

The earth moved—literally shook under Violetta's feet. At first it was mild, something they were all used to. There were small tremors often in this region, always had been. Most of the time it was nothing to worry about. So she swayed back and forth a bit but didn't think too much about it, until the massive earthquake unleashed its power.

Violetta was thrown into a stone wall and crouched down so as not to be thrown over it. She watched as windows shattered and buildings shook. People were screaming all around her, running out of their homes and shops and into the streets for safety.

Then, a great cacophony as bricks from the castle tower came tumbling down, hitting the stone streets like rain.

Violetta curled into a ball, draped her arms over her head, and held her breath. The noise was deafening, as if buildings were exploding all around her.

And then, silence for a long moment, until people started shouting. And screaming.

Violetta was covered in a fine ash. She scrambled to her feet and shook out her skirt, looking around her, taking stock of the scene. A portion of the castle tower had fallen, its bricks strewn like so many autumn leaves.

She staggered out into the piazza and saw that one of the massive pillars outside the church had toppled to the ground. Angelina, the mayor's wife, was kneeling beside it, wailing. Then Violetta saw the body.

Violetta rushed over to her and realized it was the mayor lying in a heap, his head crushed. She saw other people, hurt or dead.

"Signora," Violetta coughed out.

Angelina looked up, her eyes wild with rage. "Get away! Get away from us, witch! Haven't you done enough?"

People were closing in, all of them looking like stunned shells of themselves.

"First my son, and now my husband!" Angelina shrieked. "Stay away! Leave us alone!"

Angelina turned back to her husband as people came to help her. Men began moving the bricks that had fallen; women were tending to Angelina, leading her away from her husband. All of them were looking at Violetta with rage-filled eyes.

Violetta wanted to stay and help but then she thought: Mama. Auntie. She had to find her own family.

Where did they say they were going? The barn? The meadow? She hurried across the piazza and burst into the shop, just in case they were there. Broken jars lay oozing on the floor. The table was upended. Shelves were broken.

"Mama! Auntie!" Violetta cried, running through the house. But neither were there. Good, she thought. They would be safer in the barn and meadow.

She was about to run out to find them when Fiora and Florencia burst through the door, one after the other. The three women hugged each other for a long moment.

"Are you okay? Were you injured at all?" Fiora asked her daughter.

"No, and you?"

"We are fine. The bees were shaken up, but the hives still stand."

"The barn was the safest place to be," Florencia said. "Everything shook but held fast. Bianca and Freddo are fine as well."

"The mayor is dead," Violetta said. "I saw it, in the piazza."

Fiora's hand flew to her mouth. "No!"

"The castle tower was damaged," Violetta said. "Pillars in front of the church came down—I think that's what killed the mayor. But the rest of the buildings look—"

Violetta's words stopped in midair and she let out a strained cry.

"What is it?" Fiora asked.

"Gio was supposed to be traveling up the mountain road in a coach. This morning."

The women looked at each other in stunned silence. If Giovanni had been in a coach on that treacherous mountain road when the quake hit . . .

"Go," Fiora said to Violetta. "Run down to the barn and get Bianca and ride down the road, looking . . ." She couldn't say it. Over the cliff. Fiora knew there were sheer drops in some places on that road.

Violetta took her mother's hands. "Not Gio," she said, shaking her head violently. "Please. Not Gio."

Fiora gripped her daughter's hands, hard. It was too much, she knew. First Giuseppe and now this. But Violetta had to stay strong now to get through this day.

"You go find him," Fiora said, with more strength than she felt.

A knock at the door then. And another, louder.

The three women exchanged a worried glance—what was this, now? Florencia summoned the same confidence her niece had exhibited when the angry women had come to their door, and she opened it.

But it was only Sofia Moretti standing there, in traveling clothes. She looked past the two older women to Violetta.

"Good. You're here. I have my coach and driver. Geno is in the coach, too. Let's go."

Violetta didn't have to be told where, or why. She and Sofia were going down that mountain road to look for their husbands.

"Wait a moment," Fiora said, hurrying across the room to fetch a satchel that sat in the pantry. She handed it to Violetta and then turned to Sofia. "There are balms, healing ointments, cloths, alcohol. Things to dull the pain. Anything you might need if you find them injured. Violetta knows what to do. Now, wait just one moment."

She poured a few drops of olive oil into a small bowl, added some dried sage, and mixed it, whispering something under her breath. She dipped a finger into the bowl and drew it across her daughter's forehead. She did the same with Sofia.

"May this protect you," she said.

Sofia clasped Fiora's hand. "Will they be alive?"

"I don't know," Fiora said, not revealing the gnarling in her stomach. "But you need to go now."

Sofia turned to go but then, over her shoulder, said, "You should know, I heard people talking in the piazza about 'the witches' causing this earthquake. Something about the ritual of the witch, Angelina's son being cursed. It's nonsense, but I wanted you to be aware."

"It's true, Mama," Violetta said. "I tried to help when I saw the mayor on the ground, but his wife shouted at me and started calling me a witch. First her son, and now her husband, she said. Many people heard it."

Fiora closed the door after her daughter and Sofia Moretti were gone and turned to Florencia.

"I know," Florencia said. "We need to start packing."

CHAPTER 37

Cassandra

Back at my place, we paged through my ancestors' lives once again. I'd go back and read all of it again, what I could understand of it, but I was anxious to see the end of this journal. What happened to Violetta, Fiora, and Florencia? Maybe it could tell us why Violetta had come to the United States and unlock the mystery of those death certificates.

And what of this supposed curse?

We read of their early life in Santo Stefano, setting up the hives, tending to the bees. We read of the white dog Freddo, who bore a strange resemblance to the dog that kept popping up at my door. A shiver went through me as I thought of it. We read of the patient donkey Giuseppe.

One passage caught my eye. "Bianca," I said to Dante. "That means 'white,' right?"

He nodded, looking closer at the passage. "Yes, it says Violetta had been talking to her mother and aunt about a pure-white donkey, and then it mysteriously appeared out of nowhere one day. Bianca, they named her."

Another chill shot through me, remembering the vision, or visitation, or whatever it was, from what seemed to be a white donkey a few days prior.

"There is a lot of lore and legend about white donkeys and donkeys with white stars on their foreheads," Dante said. "They were considered magical, bringing good luck and protection and a sense of welcoming to those who encounter them."

Anna had said as much. My rooms were fashioned from an old barn. Could it have been their barn? Were their spirits still here, somehow?

We turned more pages until we found another name, starting another new chapter.

Violetta

It brought tears to my eyes. The connection to me, the thread that bound us all, was getting tighter. These weren't just names in a book anymore—this was my great-grandmother. I knew how her story ended. In Wharton, owning an inn.

But Violetta's section of the book wasn't very long. Several pages of logs, a few journal entries, all of them featuring Giovanni and the animals.

"So she knew him when they were children," I said to Dante, imagining it.

I could see them, running in the meadow, chasing Freddo, while the donkeys patiently watched. It was so clear to me, it was almost as if I was living it myself.

"Here," Dante said, pointing to a passage. "She's writing about tending the bees." He read in silence for a moment. "She writes in much more detail about their technique than her mother or grandmother did. It is similar to mine. That art hasn't changed much in one hundred years."

He looked up at me. "I'd love to study this journal again, if you'd allow it," he said. "We were going through it pretty quickly, and I'll bet there's a lot more about beekeeping that I could learn from this. Maybe I can pick up some tips and tricks from your ancestors."

I liked that idea. "You're tending their colony," I said. "It's only right."

We turned a few more pages, until Dante stopped on a passage.

"Here," he said, again pointing to the words. "Violetta married Giovanni Moretti."

He read the passage aloud to me, about her riding on Bianca in a procession through the streets. Her gown that made her look like the night sky.

Tears, again. It sounded breathtaking. "I wish we had a photo of that," I said.

"Maybe the Morettis do," Dante said. "They said they had more photos to show you. The town banker certainly would have a photograph of his son's wedding."

I made a mental note to ask them about it when I saw them next.

Dante read another page. "Violetta is writing about the curse on the women of their family." He looked up at me. "Your family."

Here it was again.

He read it aloud. "Mama told me of the curse on our family, about our true loves being taken from us. She said her mother broke that curse. I'm glad of it! I know my true love is Gio and we'll grow old together."

A chill ran through me. They did not grow old together.

Dante turned another page and gasped aloud. There was only one paragraph. Just a few hastily scrawled lines. He read:

Earthquake. We are unhurt. Violetta has gone to find Giovanni, who was traveling up the mountain road when the quake hit. She is with Giovanni's mother, Sofia Moretti.

The people of the town are turning against us. People we have helped, all of these years. Calling us witch. They were here two nights *ago, saying Violetta put a curse on a boy in town. She scolded them and slammed the door in their faces. But now, the mayor is dead. Rumors are circulating that we caused this terrible quake. This is no longer about a little boy with a fever. A town elder has been killed.*

We are leaving Santo Stefano, as quickly as we can.

Dante reached over and took my hand. "That's the last entry," he said.

"The people were calling them witches," I whispered. "Your grandmother knew about that. You don't think they were harmed . . . or worse?"

Dante shook his head. "I can't believe it. Nothing like that would have happened in Santo Stefano without it going down in history. We would all know about it."

There was an earthquake, which we now knew was devastating for the region, but most of the buildings in Santo Stefano sustained only minimal damage, if any. We know my family survived the quake. Violetta was out looking for Giovanni. And the townspeople were calling them witches for various reasons.

And we knew Violetta's death certificate said she died in that year of witchcraft and, from the Morettis, that Giovanni died the same year. I knew both of those were wrong. Or . . . had Giovanni died in the quake, with Violetta carrying his child? Did history repeat itself with mother and daughter?

I ran a hand through my hair and leaned back in my chair. "Are we not going to find out what happened to them? Is this all there is?"

But then, I thought, no. There was one more place to look.

CHAPTER 38

Violetta

On the way out of town in the Moretti carriage, Violetta saw that the damage to Santo Stefano was minimal. Those medieval buildings had stood fast for hundreds of years in an earthquake-prone area for a reason, she thought.

But as the carriage made its way down the road to town, Violetta saw a different story. Boulders had fallen from the cliffs, making passage difficult. Whole sections of the road on the cliffside had fallen away.

The horses knew to step carefully, and it was very slow going.

Giovanni's brother Geno sat on top of the carriage, scanning the hill below. Inside the carriage, Violetta and Sofia clasped each other's hands, both women silent. Violetta's stomach was in knots.

It felt like an eternity until Geno called, "There!"

~✻~

Back at the shop, Fiora and Florencia were hurriedly stuffing clothes into their bags, only what they could carry. They could hear the shouting in the streets. *"Witch! Witch!"* The sisters didn't know what this crowd would do but were not about to stay to find out.

"This is unbelievable," Florencia said, her voice a harsh whisper.

"And yet, familiar somehow," Fiora said. "Our people have heard these cries for generations."

Florencia looked at her sister. "But our outcome will be different."

Fiora didn't know that was true. She wasn't sure how they would get out of town, undetected by anyone.

A thought stopped her packing for a moment. "What if Violetta comes back with the Morettis and we're not here?"

"No," Florencia said. "We can't miss her. There is only one way down the hill and one way up. We will meet her if she is on the road coming back. And we will catch up with her if she isn't."

Her sister was right, Fiora thought. As always. What would she have done without steady Florencia over the years? Her eyes filled with gratitude as she looked at this fortress of a woman.

Then, a knock at the back door. A soft rap. Not an angry mob. Florencia opened it to find Claudio there. He took Florencia into his arms—all pretense was over.

"Thank God you are unhurt," he said.

"And you," she said, her voice wavering.

He pulled back and looked from Florencia to Fiora. "Come," he said. "Both of you. We must go."

Florencia and Fiora exchanged a glance.

"The word is spreading quickly that the Rossi women caused this earthquake," he said. "Cooler heads might prevail. But they might not."

"We were just packing," Florencia said. "We have been thinking about this for a few days now, since the ritual. The women came here, an angry mob. Violetta sent them away. But what if their husbands come next time?"

"I will make sure you get out of town safely," he said.

So, with Freddo at their heels, the Rossi sisters left the shop in Santo Stefano—the place where they had raised Violetta, tended the bees, and built a wonderful life—for the last time. Claudio led them out the back door and down the stairs to the barn—they were almost there. Almost safe.

Bianca was waiting, bridle on, wagon hitched up, and ready to go. Claudio smiled. "I stopped by here before I came up to get you."

The sisters tossed their bags into the wagon and climbed in, along with Freddo. Claudio led them out of the barn, but not before Fiora looked back one last time and offered a prayer of thanks.

"Protection to all who dwell here," she whispered.

That it was a bright, sunny day and nobody saw Claudio, the Rossi sisters, a large dog, and their pure-white donkey pulling a wagon as they stole out of town, Fiora could never explain. But she had a hunch her mother and grandmother had something to do with it.

They were about halfway down the road to town when they saw the Moretti carriage. Florencia grasped her sister's arm. Bianca stopped. The sisters jumped off the wagon and hurried to the edge of the cliff. What they saw made them take a collective deep breath and say a quick prayer.

The carriage that had carried Giovanni and his father had gone over the side, and it looked as though it had toppled over more than once. The horses, tragically, lay silent and still. Fiora whispered her blessing for a safe passage to the other side for those beautiful creatures.

The carriage driver was sitting on the ground—he looked bruised and shaken, but otherwise unhurt.

Sofia was tending to her husband, who was lying on the ground beside her. She caught sight of the sisters and called out to them. "I think he has a broken ankle," she said. "Maybe ribs, too. But please, come down and see to Gio."

Fiora and Florencia scrambled down the hillside and found Violetta kneeling beside Gio, who was laid out on the ground, his face bloodied.

"He's alive," she said, her voice steely and strong.

Fiora saw a poultice on his forehead, and one on his arm. She hurried to his side. Fiora held a hand to his cheek and one on his wrist. She felt his ribs and stomach and down his legs as he let out a soft groan. She nodded to Violetta.

Fiora turned to Claudio, Geno, and the carriage driver. "We need to get him onto the wagon and take him to the hospital in town."

"And my husband?" Sofia said, her face dirty and stained with tears. Fiora knelt beside him. "How do you feel?" she asked.

"Fine, considering," Silvio said, with a weak smile. "My ankle is killing me. And I'm very sore everywhere. But otherwise, I'm okay."

Fiora felt his arms, stomach, ribs, and down his legs. "Forgive me, *signore*," she said. He waved his hand as if to bat her comment away.

Florencia appeared at her side with two small, sturdy pieces of wood. Fiora knew they were from her satchel. Splints.

She put the pieces on either side of Silvio's calf and secured them tightly with linen. "Ask the doctor to check in on you," she said. "I'm sure he'll be visiting Santo Stefano soon, making the rounds after the quake." Then, turning to Sofia. "He needs to stay off of this for it to heal. But if any fever erupts, or if his leg seems to be getting worse, put him in a carriage and take him to the hospital in town immediately."

She and Sofia got on either side of Silvio to help him up the hill toward the waiting carriage.

With Gio laid out in the wagon, still drifting in and out, and Silvio settled in the carriage, it was time to go their separate ways.

Sofia asked when the sisters would be returning to the shop, and they looked at each other in silence for a moment before Fiora answered.

"I think we have overstayed our welcome in Santo Stefano," she said.

Sofia shook her head. "Understood. Go with God."

"I will send word from the hospital about Gio's condition," Violetta said, enveloping her mother-in-law in a hug.

And the sisters, Violetta, and Claudio climbed into the wagon as Bianca walked slowly and carefully down the road.

CHAPTER 39

Fiora

Nearly a month later, Giovanni Moretti was released from the hospital with a clean bill of health. He still needed help getting around, but Violetta was more than happy to provide it. The sisters and Violetta had been staying with Claudio in his cottage on the outskirts of L'Aquila, helping him tend the sheep. Bianca and Freddo took their turns herding.

It was clear to Fiora that it was not her sister's first time at Claudio's cottage. Her apron hung in the kitchen. She knew where everything was. Fiora was aware this had been going on for some time—years, likely—but let Florencia decide to tell her about it in her own time.

Word had come from Sofia Moretti that her husband was doing fine as well, if cranky that he couldn't put weight on his broken ankle.

She also reported that, in Santo Stefano, people had cleaned up the rubble, dusted off the piazza, and life went back to normal, albeit a new normal. The mayor was the only casualty of the quake, but many people had been hurt. Some, quite badly.

Long-held beliefs ran deep, and although people were reticent about it and backtracked when they said it out loud, there was a current of blame wrapped around the Rossis slithering through the town. First Alessandro falls ill, and then the mayor was killed. It was too clear to be a coincidence, wasn't it? Part of it could be the fault of the women in town and their ridiculous ritual, the burning of the clothes—or was it so ridiculous? Alessandro recovered that very night. And after the angry confrontation at the Rossi shop, the earth itself moved and took down his father.

And what of poor Giovanni? Was the witch targeting him, too? Certainly she had bewitched him into marrying her—that had been clear to all the more eligible women in town all along.

And now, the Rossi sisters, Violetta, and Giovanni had disappeared.

Had they been living among witches all this time?

Because of the sentiment in the town, Sofia neglected to tell anyone that Giovanni was being treated in the hospital in town, mainly because the Rossi sisters and Violetta were with him. That, she said, was family business, and nobody else's.

When the sisters read the letter, it solidified their intention to leave. Would there be consequences if they returned? Certainly nobody was going to be burned as a witch in 1911. This was the modern age. But there was so much ill will. Nobody would patronize the shop. Friendships would dry up. And there might well be retaliation in some form or another.

During the weeks Giovanni was recovering, Fiora had written to Rosa and Constant—Cecile had long since passed on—in New Orleans and had already received word back.

"Come home to us," Rosa had written. "We will be waiting for you. We cannot wait to see you."

One night, the family sat at Claudio's kitchen table. As Florencia served the stew she had been simmering on the stove all day, they talked about their future.

"My parents wrote that we should go south, to Portofino, and travel to America from there," Fiora said. "New Orleans. That's where our people live. When we are ready to leave, I will write ahead and book passage for us."

Giovanni and Violetta had talked endlessly about what they would do. Go back to Santo Stefano—but what would people do to the wife of the banker? Make a home in L'Aquila? Go to Rome, where Violetta's family had come from all those years ago?

In the end, they decided to go to America, to make a new life. It sounded like a grand adventure, as Rosa thought it would be. He knew his parents would not be happy about this decision, and he had trepidations about it as well—leaving Italy?—but Violetta was his family now.

It was all settled, then. Until Florencia cleared her throat. She looked from her sister to her niece and back again. Fiora knew what she was going to say before she said it.

"You are going to stay here with Claudio," Fiora said, tears brimming in her eyes. Tears of sadness at the thought of being apart from her twin soul, yes. But also tears of joy for her sister, who had steadfastly stood by her, helped her, supported her for a lifetime. Now it was Florencia's turn to find happiness.

Claudio stood next to Florencia and put an arm around her waist. "I asked her to be my wife," he said. "As I have done countless times over the many years we have known each other. Only this time, she said yes."

Fiora and Florencia embraced each other then, whispering a lifetime of love, blessings, and gratitude into each other's ears.

As the family was preparing for their journey, the Morettis, Sofia and Silvio, knocked on Claudio's door.

It was the last time they would see each other for a very long time, they all knew. So they did what Italians, and all families, do. They sat around the table, full to the brim with pasta and fish and breads and cheeses and wine, and shared memories, family stories, and laughter, tied together with the meal Florencia and Fiora conjured up in the kitchen.

When they were enjoying a sip of grappa after the meal, Silvio got to his feet, careful of the ankle, and raised his glass.

"To the Morettis and the Rossis," he said. "Two great families, now one. We send you off with love and wish you safe passage on your journey."

They all raised their glasses.

Later, Sofia took Gio aside. "People in the town are speculating you died in the earthquake," she said. "We're going to just let them speculate. We have been 'in mourning' and have not spoken of it. Nobody needs to know your business, where you're going, not with them whispering about Violetta. Especially now. We are going to let you 'stay dead,' if that's what you want."

Gio nodded, a pang of grief inside his heart for leaving the village he loved so much. But he loved Violetta more.

"The new mayor has already declared Violetta dead," Sofia said, lowering her voice so no one else could hear. "Witchcraft, they've said."

"Why? That's . . ."

Sofia held up one finger. "That's not so crazy. Let them believe it. It's a way to put an end to the talk, the speculation, and, the way some in town look at it, the bad luck. Let it be."

And so he did. He and his wife were both dead, as far as anyone else in Santo Stefano knew.

At the same time, Silvio was taking Fiora aside. "I have made arrangements to transfer all of your money to the bank in New Orleans you have specified. It will take a week or so. But you will have ample funds to set yourselves up when you get there."

When it was time for the Morettis to leave, Gio hugged his parents tight.

"We will visit you in America," Silvio promised, before climbing into their carriage for the long ride up the mountain road.

That was how it happened that Fiora, Violetta, and Giovanni set out in a coach on a crisp September day and headed south to Portofino, where their new life would begin.

Florencia and Claudio stood together, waving, as tears streamed down her face.

As the coach passed the meadow where the sheep were grazing, Violetta watched from the window as Bianca and Freddo, who had been playing with the sheep, stood sentinel, heads bowed. A shadow of another donkey stood beside them. As he always did. With tears in her eyes, Violetta waved goodbye to her faithful friends, thanking them for their lifelong service to her.

As the coach rocked along, Violetta rested her head on her husband's shoulder and her hand on her belly, wondering if they should make the transatlantic trip before the baby was born.

∾✤∾

As it turned out, it wasn't Violetta's decision to make. Gia came into this world in Portofino, two months early, tiny and blue as a baby bird but healthy all the same. Fiora, along with another midwife from the area, attended the birth, and as her mother was cleaning up the baby and checking her vital signs, Violetta gazed out her window and saw dolphins jumping in the sea.

She turned to Giovanni. "She will love the water," she said. "There's no better sign than this."

A few hours later, Fiora came back into the room holding a piece of paper. "A birth certificate," she announced. "They are popular in America. An important paper to have."

She handed it to Violetta.

"This says New York," she said, frowning at her mother.

Fiora nodded. "This baby will be American," she said. "Her paperwork will show she was born there."

"And what's this? Why is Gio's name not on here?"

"He's dead, remember?"

Violetta shrugged. All this subterfuge. All these secrets. Wasn't it all silly? Wasn't this the modern age? But, she thought, here they were. She was too tired to fight with her mother about it. Let the woman have her secretive ways. What could it hurt?

When Gia was a few months old, the family boarded an ocean liner for their first-class trip to America. As the ship pulled away from the dock, Violetta watched as Italy, her home, grew farther and farther away.

She brushed a tear from her cheek. She wasn't sure it was the right decision. Or what was awaiting her across the sea. But she was with Giovanni, their daughter, and her mother. Headed toward her grandparents and a new life. Let the journey begin.

CHAPTER 40

Cassandra

"Bingo," Maria said to me on the phone a few days later. She was the "one more place" I had thought of to look.

I had told her about the New Orleans connection, and she—with a better internet connection than I had here in this medieval town—spent some time researching records from the port in New Orleans.

And there it was, in black and white. Fiora Rossi, Giovanni and Violetta Moretti, and Gia Moretti came through the immigration station in March 1912.

She had also looked up Constant Broussard, a professor at Tulane University. She found records of him as well.

"I can't believe we have roots in New Orleans," she said to me. "I'm totally blown away by all of it."

"I know," I said. "I think a trip is in our future." I wanted to know more about my ancestors there, too.

"Absolutely," she said. "And I can't wait to get a look at that journal you found. So, when are you coming home?"

I didn't quite know how to answer that. I still had the barn for another few weeks, or longer if I wanted it. I hadn't talked to the Morettis again, and I really wanted to see if they had photos or any other stories about Giovanni and Violetta. Luna and Renzo and Anna were becoming fast friends of mine. Tony at the restaurant, too. And Dante . . . the possibilities floated in the air between us every time we were together. We had begun to stay at either his place or mine each night, and exactly nobody in town was surprised.

I had been quietly building a life here.

I knew that my ancestors had left this place. But I was called back to it. And it welcomed me and wrapped itself around me. I found friendship, family, and even love here in this medieval town where Fiora, Florencia, and Violetta had made a home. Where Violetta had had a wedding procession, riding on a white donkey. Where she had fallen in love.

These were my people. This was my place, where the roots of my family tree were woven into the soil and the trees and the meadows. Where the bees still remained.

I still had questions. What of Violetta's death certificate? I felt as though, given the sentiment of the townspeople after the earthquake, someone had concocted it. Giovanni's death, too. They left this village, and this country, together—maybe that was the subterfuge they used. I would never know for sure, but I felt, deep in my bones, it was true.

I felt something else, too. That second sight my grandmother always told me I'd had. My "women's intuition." How I knew things. Felt things. Anna had been right—it was growing. All of it finally made sense in a way it never had before.

I thought about the journal constantly and was diligently improving my Italian so I could read it for myself. But one thing nagged at me. The curse.

I turned that over in my mind. Violetta had certainly found the love of her life, but it was short-lived. She did not have him for long. My grandmother and grandfather had had a great marriage, though, as did my parents. In the journal, it said something about love in Italy. Was that the difference?

But . . . both my marriage and Maria's had ended badly. Did it skip a couple of generations, or were we just the product of modern society, when divorce was more common? Not everything was a curse. Maybe both of us just picked the wrong men. I didn't know, but I was planning to ask Luna and Anna if they knew anything about curses. Better safe than sorry.

The three of us had been sitting at a table in the piazza, sipping wine and sampling some pastries Luna had made, when I finally brought it up. I told the women what I had read in the journal about the curse, and indeed what the women in my family had experienced.

Anna squinted, looking off into the distance. Then she turned her gaze to me. "Curses can be broken," she said, nodding. "Or diluted. I've no doubt your grandmother and mother found their loves, with Violetta standing between them and this curse. Intervention is a powerful thing. But you and your cousin didn't have her to protect you, so it gained strength again. It could be why it seemed to have skipped a generation."

It made a strange kind of sense.

"It could also be tied to Italy, as you suspected," Luna said. "There's no way to truly know."

"We can try to extinguish it once and for all," Anna said, raising her eyebrows. "What do you think?"

That is how, a few nights later, I found myself standing in "my" barn with Anna and Luna. They had brought dozens of candles with them, and the flames were flickering in the darkened room like stars in the night sky. The sweet smell of incense wafted through the air as moonlight streamed in through the window.

Luna had filled a silver chalice with wine infused with rosemary and flower petals and handed it to me. I drank it down, set the goblet on the table, and the three of us joined hands.

I took a deep breath and said the words Luna had instructed me to compose for the occasion. Breaking the spell couldn't come from a book, she had said. You couldn't look this kind of thing up on the internet. It had to come from me, from the bloodline. From somewhere deep inside.

As I sat down to write the spell, I was surprised by how easily it came. How powerful it felt. How natural it was to craft the words. It was almost as though someone else was guiding my thoughts.

And that night, I said it aloud for the first, and hopefully last, time.

"From mother to daughter, the curse was passed
    down,
From a jealous hex, love's fire did drown,
Be it death of beloved or love's own demise,
Grief did surround us, and wore no disguise.
By the light of this moon, I call on these souls,
The women, my bloodline, whose grief was
    foretold
Stand together we shall, against this dark spell
To summon our power, dip into its well.
With the magic of women, command I shall take
I call on these souls, the curse we will break.
Love will be freed, from now throughout time
Our soul's desire shall live on, in the sublime."

With that, the candles whooshed brighter. And I could have sworn I saw the shadows of women, seven of them, on the wall across the room. I recognized two—my mother and grandmother—and my eyes filled with tears.

❧

I didn't know whether the spell worked or not. Or if any of this was real. But I did know that I felt lighter somehow. Maybe that was the whole point. Doing something to take control of what you thought you couldn't control.

A few weeks passed after that, and I had been making plans. Henry was coming for an extended visit when the school year ended. While he practiced some basic Italian and brushed up on his manual-transmission driving skills, I made reservations for us in Rome and Venice and Siena. I couldn't wait to introduce my son to Italy and all the wonderful friends and family I had found here.

Maria, too, was buying a plane ticket for a trip in late summer. We would drive down to Portofino and spend some lazy days sipping Aperol spritzes by the sea where our grandmother had been born.

I actually dared to think it—I was happy.

One afternoon, sitting at a table in the piazza with a cold glass of Abruzzo wine, the white dog sleeping at my feet, (whose presence I still couldn't quite explain but whom I had named Giuseppe and intended to keep) I opened the journal in which my ancestors had chronicled their lives and turned to the first blank page. I picked up a pen and wrote one word.

Cassandra

EPILOGUE

Cassandra

Hundreds of people, maybe more, roamed the ancient streets, lit by the full moon, candles, and the bonfire in the piazza. Woodsmoke hung in the air, mingling with the scent of incense and herbs, and wrapped itself around me with a familiarity I couldn't quite explain.

Spring had turned to glorious Italian summer, and on a warm August night, I was in the neighboring village for their annual Festival of the Witch.

During the day, there were local vendors and food and music and dance, people laughing and drinking delicious Abruzzo wine. But as night fell, the entire town became a stage as people dressed in costume, either as townsfolk or witches, and marched through the streets, some carrying torches, others speaking an ancient Italian dialect preserved through the ages, all of it culminating at the bonfire in the piazza. They were reenacting an ancient ritual meant to rid the children of the town of a witch's curse . . . or evil eye.

I had tried every flimsy excuse to beg off—I was tired, I had writing to do, I wasn't feeling well—but Dante and Renzo and Luna had worn me down and convinced me to join them.

As we walked the cobblestone streets filled with revelers, my eyes blinked back the smoke that hung in the air. I reached down into my purse for a tissue and was jostled back and forth by the crowd. *"Scusi! Scusi!"*

When I looked up again, I had lost my companions in a sea of strange faces. I couldn't tell one person from the other—everyone seemed to be wearing black cloaks or jackets. They all looked the same. Where was Dante? He was here just a moment ago, wasn't he? Where were Luna and Renzo? People were shouting in a language I didn't understand. But one word rose above all the others: *strega*.

Were they hissing at me? Why were they all looking at me? An ice-cold fear sizzled through my veins as the crowd seemed to surround me, angry faces shouting in mine. I had to get out of there.

I turned and pushed my way out of the crowd and ran down an alleyway, gasping for breath. I heard angry voices shouting, *"Strega! Strega!"* Were they behind me? Were they following me?

My heart was pounding as I hurried under an archway, which led to another passage. Another archway. Another passage. And still the voices followed, echoing off the ancient stone. *Or maybe coming from it.* It was like I was lost in a maze, created for—or by—witches to escape angry townspeople whose children had fallen ill. I was taking the steps they had taken hundreds of years before.

"This way." A woman in a hooded cloak was standing in an archway ahead, beckoning me, crooking her finger. "Come this way."

I followed as she wove through the dark, dark streets, disappearing around corners and down slim passageways, slowing her pace just enough for me to keep up.

Finally, I saw light at the end of the alleyway. Music. People. But not the angry crowd from before. These were just revelers, taking part in the festival. I heard laughter. I walked slowly down the alley and saw I was entering the piazza.

"Where have you been?" Dante enveloped me in a hug. I could feel my beating heart begin to calm.

"I don't know," I said.

Wanting to thank the woman for leading me back to the piazza, I glanced toward the alley. She was gone.

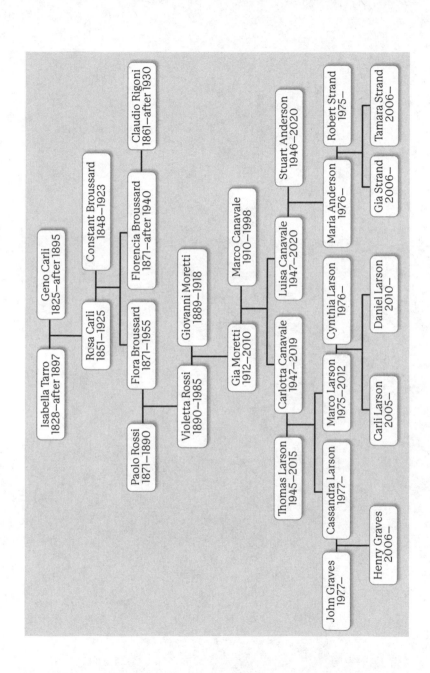

ACKNOWLEDGMENTS

Readers always ask how I get the ideas for my books. The truth is, I don't know. Something floats into my orbit and sparks my imagination . . . and I grab it. The idea for this book happened just that way.

A friend I've known for a couple of decades bought a home in Santo Stefano di Sessanio, Italy, a perfectly preserved, eight-hundred-year-old hill town. Complete with a castle built by the Medici family; a maze of arched, cobblestoned alleyways; little shops, including one that sells local honey; and a dramatic view of the Apennine mountains.

"What a great place for you to write your next book!" he said. And that magical something, that spark inside me, ignited.

Before I knew it, I was on my way to Italy for the adventure of a lifetime. And you just read all about it. With a few embellishments, of course.

Many parts of this book were taken directly from my experiences in Italy—the warmth of the people, the beauty of the landscape, the breathtaking history. The food!

But the central plotline about Cassie discovering she is descended from a long line of witches—that comes directly from my imagination. I pulled it out of thin air without even thinking about it when my publisher asked what this new book set in Italy was going to be about. As my agent likes to say, my thin air is different from other people's.

So many strange coincidences about witches were swirling around me in Italy, I could fill a book with just that. Truly, in a life in which odd, otherworldly things happen to me constantly, this was by far the oddest. Here's one example.

You have just read a scene in which Cassie is sitting in an ancient restaurant talking with the bartender. That happened to me. Word had gone around about an American author who was in town, and this adorable bartender sat with me, wanting to practice his English. He knew only that I was an author, not that I was writing a book set in the town, certainly not that it was about witches.

Pointing out of a window toward the mountains, he said, "See that hill town, just over there? You should visit it. It's just like this, but there, it's only witches."

Um, what? He went on to explain that once a year, *on my birthday*, they hold a famous witch festival, where they re-create the ritual of the breaking of a witch's curse.

You'll notice this book starts and ends with that very ritual.

That's not the end of it, though. Back at home in Minnesota, at the very moment when I was writing the scene with that bartender in it, I got a ping on my phone. It was a text from him, the real-life guy! I had just popped into his head, and he thought he'd reach out to say hello.

I told him I was *just writing about him* at that exact moment. He said, "Remember, I told you this place is all about synchronicity. Now you see it's true."

Yes, it is.

The first people I need to thank for making this book possible: Rod and Katrina Raymond, who so generously opened their home in Italy to me. Let's do it all again soon! Even getting lost on the way home from the Adriatic and stumbling upon the restaurant with the best pizza in Italy. Especially that.

To the wonderful, warm people in Santo Stefano di Sessanio, I hope you can feel the love I have for your magical, beautiful town, and for you. Laura, Francesco, and Kokuu—I'll see you again.

To my agent, Jennifer Weltz, thank you for your wise counsel, your inspired (and a little magical I'll just say) help in brainstorming, and for being the best partner in world domination a girl could ever have.

To my editors Alicia Clancy and Faith Black Ross—I love working with you! Your ideas and insights made this book, and every book, better. To everyone else at Lake Union, including Carissa Bluestone, Karah Nichols, and everyone else I forgot to mention—you're awesome. I am so, so lucky to have you all in my corner.

To all the librarians and booksellers who have supported me, suggested my books, and hosted events with me—thank you for giving me the opportunity to come out of my hobbit hole and meet readers! I am so grateful to you for your unwavering support!

To Pamela Klinger-Horn, every author's fairy godmother—the events you organize are legendary. We all owe you a huge debt of gratitude. I hope you know how beloved you are in the book community. And I am so fortunate to call you my friend. (Plus you make the best madeleines I have ever tasted.)

To my dad, Toby Webb, for telling stories around our dinner table, especially the tales of your exploits in Italy. Those stories live in my brother and me, and in my son, and will live in his children when that day comes. These stories make up the fabric of our lives and will not be forgotten. And neither will you.

And to you, my readers. I am grateful beyond measure for you. Thank you for reading my stories, for coming out to my events, and for emailing me with your thoughts. I truly do write with you in mind, hoping you'll love the tales I spin.

Now, I'm on to my next one. What will it be?

BOOK CLUB QUESTIONS

1. Were the women in Cassie's family really witches, or were they healers?
2. Is there any difference?
3. Is Luna a witch? What about Anna?
4. The sense of place is a major part of this story. Could you imagine being there?
5. What is the significance of the animals in the story?
6. Wendy often includes animals in her books. Would you? And if so, why?
7. Do you agree with forging the birth certificate? Why did they do that?
8. Were Giuseppe and Bianca spirits?
9. Can you explain the spider dream?
10. What would you do if you had that dream?
11. Is the dog in the present Freddo?
12. What is his role in the story?
13. Will Cassie and Dante end up together?
14. Italians have a superstition about the "evil eye." What do you think about that?
15. Where do these superstitions come from?
16. What sorts of lore and legend do you think have a basis in truth?

17. Would you leave your home and go live in a small Italian village?
18. Would you travel overseas alone?
19. Have you ever traced your ancestry?
20. What would you do if you found a mystery in your family tree?

ABOUT THE AUTHOR

Photo © 2020 Steve Burmeister

Wendy Webb is the #1 Amazon Charts and Indie bestselling, multiple award–winning author of nine novels of gothic suspense, including *The Stroke of Winter, The Keepers of Metsan Valo, The Haunting of Brynn Wilder, Daughters of the Lake, The Vanishing, The Fate of Mercy Alban, The Tale of Halcyon Crane,* and *The End of Temperance Dare,* which has been optioned for both film and television. Her books are sold worldwide and have been translated into a dozen languages. Dubbed "Queen of the Northern Gothic" by reviewers, Wendy sets her stories on the windswept, rocky shores of the Great Lakes. She lives in Minneapolis, where she is at work on her next novel when she's not walking a good dog along the parkway and lakes near her home. For more information, visit her at www.wendykwebb.com.